THE LOOSE END

Also by A.J. Cross

The Dr Kate Hanson mysteries

GONE IN SECONDS
ART OF DECEPTION
A LITTLE DEATH *
SOMETHING EVIL COMES *
COLD, COLD HEART *

The Will Traynor forensic mysteries

DARK TRUTHS *
DEVIL IN THE DETAIL *
A DARK, DIVIDED SELF *
REFLECTIONS OF DEVIANCE *

* *available from Severn House*

THE LOOSE END

A.J. Cross

SEVERN
HOUSE

First world edition published in Great Britain and the USA in 2024
by Severn House, an imprint of Canongate Books Ltd,
14 High Street, Edinburgh EH1 1TE.

Trade paperback edition first published in Great Britain and the USA in 2025
by Severn House, an imprint of Canongate Books Ltd.

severnhouse.com

British Library Cataloguing-in-Publication Data
A CIP catalogue record for this title is available from the British Library.

ISBN-13: 978-1-4483-1474-4 (cased)
ISBN-13: 978-1-4483-1699-1 (trade paper)
ISBN-13: 978-1-4483-1539-0 (e-book)

MIX
Paper | Supporting responsible forestry
FSC
www.fsc.org
FSC® C013604

Typeset by Palimpsest Book Production Ltd., Falkirk,
Stirlingshire, Scotland.
Printed and bound in Great Britain by
CPI Group (UK) Ltd, Croydon CR0 4YY

The manufacturer's authorised representative in the EU for product safety is
Authorised Rep Compliance Ltd, 71 Lower Baggot Street, Dublin D02 P593
Ireland (arccompliance.com)

Praise for A.J. Cross

"Plenty of unexpected twists sure to set pulses racing"
Booklist Starred Review of *A Dark, Divided Self*

"A suspense-filled police procedural with engaging but flawed lead characters and well-researched insights into modern policing"
Booklist on *Reflections of Deviance*

"Cross builds tension while keeping a diverse cast of characters sharp and sympathetic"
Kirkus Reviews on *Reflections of Deviance*

"Full of bizarre turns and tantalizing red herrings . . . Gripping and entertaining"
Booklist on *Devil in the Detail*

"Readers will find themselves warming to Watts, Traynor, and Judd in this clever and absorbing rollercoaster of a procedural"
Booklist on *Devil in the Detail*

"A skillfully written police drama with plenty of twists"
Booklist on *Dark Truths*

About the author

A.J. Cross is both a court-appointed expert witness and a forensic psychologist with a masters degree and PhD from the University of Birmingham and over twenty years' experience in the field. She lives in Birmingham with her jazz-musician husband and is the author of five Kate Hanson Cold Case mysteries and four previous Will Traynor mysteries. *The Loose End* is the first title in the Teigan Craft forensic mystery series.

This book is dedicated to two very special children in our family:

Thea, who has learned how to make friends and now has lots of them; who sings, dances, loves drama and has blossomed with confidence.

And Evan, her brother, a great chess player and speedy Lego builder, who is also the bravest boy we know. He finds school a challenging place to be, yet he still goes there every day and does what is asked of him.

ACKNOWLEDGEMENTS

My grateful thanks go to Dr Joshua Muggleton, clinical psychologist, for his invaluable insight into what was for me and the book a key aspect of Professor Teigan Craft's thinking.

Late September 2023

She watched the tall man move calmly, methodically around the room, his suitcase a cue to her panic, her loss of control. 'When shall I see you again?'

'In about four days. I'll ring you.'

'Oh.'

'What's wrong?'

'I've run out of bread . . . the dishwasher is full and the—'

He came to her. 'Tell me your real worry,' he said softly into her hair.

More words poured from her mouth. 'What I've agreed to do! It's a terrible mistake. I can't do it. What if I don't understand something? I should never have agreed. I must tell the police—'

'Ssshh. Easy . . . easy. Right now, there is nothing for you to do—'

'But there is!'

'When you are in the situation, you will know what you need to do. I know you will.'

She looked at him, tears coming. 'I'll get it wrong! I'll get the wrong idea, the wrong answer' – she pulled air into her chest, panic rising – 'and everyone will be looking at me, knowing there's something—'

'When you are in that situation, all they'll see is you, doing what you know you can do.'

She watched him walk away, hefting the small suitcase.

'My taxi has arrived. I'll phone you.'

She came to him. 'Promise?'

He put down the suitcase and hugged her. 'I promise.'

ONE

Wednesday 16 October 2023, 8.10 a.m.

The flatbed truck moved quickly along Forrest Road, stopped close to number three and began reversing into a nearby space.

'*Oi! You!*' A belligerent male in an orange hard hat came quickly to the truck and banged his fist against the driver's window. 'You can't leave this here!'

'Who says I can't!'

'*I* do!' He pointed to the house. 'I'm the project manager on this refurb and I'm expecting a delivery any minute.' He looked up at a large lorry approaching, then back to the irate-looking truck driver. 'You heard me! Move it, *now.*'

On a crunch of gears and engine roar, the truck pulled out, quickly replaced by the lorry. The project manager went to it, signed for the delivery, and looked over at the site.

'*Wes!* You and the other three with you doing eff-all – start unloading this lot, *now*.' He headed for the large, double-fronted house, glancing along the side of the road at similar Victorian, detached properties screened by mature trees.

All right for them as can afford it.

Coming inside what was now the gutted shell of the house, he headed to the original kitchen at the rear, located a more-or-less clean mug, poured himself strong coffee from one of four large thermoses, added three heaped spoonsful of dried milk and a similar amount of sugar. Noise from outside was still audible. If he and his lads did not make up for lost time in the next couple of weeks, they could be facing a big problem. Taking a fistful of biscuits from an open pack, wolfing them, interspersed with gulps of coffee, he stared out of the window at the rear garden. He was thinking about the owner of this house and what he would like to say to him. He reached into the pocket of his hi-viz jacket, pulled out his phone, looked at the caller's name and rolled his eyes. *Talk of the devil.*

'Morning, Mr Baxter!'

'How's that plasterboard in the basement looking?'

'Superficially, OK, but there are some cracks in—'

'How much to get rid?'

'It all depends on what's behind it and how you want it finished off. I'd have to get back to you on that.'

'See that you do. I'm keeping tabs on all these extras.'

'You're saying you want the plasterboard gone?'

'Yes. *Today*. I'll be over soon. Another thing. All the trees in the front garden. Get rid of them as well.'

'That could be a problem, Mr Baxter. This might be a conservation area and if it is—'

'Once they're gone, they're gone, *right*? I'm not spending a fortune on that house to have it hidden away where nobody can see it! Get rid of 'em. End of.'

'I'll see what can be done, as long as you know that all these extra jobs are using up time as well as . . .' Realizing he was talking to himself, he muttered, 'Twat.' Ending the call, he left the kitchen munching the last biscuit, went down the curving stairway off the hall and entered the massive basement with a glance at the plasterboard. He was thinking how much he detested people like Baxter, all credit card and '*now-now-now!*'. He went to the other end of the huge room, low morning sun streaming through the massive bifold doors, and looked out, getting a rare moment of pride in this job. His lads, plus a mechanical digger, had moved God knows how many tons of earth to reduce the level of the rear garden. This room was destined to be a large, modern family kitchen with access to the rear garden. He went back to the plasterboard, nudged it with the toe of his boot, watched pieces fall on to the floor. Hearing heavy footfalls above, he raised his head. 'Mick? *Mick!*'

'Wha'?'

'Baxter's just phoned. He wants the plasterboard down here gone. Get down here and we'll do it.' Picking up grousing, he listened to heavy footfalls starting down the stairs.

Thirty minutes later the plasterboard was gone. The project manager and his mate were eyeing what had been revealed. Mick shook his head.

'Why would anybody want to cover *these* up?'

'I'm asking that same question.' The project manager's hand moved slowly over the smooth, dark wood surface of the double doors which were now revealed. 'You know what this is? It's solid mahogany, mate. Must have cost a packet, even back when this place was built.'

'What do you want done with them?'

'We wait till Baxter gets here. It's his call.'

8.45 a.m.

The dark red Lexus convertible thrummed along Forrest Road, swung in a wide arc spitting gravel and came to a sudden stop outside house number three. One of its doors was thrown open and a man got out, slammed it, headed up the path and into the house. '*Hey!* Where is everybody! *Chop-chop!*' Hearing voices coming from below, he hurried along the hall and down the basement stairs to where the project manager and two of his workers were standing. He followed their gaze to the wall from which the plasterboard had been removed. 'What's all this?'

'Mahogany doors to what looks to be a storage cupboard—'

'You heard what I said. Get *rid*.'

'We thought you might want to see it first. Back in the day it would have cost—'

'I don't care. My wife's set on an ultra-modern kitchen down here, stainless steel two-door fridge-freezer, a range with three ovens, a dishwasher with *drawers*, for God's sake!' He shook his head. 'Know what I took delivery of this morning? A chrome peppermill with a bill for a hundred and five quid! We only ever have black pepper when we eat out!' He looked around the vast room. 'Who knows, she might even do some real cooking down here, once it's finished.' They watched as he headed back to the stairs with a finger-jab for the cupboard doors. 'I'll be in my car, making business calls for the next fifteen minutes while you start ripping that lot out.'

The project manager watched him go then turned to his workmates, his voice low. 'I want these doors removed with zero damage. Got it?' His two workers exchanged glances and set to work, opening both doors with minimal resistance following initial high-pitched shrieks from their hinges. After several minutes the heavy doors had been lifted away, revealing what had once been spacious storage. 'Well done, lads.' He watched as they carried the doors across the room. 'Lean 'em against the wall to the left of the bi-folds— *Careful!* Don't damage 'em.'

One of his colleagues glanced back at him, grinning. 'Got 'em earmarked for something, boss? Half the stuff at your place is from jobs.'

The project manager shrugged. 'Let's say I'm a big fan of recycling.' His attention turned to several shelves now visible inside the cupboard. He went to them, took hold of one. 'These are solid wood – and they slide out, dead easy. I want them as well.'

In a matter of minutes, the shelves had been removed and stacked on end close to the mahogany doors. The project manager's eyes moved over the large, deep space now exposed. 'Baxter needs to instruct us on what he wants done with this.' He approached it, lowering himself on his haunches. 'I'll check if there's any damp inside here.' He knelt before the cupboard, pushing his upper body towards the back of it, feeling light, cool air on his forehead. 'There's a bit of a draught coming from somewhere! A good sign that there's no damp' – he leant further inside, reaching out his hand – 'and there's a bit of movement to this rear wall.' Hs hand appeared. 'Pass me a small hammer.' Taking it, he gave the wall a light tap. 'Would you *believe* it? Sometime in the last hundred years there were cowboys working on this place! Pass me a Stanley knife.' Taking it, upper body straining, he reached further into the space, eyes fixed on the back wall. 'This is just a flimsy fill-in!' The two workers came closer, waiting out several seconds of grunts, low tearing sounds, followed by silence . . .

'What you got, boss? Boss?'

An explosion of flailing limbs scattered them as he scrambled backwards out of the cupboard, all colour gone from his face, coming to a sudden stop several feet away, eyes wide, his hand at his mouth. 'Jesus . . . *Christ*!'

His men exchanged looks, one saying, 'What's up, mate? You don't look too clever—'

'Phone.' The project manager patted his jacket pockets. '*Phone!* Don't just stand there, gawping! Somebody, give me a *phone*!' He snatched at the one handed to him, jabbed numbers, heard words.

'Emergency services. Which—'

'*Police!*'

1 p.m. West Midlands Police Headquarters

Hearing footsteps coming down the stairs, Detective Chief Inspector Steve Thompson smoothed his hair, straightened his tie and assumed a look of confidence mixed with determination. A face to be relied upon. Which about summed him up. Twenty-one years on the job had gone fast. He had enjoyed it. Except for the paperwork. And the hours. He had a reputation as a steady pair of investigative hands. A call had come through two days before from Superintendent Graham Holdsworth of West Midlands Police requesting Thompson take charge of a vehicle-cloning investigation in Small Heath. This was the kind of case Thompson welcomed. According to what Holdsworth had already told him it was a contained scene, namely a large garage lockup with a limited number of potential suspects already known to the police. He was here to get the details so he could get started. He liked jobs which were clear, simple. Both led to quick results. The footsteps on the stairs went past him. He relaxed. He knew other DCIs who regularly worked high-profile investigations, such as homicides and the like. They were welcome to the long hours, the high blood pressure and ulcers that often went with them. He glanced out of a nearby window at terraced houses, the value of which was stratospheric, according to his wife, who made it her business to know these things. The houses, some with Teslas, BMWs and Audis parked on tarmacked front gardens, looked back at him, smug. Thompson lived to the north of the city, which was no quick commute here during rush hours, but he had already spotted a quiet-looking pub just off the High Street where he might have a half lager as he waited for the traffic to slacken. A time to wind down . . .

'Steve!'

He shot to his feet, recognizing Superintendent Holdsworth from past meetings they had both attended. 'Sir!' They shook hands.

Holdsworth indicated the stairs. 'Good to see you again, Steve. Let's have a chat, shall we?' They reached Holdsworth's office. 'Have a seat. We've been landed with an unusual case which needs a safe pair of hands. Which for my money is you. Do you know the Forrest Road/Forrest Park area three, four miles from here?'

Thompson shook his head, trying to figure out from what Holdsworth had said how they connected to inner city car crime in Small Heath.

Seeing his confusion, Holdsworth nodded. 'That car-ringing job is still on but before we get into any of that, I want you to take a quick look at this other case.' He slid a photograph across the desk.

Thompson looked down at a substantial house, probably Victorian, partially obscured from view by trees. Thompson's police officer and property-owner interests suddenly coalesced: the house had been burglarized because of the trees, which would all have been gone if it was his place.

Holdsworth tapped the photograph and told him what builders working on the house had found. 'Human remains, Steve. *Mummified* remains, to be precise.' Holdsworth was eyeing him, waiting for a response.

Maintaining his facial expression, Thompson did a quick, desperate search in his internal lexicon and came up with: 'Interesting,' not liking how this conversation was going.

Holdsworth nodded. 'I knew you would be up for it. It needs a practised eye from you and the pathologist. From what I've been told so far, it sounds historical, say a couple of decades, in which case it'll go straight to our cold case team here and you're on your way to Small Heath and the car-ringing.'

Thompson received these details relating to human remains with growing alarm. 'I'm very keen to get started on that car-ringing, sir—'

'Of course, you are, but first, get over to Forrest Road and see what's happening there. Nobody's living in the house, which is in the process of radical refurbishment, so I'm told.'

Thompson nodded, his mood now hovering somewhere in the vicinity of the floor.

'The builders working there located the remains this morning and Lucia Russo, the pathologist, is already there. I think you know each other from previous jobs?'

Thompson nodded, thinking of the small number of homicides he had investigated, and preferred to forget. 'Homicide' meant hard work, long hours, plus the very real possibility of failure-to-solve. Thompson had no wish to head such an investigation.

Holdsworth was speaking. 'As I said, it sounds to me very much like an historic matter – those houses must date from Victorian times, but for now, I want your eyes on it.'

Thompson was searching his head for anything similar he had worked on. He managed to dredge up one possibility. 'I was the DCI on the Betty Wilson homicide—'

'I know, but this is no "wife-under-the-hydrangeas" job by a husband who fancies being with somebody else.' A second black and white photograph slid towards Thompson of a large cupboard set into a wall, inside it something folded, odd-looking.

Grimacing, leaning away from the image, his eyes moved over a pale, dry-looking shape in a cramped enclosure close to the floor. trying to come up with a reason why, regretfully, he could not be part of this investigation. He suddenly recalled his GP's recent opinion that he required a hernia operation. The doctor had not referred to it as urgent and, given the state of the health service, a date arriving any time soon was unlikely. He would tell Holdsworth it was imminent and pay for it himself.

Opening his mouth, he was beaten to it. 'The remains were discovered in the cellar of the house.' He tapped the photograph. 'It's still in situ, but if you look here' – Holdsworth's thick finger was indicating the pale, dry object; Thompson gave it a brief glance, then away – 'you'll see how well-concealed it is. Any experience of mummified remains, Steve?'

Thompson managed a headshake.

'No. I didn't think so. On the bright side, like I said, they probably date back decades. In which case you're off the hook and on your way to Small Heath.' He stood.

Thompson did the same, looking for a way to emphasize his interest in Small Heath and not finding one.

Holdsworth's focus was still on mummification. 'Good man! I can see your determination to get going on it. As far as I know, Russo has barely started so get over to Forrest Road. You'll find Detective Constables Dean Ashton and Gary Sullivan and PC Naz Sandhu already there. The other two officers I would have sent are both on long-term sick leave.' He raised both hands. 'And before you ask, Steve, I don't have the capacity to replace them.'

Holdsworth was beaming at him. 'Let's keep positive, shall we? If it does turn out to be a modern homicide, there's a possibility I could give you some expert specialist help.' Thompson's mood dropped even further. 'Although she might not be expert on mummification, but let's not jump ahead of ourselves. Get over there, there's a good chap. Have a look at what's happening . . . Oh, and ensure the builders are out of that house and *stay* out.'

Thompson went down the stairs and out of Headquarters, guessing that Holdsworth was already on to the three named officers to tell them that they now had a senior investigative officer. He thought over the conversation, of which he had been a very small part. He pressed his abdomen, seeking a familiar ache, feeling nothing at all. An operation and long-term sick leave might be a welcome alternative for which he was willing to pay. Which itself presented a problem: his wife had booked an expensive cruise for the following year.

TWO

2.15 p.m.

Guided by his satnav, Thompson drove to Forrest Road and was now moving along it, sending quick glances to the row of large, double-fronted detached properties and vigorous trees on his right, to his left an unbroken line of still more trees, beyond which, according to his satnav, was Forrest Park. He slowed, realizing that the road was a dead end. In more ways than one. On a quick three-point turn he parked next to the black pathology vehicle and headed across the road to house number three. Finding the front door open, he went inside and started along the hallway.

'*Hello?*' A sudden flurry of movement, some low voices starting up and a workman appeared from a room at the back of the house.

'Who the hell are *you*?'

In no mood to be messed about, he produced his ID and held it up. '*My* turn. Who are *you*?'

'I'm the project manager on this job and' – he jabbed a thumb in the direction from which he had come – 'my lads are in there having a break.'

Thompson eyed him. 'I'm about to make it an extended break. I want all of you outside *now.* Who else is here?'

The man gestured towards a stairway going downwards. 'A woman went down there but she never said anything to us about having to go outside.'

'Probably because she's not the senior investigative officer. *Out.*'

'Hang *on*! We've got work to do here—'

'I'm the one with work to do, so move it! Nobody's allowed back in here till I say so.' He waited, picking up a muttered 'fascist' as several surly-looking workers appeared, filed past him to the front door and out. He followed them, seeing a squad car arrive and a young, non-uniform officer get out of it. He went to her, trying to recall her name . . . Sand-something. 'You're from Headquarters?'

'Yes, sir. PC Naz Sandhu. I was told to report to DCI Thompson—'

'You've found him. I was expecting two other officers to be here.' He consulted his notebook. 'DCs Ashton and . . . Sullivan. Where are they?'

Sandhu's eyes slid from his. 'Don't know, sir. I was delayed by a childcare issue which Superintendent Holdsworth knows about.'

'Until these other officers arrive, I want you outside this house stopping anybody going in, while I see what's what.'

'Sir!'

He went back inside the house and down the flight of stairs leading to the basement. Reaching it, he took gloves and a mask from his coat pocket and headed across the expanse of space with a glance towards the expensive new kitchen fittings along one wall, and on to the robust shape of Dr Lucia Russo on her knees examining a low area in the recessed wall to his left. They had met on two previous and mercifully straightforward homicides. His spirits rose slightly. Russo was a straight talker with none of that Latin claptrap pathologists usually indulged in. If things did not go as he wanted and he was stuck with this homicide, at least he could expect clear, concise details from Russo, plus what looked to be a neat, contained scene.

Upon this slight rise in mood, he lowered his head and his voice. 'What've we got, Lucia?' He crouched beside her bulk and leant forward, his eyes moving slowly over the recessed area in front of him. 'I can't make out what I'm seeing—'

She activated a forensic light source, flooding the whole space in bright white. He pulled away, wincing. What Holdsworth had shown him was tame when compared to seeing it in person. 'Bloody hell, Luce!'

'I doubt blood is a feature we need to concern ourselves with. Give me a hand up, Steve.'

He did, thinking that at around five-three, a few less pounds might not hurt. He picked up sounds from the upper floor.

She called, 'That you, Oliver?' Quick footsteps coming downwards were followed by the appearance of a thirtyish male with ear studs and tattoos to the backs of both hands.

Thompson gave Oliver Flood a disapproving once-over as he moved over to them and lowered his head. 'Holy *Karumba.* Never seen anything like *this*.'

Russo, bent from the waist, generous rear out, and stretched out her hand towards the huddled shape. She looked back to Thompson. 'There's a draught in here. You'll feel it if you get down—'

'I'll take your word for it.'

'That subtle air circulation has produced what we're now seeing.'

'And we're talking "old", right?' he pushed. 'As in, historic?'

'I seriously doubt it.'

Mood plummeting, Thompson made room for Flood, now masked as Russo handed him the light source. Thompson watched its slow progression over the internal space as Flood whispered, 'Holy *shit.*'

Thompson's eyes were moving slowly over the huddled mound of off-white-to-mid-to-dark-grey something, a sprinkling of what looked to be shed fingernails, a mouth in a rictus shriek, teeth fully exposed. Averting his eyes, he was also seeing long investigative hours ahead, none of which would be anywhere near Small Heath.

Flood murmured, 'I see problems, Doc.'

'Same here,' said Russo. The pathologist glanced at Thompson, wondering how long it would be before he looked at his watch.

Pulling out his phone, Thompson glanced at his watch, then at Russo. 'Holdsworth says he can't assign extra officers to this job, but I'm still hoping he'll find some.'

'To speed up this process? In your dreams, Steve. For evidentiary purposes, what we have here must be brought out very carefully and as fully intact as possible.'

'I'll tell them to be careful. That this is no "bull-in-a-china-shop" set-up—'

'It's not that straightforward. Mummified remains can be extremely friable. Once we get them out of this cupboard, we still have a problem.'

Wishing that he had never heard of Forrest Road, Thompson watched as she took out her phone, scrolled, tapped a number, and waited.

'Hello, *Michael*? Lucia Russo! . . . Yes, you too. Listen, I need your assistance.'

Thompson was picking up her half of the exchange, Latin words here and there, his irritation climbing. He began pacing as Russo continued, 'At this stage, given what is visible, the mummification process looks complete, but I need you to scan it for pre-mortem injuries and . . . You *can*? Thanks, Michael. I am obviously concerned about freeing the remains and transporting them to you with minimal damage so it's going to be a slow process. I'll proceed on a similar basis to that for an incineration case . . . Yes, OK. I'll see you later.'

Call ended, she said, 'Dr Lambert has agreed to wait for us at the Queen Elizabeth Hospital where he's going to conduct a CT scan of the remains.'

And to Flood, she added, 'I need your help with removal and we have two hours to do it.' Seeing Thompson move towards the stairs, she called, 'Steve! As SIO, I need you to stay here whilst we accomplish this move, then accompany us and the remains to the hospital.' She waited, guessing he was trying to estimate the time-scale when he would be finished and on his way home.

He said, 'At least it'll be warmer at the hospital than down here.'

'You should be grateful for the low temperature and the coolness within this cupboard.' She turned to Flood. 'It's time we made a start.'

Thompson headed for the stairs again. 'Give me five to ten minutes. I'll be right back.' He went up the stairs, catching sight of two uniformed officers he assumed to be Ashton and Sullivan hanging around outside the house, chatting to the female police officer. Reaching them, irritation surging, he snapped, 'Where the *hell* have you two been hiding!' He pointed into the house. 'Get yourselves down to the basement and await instructions.'

Within the hour, the remains had been brought slowly to the front of the cupboard, Russo and Flood flushed and perspiring from their efforts, the two officers standing some distance away, arms folded. Moving a light slowly over the remains, Russo said, 'I can't see any indication of active insect life which suggests that the remains are in pretty good shape. The body bags in the van, Oliver – fetch the largest one, please, the one with several handles.' As Flood left, she turned to Thompson who was ending a phone call to his wife. 'We'll transfer the remains to the van. You, me, Oliver,' she indicated Sullivan and Ashton, 'plus these two officers here. During the journey to the hospital, I'll alert Michael. He's arranging assistance for us at that end.' She turned back to the remains. 'OK. Let's take a look at what we have here . . . From what I can see, it appears to be minimally clothed.' She studied what looked to be a small area of pinkish-red, sparkly material. 'The victim appears to have been entertaining when death called.'

Flood returned with the body bag, placed it on the floor and opened it fully. 'I've also brought some linen sheeting in case you want to wrap it prior to it going into the bag.'

'Good thinking. Start the form-filling, please.'

'Will do.' He took out his phone, plus forms from a plastic wallet. 'I'll sort out an identification number.'

Russo studied the remains for several seconds. 'Hopefully, I'm not tempting fate when I say it's going well so far.' She signed the now completed form. 'OK, now I need help to move the remains further forward to the edge of the cupboard – yep, that's fine . . . *slowly* does it. It isn't as heavy as I might have anticipated. A good sign that it's fully dried.'

Thompson experienced a sudden roiling sensation in the pit of his stomach as she and Flood brought the remains out of the cupboard and on to the sheet spread over the open body bag. He crouched close to where the remains had been, his eyes moving over the small space. 'There's something else in there.'

Russo came to him, following his finger-point into the small void. 'I see it. Can you bring it out?'

A quick nod and he reached out his gloved hands and brought out a plastic bag by one of its tied-together handles. He peered inside a tiny gap at the mouth of the bag. 'It looks to be empty but I'll bag it.' He took a brown paper evidence bag from Flood and Russo checked her watch.

'We're not doing too bad, time-wise, but we need to get it up to the ground floor which could take a while.'

Russo moved to the bifold doors at the end of the room and looked out at the damp earth of the rear garden.

'We can't risk removal via those curved stairs. We'll take the remains through these doors and around the side of the house to the van,' she said.

Flood pulled keys from his pocket, heading for the stairs. 'I'll move it so its directly outside the house.'

The remains were transported without incident to the hospital's Imaging Department. Thompson was now pacing the corridor outside the department, having just received a phone call from his wife that she would microwave his dinner when he arrived home. After a further forty minutes the door opened and Russo appeared, beckoning to him. He followed her into the room where a man was seated at a screen.

'This is Dr Michael Lambert,' said Russo, and to Lambert, 'Detective Chief Inspector Steve Thompson, Senior Investigative Officer. What can you tell us, Michael?'

Lambert went to a nearby printer, returning with several printed sheets. 'This is a copy of the CT scan tomography in the form of a 3D image.'

He handed them to Russo who looked at them and passed one to Thompson.

'In my opinion, what we have here are female mummified remains. Given the foetal presentation it is difficult to be precise on height, but age is a little easier: I'm guessing mid-forties from bone density. The remains have been subjected to natural exsiccation – the drying of tissue within a dry, enclosed but ventilated environment.' He pointed to the image and a small, darkened area. 'See this shadow here? It suggests that the deceased had a somewhat enlarged liver at the time of death, possibly indicative of excessive alcohol use.' He moved his finger. 'And here is evidence of skeletal injury. She sustained that injury some time prior to death: a broken right femur, to be exact, partially healed.' He looked at Thompson. 'All clear, so far?'

Thompson nodded, continued writing.

Lambert struck a key on his laptop and a massive wall-mounted screen brightened, displaying a representation of the remains which he laser-pointed. 'Dr Russo has already indicated what look like narrow lines here around the lower legs and here, around the forearms.'

Thompson tilted his head to study the foetal positioning, the legs folded, drawn up close to the chest, the forearms together, hands clasped below the silent shriek of mouth. He diverted his attention to the stark, narrow lines. 'I'm guessing ligatures?'

'Exactly, and if I rotate the 3D image like . . . so . . . see the neck?'

Thompson nodded, now seeing a substantially thicker line.

'Strangulation appears to be the likely cause of death. These ligatures around the arms and legs . . . I can't identify what material they're made of, but given Dr Russo's description of the limited space within which the remains were located, their likely purpose appears to have been to render them as compact as possible.'

The pointer was back at the neck. 'This looks to me to be cord of some kind, possibly pale in colour, of a type used domestically, say to hang pictures. Whoever applied it to the remains meant business but that is all I can tell you without straying into your territory, DCI Thompson.'

'What about identification?' he asked.

'The fractured femur may help with that. As it was not fully healed, my guess is that the deceased received medical treatment for it not long before she died. First chance I get, I'll have it checked against our A and E records. It might take me a while, but if it yields an ID, I shall immediately inform you and Dr Russo.'

Thompson was on the phone to Holdsworth, delivering the information gained from the hospital CT scan. 'We might have an ID for the deceased as it looks like she was treated at the hospital's A and E department, but we'll have to wait on that. The likely cause of death is strangulation. Lambert's estimated timescale fits with Russo's, which is approximately four years ago. The ligatures on the remains and another item located with the remains are now with our forensic department, which is under pressure, but they have agreed to prioritize them.'

'That's probably the best we can hope for right now.' Holdsworth sounded downbeat. A silence formed between them. 'This is complex, Steve.'

'Sir, there's a potentially strong lead found with the remains – an item of clothing, which could yield a label—'

'Yes, and we both know how "strong leads" fail to pan out.'

Thompson said nothing. He understood the tone. Despite officer shortages, or possibly because of them, there was currently significant pressure on policing for results, added to which, the likelihood of media interest was high, which in turn would need handling and come with costs. He waited, sensing a shoe about to drop.

Holdsworth said, 'This is a high-category homicide, Steve, and I want you on it.'

Thompson had been anticipating this. *Goodbye, car-ringing job in Small Heath.*

'But your luck is in, Steve. I talked to the vice chancellor at Central University an hour ago and he's confirmed the specialist help I mentioned earlier, from a professor-researcher who's also a forensic psychology expert, no less.'

'Sounds hopeful, sir,' said Thompson, thinking entirely the opposite.

'Glad you agree. The vice chancellor is very positive about this being a strong source of investigative help.'

Thompson frowned at the second reference to 'help'. Being landed with this investigation was bad enough, a thankless task in the making, without his having to put up with some beardy academic, 'right-on' type hanging around the place, full of enthusiasm and theories which had zero relevance to real-world policing. Once Holdsworth had stopped talking, he would swiftly point out the inherent difficulties of working with civilians.

But Holdsworth was still droning. 'Most investigations don't have that luxury, Steve. Given what we know so far, this homicide appears complex' – Thompson got a sudden vision of long days and no weekends – 'and you're going to need all the help you can get, so. I've taken up the vice chancellor's offer on your behalf. There is a quid pro quo in it for all of us: we stand to get a possible quick arrest, and this researcher-forensic psychologist gets some research data. How's that sound?'

'Like a plan, sir,' said Thompson, staying non-committal, thinking that it sounded like a potential car crash in the making.

'Good man! I've already contacted the VC with a tentative yes, so I'll let him know it's definite. What's your immediate plan?'

Not having anticipated the question, Thompson quickly found one. 'I'm on my way back to the crime scene to make sure it's secure and SOCOs are there.'

An hour later Thompson was at the scene, Holdsworth's reference to academic support still inside his head. His hands pushed deep inside the pockets of his heavy coat, he gazed across at number three Forrest Road, the sun's weak October rays dying on its frontage, leaving it shadowed and unwelcoming. Whoever was spending big money on it was more than welcome to it. Getting vibrations from his phone, he reached into his pocket and pulled it out, his other hand against his ear, blocking the sudden noise of a digger starting up and shouts from builders. It was Holdsworth.

'Just to confirm I've fixed up a meeting at Headquarters tomorrow morning at nine thirty for you to meet Professor Craft.'

Thompson's eyes were now fixed on the sudden arrival of a red car swooping into a space in front of number three.

'That's the name of the researcher-forensic psychologist I told you about.'

Sounding upbeat but not feeling it, Thompson gave a brief response and ended the call, thinking of his daily, manic, early-morning commute over Spaghetti Junction to Headquarters. Now he had another unwelcome possibility to add to the little he knew of this academic. Kraft. German? With a strong accent? He headed across the road to the red car, a man climbing out of it, giving him an irritable look. 'Who are *you*?'

Thompson produced ID. 'I'll ask you the same question.'

'I own this money-pit! I just took a call from one of my idiot builders saying that there's been a serious accident here or something.' He pointed at Thompson. 'Make a note! Whatever happens when the builders are in charge here is *their* responsibility.'

'Mr . . .?'

'Baxter. Brad Baxter.'

'I'll bring you up to speed, Mr Baxter. Your builders have removed plasterboard from the basement—'

'Yeah. yeah, I know all about that. I sanctioned it.'

'Here's something you don't know – behind a flimsy partition were human remains.'

Baxter stared at him, open-mouthed. 'You're having me on!'

'This is now a crime scene. You cannot have access to it—'

'Did you hear what I just *said*? I *own* this bloody place!'

'And I'm the senior investigative officer on what is now a full-scale homicide investigation.' Thompson left him and moved towards the house, Baxter coming after him.

'Hang on! This is a bloody disaster, this is! I don't want the newspapers getting hold of this. If my wife gets to hear about it, she won't move in here! I've got two hundred thousand quid tied up in this refurb which is climbing as the clock ticks and delays are doing nothing to help!'

Reference to the press further reduced Thompson's mood further. 'That's your problem. I'm about to close this site down and' – he pointed to a large police van coming towards them – 'here are the scene of crime officers who'll be thoroughly examining the interior of the whole place.'

Baxter's eyes gleamed. 'What about overnight? There are a lot of pricey fittings inside.'

Thompson eyed him. 'Who do *you* employ for overnight security?'

Baxter's eyes slid away.

'Mr Baxter, I'll be arranging for a couple of officers to be here overnight for one purpose only, which is to protect potential evidence.' He raised a hand to the digger operator then moved it across his throat. The digger noise stopped.

'What about my house! My builders!'

'All stopped, as of now.'

'What! For how long? Delays cost money!'

'Long enough for the scene of crime officers I just mentioned to process the whole place. Possibly longer. My advice to you is to keep what is happening here to yourself. You might have your property back in a few days.'

'A few *days*!'

Thompson was now more than fed up of listening to Baxter's voice and wanted rid of him. 'Who did you buy the house from?'

'I bought it at auction.'

'Who lived in it before you bought it?'

'Not a clue and I don't bloody care.'

'Was an estate agent handling the property when you first got interested in it?'

Irritable, Baxter reached inside his coat, brought out a thick wallet, searched it and handed Thompson a business card. 'This is them. A right bloody shambles, they are. I missed out on buying this place when they were handling it. *I'll* be giving them a ring later.'

Thompson looked down at the local details. 'Like I said, Mr Baxter, I advise against discussing this situation with anybody.'

Baxter turned quickly away. Thompson watched him stride over to his car, get inside, slam the door, drive the length of Forrest Road, turn left and disappear. He was confident that Baxter would not act in any way which might attract attention to recent events here. It would come anyway, given time. Thompson visualized the scene when Baxter's wife finally learned what had happened here four years back and gave her husband hell. It would be worth good money just to see it. He looked again at the estate agent's card, then up at the house. How many houses as pricey as this one stayed vacant all this time? He turned from it. Strictly speaking, it had never been vacant.

Alerted by the sound of a vehicle some distance away, he quickly went along the road to a large van bearing a three-letter logo, a woman, plus two men in baseball caps, getting out of it. One of the men reached into the van and brought out a camera, the other an item covered in light-reflecting foil and placed it on the ground in front of the woman who fluffed her hair and straightened her coat collar.

Thompson reached them. 'This is an active crime scene. Pack that stuff away and leave, *now*.'

The man with the camera said, 'We've got a job to do here. Who are you?'

Thompson brought out ID and got a shrug.

'We came into the road without being stopped—'

'I'm stopping you now,' he snapped, wondering where the hell Sullivan and Ashton were. 'I'm telling you to leave.'

'OK, OK, but now we are here, how about a short statement from you to camera?'

Thompson weighed up his options then relented, guessing that they would be back once he was gone. He gave a short statement of basic details.

The woman turned to the camera again. 'That was Detective Chief Inspector Steve Thompson in charge of the investigation here at . . .' She turned to her colleagues. 'Where are we?' A quick nod. 'The Forrest Park area where gruesome remains have been discovered in a nearby house . . .'

They packed their gear and left, telling Thompson it would be on the nine p.m. local news.

He walked back along the road, absently smoothing his hair, anticipating hoots of laughter from his daughters, and his wife's. 'How many more times, Steve! Check your hair when there's press about!' House number three was coming into view, Ashton standing in front of it.

'Where were you this last half-hour and where's—'

Sullivan appeared from the shadows between the houses. 'I was just having a convenience break, sir.'

'You two's job is monitoring this house and patrolling the road, so get to it!' He walked away from them, checking his watch. So much for the leisurely half pint he had planned. All he wanted to do now right now was put several miles between Forrest Road and himself.

THREE

Thursday 17 October, 8.05 a.m.

Thompson joined the queue in a High Street coffee shop local to Headquarters, ordered an Americano-to-go and glanced around as he waited, his attention caught by pleasant laughter drifting towards him. It was coming from two women who were sitting together. One of them immediately claimed his attention, her short blonde hair in a smooth pixie cut. He knew this only because he had two daughters. The woman herself was very striking, her white teeth in a full smile set off by shiny red lips. He watched her stand, tall and slender, walk towards him and the queue, on her way to the door, almost matching him for height. He did not make a habit of watching women, but this one . . .

'Three twenty-five, *when* you're ready,' said a bored voice. Thompson paid the barista, took his coffee, left the coffee shop and headed to his car.

9.17 a.m., Headquarters

Thompson was inside Holdsworth's office with the three officers assigned to work with him on the Forrest Road investigation, Detective Constables Dean Ashton, Gary Sullivan and Constable Naz Sandhu, all of whom he had met the previous day. Holdsworth was looking irritated. 'As SIO on this investigation, Steve, I appreciate your getting stuck in already, but be mindful of the media. This Forrest Road business was on the news last night and I got on to them this morning to spell it out that there is now *zero* access into Forrest Road for non-residents. Make sure you all take note.' He took a breath, glanced at his watch. 'The investigation is now up and running and the good news for *us* – well, you, Steve – is that Professor Craft is due here any minute. It looks to me like we're going to need that help.'

Thompson nodded, wondering when this feeling had become

mutual. There was a sudden knock on the door. It opened and a uniformed woman leant inside. 'Professor Craft, your nine thirty appointment is here, sir.'

Holdsworth stood. 'I'll come down.' He left his office and they waited in silence.

After a minute or so, Ashton said to Thompson, 'Sir, an officer sent to take over from us phoned at half-seven this morning from Forrest Road, saying that the builders were sitting in their vans at the site, watching them and looking dead narky.'

'I feel their pain,' snapped Thompson, 'and I haven't forgotten that you two were making yourselves scarce last—' The door opened and Holdsworth reappeared, holding it open for a tall, striking-looking woman. Thompson got an immediate jolt of recognition. It was the smiling woman in the coffee shop earlier. There was no sign of a smile now. She was looking down at them, Thompson guessing that behind her face she was highly irritated.

Holdsworth was sounding upbeat. 'Come in, Professor Craft! Have a seat and I'll do some introductions.' She took two steps into the room. Holdsworth held out his hand. 'This is Detective Chief Inspector Steve Thompson, Senior Investigative Officer, and these are his three key officers on this investigation, Detective Constables Dean Ashton and Gary Sullivan, and Constable Naz Sandhu—'

'I understood this to be a meeting with you and DCI Thompson only.' Craft's voice was firm, her tone crisp.

Holdsworth nodded. 'Yes, it was, but I thought it would be a good opportunity for you to meet the team.'

Her eyes moved over them as Holdsworth said, 'Of course, there will be other officers you'll meet in due course.' He turned to those he had introduced. 'This is Professor Teigan Craft of Central University.' He indicated a vacant chair. 'Have a seat, Professor Craft.' After some hesitation, she sat, her facial expression remote, unreadable. 'Professor Craft has worked as a researcher at London University-Goldsmiths and has been called in to assist forces with several high-profile cases in the south-east—'

'Those were paper evaluations,' she snapped. 'I prefer to work alone.'

Holdsworth continued, 'All of which she advised on and brought to a satisfactory conclusion. She is now based here in Birmingham and *extremely* keen to assist on the Forrest Road investigation.'

Thompson's quick glances at her were indicating zero keenness or anything else. Something must have happened since he saw her earlier inside the coffee shop. One thing was obvious to him: she did not want to be here. Or to be a part of what Holdsworth was pushing. In any event, 'paper evaluations' were nowhere close to the direct involvement in homicide investigations which Thompson had been anticipating. His own irritation soared. He already had enough on his plate, with the pushy owner of three Forrest Road and his gang of uncooperative builders, and now he had professional 'help' who did not want to be here and looked like she might leave at any moment. Which suited Thompson. He could do without her and her obvious reluctance. He glanced at the glossy red fingernails of her left hand, the thumb rhythmically tapping each finger. A clear sign, if he needed one, that she was well irritated. He gave her a direct look, the expression on her face suggesting that she might yet refuse further involvement in Holdsworth's plan. He glanced again at the blonde hair, the gleaming black boots, the expensive-looking coat and bag, nudging Sandhu to pull her eyes back into her head. Yes, it was the same woman he had seen earlier, but now with a bad attitude and a personality bypass.

Holdsworth was making the best of the situation. 'Now you are here, Professor Craft, I expect you'll be wanting to talk with DCI Thompson and his team, so how about you go downstairs with them to his office and he will give you the gist of this investigation so far. Then he can—'

She stood, tall and straight. 'I suggest that DCI Thompson email me all of the relevant details.' She reached into her coat pocket, took out a card and held it in Thompson's direction. He took it. 'Once he has done so, I shall want to view the location in which this homicide is believed to have occurred. I shall also want to see the remains. That covers all that needs to be said for now.'

They watched her turn, walk to the door and out, leaving Holdsworth open-mouthed.

On their way out of Headquarters a few minutes later, Sullivan nudged Ashton, his eyes flicking to Sandhu walking ahead. 'That professor looks like she could be a real handful, Ash. I like a woman with brains.'

Ashton pulled out squad car keys. 'You're into women, full stop.'

'Not strictly true. They need to have something about them.'

Ashton reached the car. 'Yeah. A pulse.'

* * *

Thompson was inside his office, blowing on hot, strong coffee, his three officers already on their way to Forrest Road. He glanced across at Dr Russo who had arrived minutes before. 'Have you finished at the scene?'

'More or less. I was there until five a.m., giving that whole area inside the cupboard a thorough examination. I managed to locate the last of the shed fingernails.'

Thompson grimaced.

She pointed to one of two flapjacks in front of her. 'Are you sure you won't have some?'

He shook his head.

'Suit yourself.' Half of one of the flapjacks disappeared into her mouth. After several seconds, she said, 'The scene's all yours. Got a plan?'

'I'll follow the manual.'

Russo smiled to herself. Thompson was not known for his originality.

He swallowed another mouthful of coffee. 'I've met her, this Professor what's-her-name – Craft – and she has to be *the* most unsociable academic I've come across in a long time.'

'That's rather judgemental, based on a single meeting.'

He quickly outlined what had happened. 'I can tell you right now that anybody with the attitude she's got, to come into a meeting of professionals she's never met and perform like she did won't be bothered by other people's views of her.'

'She sounds business-like.'

'I'm hoping she'll process the Forrest Road homicide by way of a paper exercise, which is all she seems to have done to date, write us a report, we'll say "Thanks a lot", she'll get back to her research and whatever else she does and that will be the end of it. If we must have an "expert" I'd prefer somebody who has direct experience of actual homicide investigations. As far as I know, this one has zero experience of the recovery of remains, the teamwork involved, the need to be across the detail as the whole case unfolds . . .' He sat up. 'Which reminds me, I need to get the details together that she asked for . . . make that "demanded".'

Russo grinned. 'I see she's already got you toeing her line. Did you say that you had met her before somewhere?'

'I was in the coffee shop on the High Street and she was there.'

'Which one? There are about eight.'

'That Italian place you like. She was there with another woman, sitting there chatting away, laughing, easy as you like.' He paused. 'She's very attractive.'

Russo gave him a sideways glance. 'That should make for a nice conversation opener when I next see your wife at some police dinner. What did young officer Naz have to say about her?'

'Impressed by her clothes and attitude, about covers it.'

Russo hauled herself to her feet. 'Right. I'm gone. I'll be at the scene for another hour or so.'

'I'll be there, soon as I get the email off to this Craft.'

An hour later Thompson was back inside the basement of three Forrest Road, watching Russo move bright white light slowly one final time over the space where the remains had been. 'Have you heard anything from the hospital on identification?'

'Not yet.'

He pointed at the ceiling and the sounds of steady activity on the first floor. 'SOCOs have nearly finished. They'll be down here soon. I've sent Sandhu to the estate agent who handled this place prior to it being sold by auction to the current owner. It makes no sense to me that if the remains found here are those of whoever once owned this place, no questions were raised by neighbours about what had happened to her. A name means we can access medical records. Right now, I'm waiting for Holdsworth to pull his finger out and get me more officers for house-to-house inquiries along Forrest Road.'

Russo got to her feet, massaging her back with both hands. 'I like listening to a man who's happy in his work.'

'If you find him, let me know. He's welcome to my job on this team.'

PC Sandhu was half a mile away from Forrest Road inside an estate agent's office, looking at photographs of properties she fancied but could never afford. She had requested available information on residents of number three Forrest Road during the last decade and was waiting for the woman dealing with her query to return. Hearing footsteps on the wood floor, she looked up. 'Any luck?'

'Some. The name "Baxter" you mentioned. He came here around twelve months ago to express an interest in purchasing three Forrest Road. There were several other people also expressing interest at the time, but when they saw the amount of internal work needed to fully modernize it, they lost interest. It had been rented out for several years, which was evident from its general condition inside.'

'Do you have contact details for whoever bought it?'

The woman shook her head. 'No.'

'The property went to auction?'

'Yes. I assume that the owner was impatient for a sale. Once it was placed with an auctioneer, our involvement ended.'

'You can't remember who owned it at that time?'

'It wasn't an individual but a property company, for which I have no details.' She handed Sandhu a slim file. 'This is all we still have on the property, just bits and pieces of information. If you find anything of interest, I'll try and chase up more details.' The street door opened. She looked at Sandhu. 'Can I leave you to it?'

Sandhu nodded, taking the file to a nearby desk. After looking at a few pages of miscellaneous information, most of which related to the general area of Forrest Road, she found the first direct reference to house number three. Turning more pages to those dated around six years previously, she stopped at a list of tenants' names. She read on, finding only one reference to a woman's name: Emma Matheson. She looked up and went over to the woman who had provided her with the file.

'Have you found what you were looking for?' she asked.

'Possibly. Does the name Emma Matheson mean anything to you?' Getting a quick headshake, Sandhu pointed to the printed page. 'What about this name?'

The woman looked at it, nodded. 'Yes, Harrison Marsh Investments. It's a London property management company. I remember now – it was involved with the house around the time it was to let, but that's all I can tell you. How about I ask my boss here and, if she knows anything, I'll give you a call.'

Leaving her contact number with the estate agent, Sandhu walking slowly back to her car, phone in hand, absorbing on-screen details of the nearest medical practice. Thinking it was worth a try, she drove directly to it, showed her ID, queried the name and was given confirmation that Emma Matheson of 3 Forrest Road had been a patient. She requested the medical records, completed the relevant form, then drove back to Forrest Road. Getting out of her car, she saw Thompson standing alone, his back to the park entrance, his eyes fixed on the house.

'Sir? I've got a possible ID for a tenant of number three approximately four years ago which seems to fit the remains. According to the estate agent's details she was an Emma Matheson. I've also been to the local medical practice and they're processing my request for her med recs which should confirm who she was.'

His eyes still fixed on the house, Thompson said, 'Good work, Sandhu. When do we get them?'

'In a couple of days, hopefully.'

'Good work,' he repeated.

She eyed him. 'There's more, sir. While I was at the estate agent, I found a reference to a property management company in London: Harrison Marsh Investments. They appear to have had some involvement with the house around the time it was let to various tenants. They might have information about Matheson as a tenant of number three. I've got their phone number.'

'Good. Follow it up.' They turned as a car appeared halfway along the road and silently approached. Thompson's eyes fixed on the immaculate Mini Cooper, all black except for a single white stripe running over its roof, over the bonnet and on to the front grille.

Sandhu watched, open-mouthed then hissed, 'Sir, it's Professor Craft! How cool is *that*. She drives like she dresses.'

'Meaning, badly?'

She eye-rolled. 'You know what I'm saying, sir – *coordinated*.'

'Let's hope we get some coordinated thinking from her on this Emma Matheson homicide.'

The car came to a stop, the driver's door opened and Craft got out, phone in hand, and approached them, red mouth in a wide smile. 'It is good to see you again, DCI Thompson, PC Sandhu! I'd appreciate a tour of the house if that's possible?' She looked across the road and pointed. 'At a guess, *that* one.'

Giving her a barely perceptible nod, Thompson walked with her to the house, his eyes on lounging builders in various parked vehicles tracking them. He shrugged. If Baxter did not have the sense to release his builders for some days of alternative work that was his funeral. Picking up the sounds of vehicle doors opening, several builders getting out, a couple of them approaching, Thompson braced himself, anticipating aggravation. Craft turned and smiled at them.

'Good morning! This is a very brief visit. We promise not to delay you any more than is entirely necessary.' Several of them smiled back at her, the first positive sign Thompson had seen.

He led the way into the house. 'No need to make any promises to that lot,' he snapped as he led the way to the basement stairs. 'My advice, ignore them. I've put a stop to them working while this whole house is being processed and they're not happy.'

Reaching the basement, he indicated the well-built woman gathering up her equipment and placing it in her case. 'This is Dr Lucia Russo, Headquarters' in-house pathologist,' and to Russo with a meaningful look, he added, 'Professor Teigan Craft, Central University, who has agreed to assist with our investigation.'

Russo held out her hand to Craft. Thompson added, 'We now have a possible ID for the remains: Emma Matheson. We're waiting on her medical records.'

Thompson watched Craft take out a small black notebook from the pocket of her coat and write in it. He frowned. What was there to write about so far?

He indicated the recessed area low down in the nearby wall. 'This is where the remains were located.'

Gathering up her long black coat, Craft crouched beside Russo who pointed, saying, 'They were way back there. Those small bits of wood you can see are what is left of an extremely flimsy partition concealing them. SOCOs have processed it, plus this whole basement area.' She took out her phone. 'If you give me your email address, I'll send you a couple of photographs of the victim in situ which will probably help you get a sense of the concealment.' She tapped in the details Craft supplied and sent the photographs to her, hearing a ping signalling their arrival. They watched her study what had been sent.

'Mummified remains?' said Craft. 'I have zero experience of anything like that.'

Ignoring Thompson's second meaningful look, Russo said, 'I've had just one case prior to this and I'm thinking that my professional career is a good deal longer than yours. I would appreciate having all your contact details.'

Thompson watched Craft produce a card from her pocket and hand it to Russo, wondering how many cards this woman carried around with her. They both stood, Craft brushing something invisible to Thompson from the hem of her coat.

He said, 'As soon as the CT scan details arrive, you'll get a copy. I've got some photos here that I took of the remains during recovery.'

Craft reached for his phone, looked at each one. Thompson

pointed out the ligatures. Before he could speak, she said, 'Those were presumably used to secure the limbs in position within this very small space.'

Very slightly heartened by her quick grasp of the situation, he said, 'Our forensic department has the ligatures but you can see here on the limbs—'

'Anything else found?' She handed the phone back.

Vexed at her abruptness, he swiped the screen and pointed. 'This plastic bag in very close proximity to the remains, which suggests it is connected in some way to them. Our forensic department is processing it.' He pointed again at his phone screen. 'See that? The remains were clothed in a short dress, bright in colour.'

Again, she took his phone in her left hand, gazing intently at it. She looked up at him. 'Rather garish, possibly a little dated?'

He shrugged. 'Could be.'

Returning the phone to him again, she walked away, holding out both her arms. 'I must walk through this entire house, this whole scene, as soon as possible, to get a sense of what happened here which ended with this woman's death.'

'The upstairs has been processed by SOCOs. I'll check with them that every ground floor room has been completed and let you know.' He watched her head for the stairs.

She was offhand, but she missed nothing. Maybe he really could have this case wrapped up in no time.

12.25 p.m.

Thompson was outside the house getting loaded glances from various builders, the project manager now heading for him looking riled.

'Listen'– he puffed out his chest – '*I'm* the boss on this project and if my lads aren't working flat out, we'll soon be heading for breach of contract!' He raised his hand and the yellow digger a few yards away started up.

Thompson took out his ID. 'It's *this* which says who the boss is here.' He pointed at the digger operator, shouting above the din, '*You!* Shut that off *now*.' The digger fell silent.

Seeing Thompson head for the house, the project manager shouted after him, 'What's the problem with them working *outside*?'

Thompson turned, seeing two large lorries parking halfway along the road, their engines idling, two of his officers heading in his direction. He shouted, 'Who the hell allowed *them* access?'

'*Sir!*' yelled Ashton. 'They just drove in! We've started the house-to-house, but it's impossible in this racket. I thought you'd stopped all the work?'

'Yes, and I'm about to stop it *again*.'

The project manager squared up to him. 'You can't do that! We're already two weeks behind. If you delay us, we'll be into contract penalties and Baxter will make bloody sure we pay—'

'*Watch* me!' said Thompson, walking away.

'Detective Chief Inspector Thompson!' He turned to see Craft. She was looking tense. 'I have done a superficial tour of the house. I am now leaving.' She turned on a swirl of coat and he watched her head to her car.

He went after her. 'No, no, no, hang on! Just a *minute*! What about your thoughts on this homicide? I want us to do a joint walk-through of the whole place and SOCOs have more-or-less finished—'

She spun to him on another swirl. '*No*. This whole scene, the noise, the shouting, the almost constant friction between you and these men, is making it *impossible* for me to focus in the way I *must*.'

'I'm about to sort it.' He eyed her, seeing how pale she was, and turned to the builders, waving his arms. 'Right! Everybody *stop*! *You!* I said *stop*.' Lorry engine noise and that from the digger stopped. The general tumult died away. Thompson was seeing real animosity on the faces of the project manager and his team. As DCI, he could do without this aggravation.

He looked at his watch. With a bit of soothing and some encouraging words to Craft, he could still do the scene walk-through with her and be finished by six. She was now at her car, looking like she was doing some heavy-duty deep breathing. He went to her. 'OK. Now we can hear ourselves think, let's go inside the house, do the joint walk-through and—'

'I told you I am leaving.' She turned away and got inside her car.

'Wait, Professor! I need to know your thoughts—'

'Not now!' she said, through the half-open window.

Thompson moved closer. 'Hang on! I'm not asking for the "I"s to be dotted and all the rest of it, just your preliminary impressions, what the scene, this whole place, is giving you in terms of this homicide—'

'I have informed you that I need to *leave*.' The window slid closed.

He watched her drive silently away without a glance. He turned to the project manager. '*One* more instance of non-compliance from you, or any of this lot, in the next twenty-four hours and I'll charge you with disregarding a police order!' He scanned the area for DC Ashton, beckoned to him. 'Leave the door-to-door along the rest of the road for today. I want you and Sullivan talking to the residents of four specific houses' – he pointed – 'numbers one, two, four and five. What do they know about a woman named Emma Matheson? Were they on speaking terms with her? What was she like as a neighbour? Did they have problems of any kind with her? Did she have many visitors? Go on, then . . . get *started*.'

DC Sullivan rang the bell of two Forrest Road and waited, quietly humming. He stopped as the door opened, his eyes fixed on a young blonde woman, probably a teenager. He grinned down at her, his hands planted either side of the doorway. 'Afternoon! I'm one of the police officers working in this road, talking to residents about something that's happened at number three.' His eyes moved slowly over her. 'You look a bit on the young side to be the householder.'

She smiled up at him. 'My mum is in the kitchen.'

Letting his arms drop, he stepped inside. 'How about I come in and have a quick word with her?' Following her along the hallway, his eyes fixed on her, swiftly assessing her likely age. He came into the kitchen and a woman working there. She looked up at him, startled. He said, 'Don't mind me, love. I'm part of the police investigation working at the house next door.'

She nodded, smiled. 'How can I help?'

He reached into a top pocket for his notebook. 'Tell you what. If you pop the kettle on, mine's a coffee, two sugars, I'll ask you a few questions and be done in fifteen minutes.'

He was out in twenty, notebook stowed. It had been the waste of time he thought it would be, except for the coffee and cake and the nice chat with the mother. He grinned to himself. A real looker. This investigation was most definitely on the *up*.

FOUR

5.59 p.m.

Coming inside the dark, silent apartment, Craft called softly, 'Percy?' And again. '*Percy?*' More a wish than an expectation. The whole place felt empty. Abandoned. Feeling drained, she closed her eyes as the wall clock chimed the hour. Going to her bedroom, she took off her clothes, let them drop to the floor and pulled on a loose black yoga outfit. Back in the sitting room, she reached for the cream blanket on the sofa, hesitated, let it drop. Going to the baby grand piano in a corner of the room, she sat, taking several deep breaths. Turning to sheet music for *A Little Night Music*, placing her fingers on the keys, she began to play, the action itself and the sounds it was producing soothing her. She played on, her eyes closed, waiting for her heart and her breathing to slow, waiting for the music to do its thing. A sudden, piercing bell-ring from the hallway shredded her head, bringing her hands to her face. She stood, went to the intercom, pressed a button.

A disembodied voice said, 'Let me in, please. My hands are full.'

Pressing the button again, hearing the door-release click, she returned to the piano, placed her fingers on the keys, took a deep breath and resumed her playing, needing the combination of notes to soothe her. The sound of the apartment's front door opening was quickly followed by rhythmic little clicks on wood floor, a voice calling, 'Tig?'

'In here.'

Her mother came into the room, preceded by a small black-brown French bulldog puppy trailing its red lead. Seeing Craft, it ran to her, little tail wagging, his forepaws on the piano stool, trying to reach her. She stopped playing. 'Ah, Per-*cy*,' she said softly. 'Need some help, mmm?' She lifted him on to her lap and stroked him. 'Sshh, you're OK, yes, you *are*.' She kissed the soft fur between his ears. Frowning at the bright light coming into the room, she whispered, 'Close the door, Ma.'

'I need light in here.' Her mother walked to the bay window

carrying a large box, set it down on the dining table, switched on lamps and closed the heavy curtains. 'You should play more often, you know. Particularly your soulmate, Mozart.' In the following silence she moved around the room, switching on more lamps. 'I'm guessing you've had a hard day.'

A statement, not an inquiry. Craft sidestepped it. 'Has Percy been good?'

'Do you remember when you told me you were getting a dog rescued from a puppy farm and I was worried that his early experience might make him difficult?' She smiled, shook her head. 'I got that wrong, didn't I? He's been excellent. We went for *two* walks today, didn't we? Per-*cy*?' The puppy licked her mother's hand. 'And both times he did a *whoops*. He also ate all his lunch, didn't you, sweetie?'

She watched her daughter put him down, her fingers settling on to the keys, the music flowing, faultless, around the room. After several minutes, it stopped. 'Talk to me, Tig. I can tell something has happened.'

Craft's gaze was fixed on the puppy siting on the floor, gazing up at her. Another short silence, then: 'I went to a homicide scene this morning.'

'I see.'

'The whole place, everything was . . . noise and . . . negativity . . . and I needed to focus on what I was seeing and . . . what I was there to do and . . .' She took a breath. 'I could not do it. So . . . I left.' She looked up at her mother. 'I made a terrible mistake, agreeing to be involved with this homicide investigation. I had already decided I would not directly assist the police. I regret changing that decision. What I do, what I want to continue doing, is research, a couple of lectures per week, the occasional paper evaluation of offences – which is doable for me. It's what suits me.' She left the piano and went to the sofa. 'Today, with all the . . . negativity, the noise, it felt like I was about to implode. I had to leave. It's no good, Ma. The more I am part of the investigation, the more they'll judge me! I have had enough of being judged. I don't need more!'

'What does the officer in charge of the case know about you?'

'From the way he was, I would say, nothing.'

'Perhaps you did the right thing by leaving?'

'He would not agree with you. He kept insisting I stay. He wanted my analysis of the crime scene.' She glanced at her mother, then away. 'My head was full of impressions, observations, but I could not give him any of it. Not today. I *had* to leave.'

Her mother laid her hand gently on her arm. 'I get it.' There was a brief silence, marked only by Percy's tiny snores. 'What about tomorrow, mmm? New day?' She watched her daughter's hand with its bright fingernails reach down and gently stroke the puppy's soft belly as he lay, his legs in the air, the fingers of her other hand restless. 'After a good night's sleep, you may feel differently. Or, how about being open with DCI Thompson? Tell him—'

'You do not know my world, Ma, so he would be totally clueless.'

'What I do know is that it's the world you have. The one you trained for over several years, but if you decide that it's an impossible situation for you, that's your decision. You'll sort it, Tig. You're an uber-smart, sensible girl—'

'A thirty-year-old *woman*, Ma—'

'—who agreed with Graham Holdsworth that you would be part of that investigation. He was a good friend of your father's, so if you are saying you are going to break that agreement, you'll need to explain why.'

'*No.* I shall go back tomorrow, give DCI Thompson the information he wants and that will be it. Another paper exercise.' She looked at her mother. '*What* is that delicious smell?'

Her mother stood, pointing to the box she had brought. 'Experience told me this *woman* would be more than ready for home-made Pizza Supreme, followed by her grandmother's recipe for Strawberries Romanoff.' She went to the kitchen, reappearing with plates, dishes and cutlery and placed them on the large dining table. Removing the food from the box, she picked up movement from the direction of the sofa, felt her daughter's arms slide lightly around her waist, almost instantly gone.

'You spoil me, Ma.'

'I know. It works for us both.'

7.50 p.m.

Thompson was staring at the television screen, newspaper unread on his lap as his wife placed a cup of coffee next to him. 'How was your day . . . *Steve*?'

He looked up.

'I asked how your day went.'

He shrugged. 'I'm still getting used to this Headquarters' set-up.'

'Is it solvable, the case? You looked very confident on the news.'

He shrugged again. 'Who knows?' It sounded better than 'who *cares*?'.

'You, presumably. It's your job—'

He let the newspaper drop to the floor. 'I'll tell you what my job is, Mel. It's being handed a four-year-old homicide of a woman nobody knew or cared about and told to sort it, tout-sweet and' – he glanced up as his elder daughter came into the room – 'I'm already feeling the pressure for a result, also tout-sweet.'

His daughter grinned at him. 'The phrase is "tout *de* suite", local TV star! Mum, have you seen my umbrella?'

'No. Take mine, it's in the hall.'

'I'm not carrying an "old lady" umbrella! I want my folding one.'

Thompson gave his wife a vexed glance and said to his daughter, 'What about schoolwork?' He got the usual *ha-ha* response as she left the room. 'If *she* thinks four A levels is a breeze, she can think again, and I don't like the look of that thing she's wearing.'

'If you liked it, she wouldn't be wearing it and she's predicted to get four A stars.' She gave him a close look. 'What's put you in this mood?'

He sighed, resting his head against the back of the chair. 'I've got no problem with investigations that are a "smoking gun" with fingerprints, a few known threats to a victim from an identified source—'

'You want an easy life.'

'What I *want* is a case that's solvable without running myself ragged and into the ground.' He looked at her. 'I like things uncomplicated, Mel. Homicides that are easy to sort, a bit of domestic violence already flagged. That kind of thing is *bish-bash* and finished.'

She reached for her cup. 'Why are you in the police, Steve?'

'I'll tell you what I'm *not* in it for: a tall blonde with a bad attitude who thinks she's God's gift, who wants to call the shots and tell *me* she's off home halfway through the bloody afternoon!'

She stared at him. 'Who on earth are you talking about?'

'A pain-in-the-backside professor of forensic psychology I've been saddled with is who. She wants everything done *her* way but has never been part of an actual investigation.'

'Surely Headquarters wouldn't appoint somebody with no actual experience?'

'I haven't told you the half of it, trust me! My guess, make that *hope*, is she won't be back after today.'

He watched his wife reach for her cup and head for the door, saying, 'I'm going to get my coat on.'

'For what?'

'A film with Mum. I told you about it.'

Five minutes later, he heard the front door close and the sound of her car engine. He reached for the TV remote and started surfing, Craft still a fixture in his head. If she did appear tomorrow, he would have it out with her. Tell her straight that we park our moods before we arrive at work and, once we're there, we absorb the details the crime scene is offering us, and we make deductions from it. What we *don't* do is get upset about noise and people and everything else which is getting on our nerves and storm off like a bloody two-year-old. His coffee cup and saucer slid off the arm of his chair and fell to the floor, the sound it made telling him that they were now two items short of the set.

FIVE

Friday 18 October, 7.45 a.m.

Thompson's attention was on the distinctive black Mini with its single white stripe parked directly ahead as he drove along Forrest Road. He pulled in alongside it. He had stopped off at Headquarters and not had the time to read an email from her, timed at four eleven a.m. Seeing her at the front door of number three, he left his vehicle and headed to it.

'Good morning, DCI Thompson!' The black coat was gone, replaced by a long, cream-coloured Puffa jacket, brown trousers tucked into brown suede boots. 'Two of your officers were here when I arrived and they let me inside. I hope that is all right with you?'

'You're part of this investigation, so yes.'

She led the way towards the rear of the house, Thompson noting how quiet it was compared to the bear garden of the previous day. DC Ashton suddenly appeared some distance away, his hand raised. 'We're in here, sir!'

Entering what looked to be the original kitchen, he found DC Sullivan leaning against a cupboard drinking coffee. Order had replaced builders' chaos. Feeling warmth around his lower legs, Thompson glanced down at a small fan heater. 'Where's all this come from?'

Craft smiled. 'Your investigative team needs somewhere comfortable for breaks and' – she pointed to boxes of quality biscuits, tea bags and coffee – 'a few treats.'

Sullivan said, 'Sir, SOCOs phoned to say they'll email their report to you, soon as.'

'Did they give any details?'

'No.'

Thompson's attention was back on Craft pouring instant coffee.

She turned to him, brows up. 'Three spoons of sugar, black or dried milk?'

'Yes, to the sugar and black.' He took the mug from her. On the way here he had rehearsed what he wanted to say to her after yesterday, the gist of which was that they should pursue their investigative roles separately. He glanced at her. 'Thanks for . . . all this.'

'Did you get my email in response to your request for my impressions of the scene?'

He pulled his smartphone from his pocket and sat on a nearby stool. 'Yes. I haven't had time to read it.' He did so now, interspersed with sips of coffee, seeing aspects in it that echoed his own thinking. Craft had identified the scene itself as 'organized', was indicating the likelihood of a male killer, the possibility that he and the victim were at the least acquainted. She was querying the concealment of the remains within the house, given the existence of a pathway beyond the property's rear fence and its gated access. According to her, the killer had rejected that route as a means of removal of the body based on the likely level of risk of being observed. Thompson had examined that pathway and thought the same.

Aspects he had not yet considered were also here. She was describing the scene and the body concealment as emotionally cool, posing the question: what does concealment of the body in this manner mean for Emma Matheson's killer? followed by two capitalized words: TIME/DISTANCE.

He frowned, not seeing the full relevance of 'time'. He read on. She was also suggesting it was likely that the killer had returned to the house to thoroughly search it. This caused another frown. For what? This place had hardly anything in it. His brows rose. She had picked up on the complete absence of paperwork or any evidence to suggest Emma had once lived at the property, and was suggesting that this indicated the possibility that the killer had removed it, taken it with him.

> One cannot exist without accumulating physical proof of one's own existence. In this homicide a likely low volume of paperwork and belongings enabled the killer to carry evidence of the victim's existence away without attracting attention. Bringing some kind of bag or similar for that purpose is further indication that this homicide was planned. If he and the victim were at the very least acquainted, it suggests that he feared the possibility of a written reference to himself.

He reached Craft's summation.

> The neatness of this scene, the disposition of the body where it has remained undiscovered for possibly four years until found by chance, indicates Emma Matheson's killer to be efficient, organized and of good intellect. Zero frenzy is evidenced. This was not a blitz attack. Not a crime motivated by passion. He arrived and he left without attracting attention so far as is known. He was fully in control of himself and his actions from start to finish. There is also indication of confidence in his behaviour. He is familiar with both the area and the house. Planning and attention to detail are both evident in the treatment of the body in terms of the folding and tying of the limbs. He had to know the house well to be aware of the existence of the basement cupboard. This investigator is sufficiently confident to state that it was he who concealed the remains behind plasterboard. Question: did any of the residents of Forrest Road witness delivery of said plasterboard, or indications of it being installed? My view is that Emma Matheson's killer arranged its delivery. The above analysis suggests that there is nothing about this individual in terms of appearance or behaviour which might alert others to his being a source of threat.

Thompson took a minute or so to absorb all the detail before continuing.

> Question: how did Emma Matheson come to know this individual and how well did she know him? I suspect they shared a history, yet it is unclear whether it was an acquaintanceship, a friendship or something more intimate. However, given the absence of emotion previously referred to, it is unlikely that that connection was one which involved a significant level of intimacy. Emma Matheson allowing him into her home suggests that she was not fearful of him. Subsequent events suggest that she should have been. Question: if Emma Matheson willingly allowed him into her home, this investigation needs to consider his bringing something for her or wanting something from her. Given indications of Matheson's health in life, the possibility is that he brought alcohol to the house. Checks of local sources of supply need to be made. The complete absence of electronic devices in the house also requires exploration via retail outlets and social media for indications of ownership.

Finding his coffee cup refilled, he sipped and continued reading.

> Question: why strangle Emma Matheson from behind? Face-to-face strangulation is an act of domination over a victim. Avoidance of face-to-face contact further supports this investigator's view that Matheson and her killer knew each other and, furthermore, that this homicide was *expedient* for him, not emotionally charged. Further investigation needs to focus on that expediency. It is unlikely that this was his only visit to that house.

Having absorbed the gist so far, Thompson glanced at a final comment, experiencing a tightening in his chest: 'The likelihood is that whoever killed Emma Matheson has killed before and may do so again.'

He looked up at her. 'This is very detailed. How sure are you about this last bit about his being a continuing risk?'

She met his gaze. 'As sure as it is possible to be. Matheson's killer knew what he was doing, what he needed to do, and he did it with confidence.'

'You're saying you know what motivated him?'

'In part, yes. He achieved both time and distance by concealing her remains in that basement. If not for the refurbishment of the house, who can say how long she might have remained there?'

Thompson's mood was taking a sudden dive. His homicide experience to date had been straightforward, no mystery to them. Just the way he liked it. He gave his face a brisk rub, blinked, seeing Ashton about to leave the kitchen. 'Ash! That plasterboard which concealed the cupboard in the basement – take a couple of measurements and visit all DIY places local to Forrest Road. See if any of them recall a similar order during the last, say, five years. Sullivan, you visit *all* local outlets selling alcohol. Find out if Emma Matheson was ever a customer.'

Ashton said, 'I've already got some intel on that plasterboard. The people at number one were no help, they moved in last year, but the people at house number four knew of Matheson, but no personal knowledge beyond describing her as a recluse who rarely left the house. The wife says she went to the house once to invite her round for a cup of tea. All she got was a "no" through the door' – Thompson's face registered irritation – '*but* she also remembered a small truck arriving at number three "a long time back". When I pressed her on it, she said it was around September time, 2019. According to her, the driver offloaded sheets of what her husband described as "wallboard" and took them inside the house.'

Thompson looked up. 'That would have been soon after Matheson's homicide, so we need to know who ordered it and who accepted delivery. Did they notice anything about this truck?'

'Yes. It had local details on it but they can't recall what they were.'

'How come they remembered any of this?'

Ash grinned. 'Their son got married at around that time. I got a lot of wedding details before I could get away.'

'And they never realized that Matheson wasn't around?'

'Not until we showed up.'

Thompson shook his head. 'People, these days! Don't they take any interest in who their neighbours are or what's happening to them?'

Ash shrugged. 'I don't know the people either side of my place. I don't have the time. It's how it is.'

'OK, you and Sullivan, get down to the shopping area closest to Forrest Road. Chase up the plasterboard and the booze. Given what we do know about Matheson, she had to be getting it from somewhere. Report anything useful to me, pronto.'

Sullivan said, 'Sir? I visited number two' – he grinned – 'and got a coffee, cake and some chat from a nice-looking mother and daughter but nothing on this Matheson.'

Thompson stared at him. 'So, nothing *relevant* to report?' He watched Sullivan smirk.

'No, sir, although women like that can brighten anybody's day, yeah?'

Frowning at him, Thompson left the kitchen, glancing at Craft who raised her cup to him, her mouth in a wide, bright smile.

SIX

Later that day Thompson left Holdsworth's office, having updated him on the investigation and current actions. His confirmation that there was little in the way of forensics, that the victim had led a solitary existence. The lack of CCTV coverage in and around Forrest Road had left Holdsworth disgruntled. Thompson headed back to his office, passing the stairs leading down to a document store. He was stopped by a sudden, sharp call of his surname. '*Thompson!*'

Recognizing the voice, he stopped on a swift surge of irritation, followed by an image of Craft forging ahead of him in this investigation. He went back to the stairs. '*Craft!*'

She was staring up at him, her face upbeat. 'Come down here!'

He did, to where she was standing at a table supporting several files. 'Make it snappy. I'm about to leave and I've just been chewed over by Holdsworth.'

She frowned at him. 'What do you mean?'

'Never mind. What do you want?'

Craft was silent for a few seconds, then: 'This is such a difficult case—'

'I always find it useful when somebody tells me something I already know.'

'—because we have no real investigative leads.'

'Funnily enough, I've noticed that as well.'

'So, why are you so irritated?'

Getting no sign that his sarcasm was hitting home, he waited. 'Well? Why did you call me down here?'

She held out both hands, looking around the room. 'This is where all the cold case files are stored. It has given me an idea.'

He waited. Getting nothing more, he said, '*And?* What's this brainwave you've got?'

She frowned. 'I would not term it a "brainwave" exactly, but I believe I can move our investigation forward.' She pointed to several files spread out on the table between them. 'I've been looking through some unsolved cases.' She looked up at him. 'There are quite a lot, you know.'

Her words caused him another surge of irritation.

'A *surprising* number—'

'You don't say.'

'I just did. One or two of them have caught my interest.'

'Is this going somewhere?'

'It is. Earlier today, I went online and looked at a couple of cases where women were attacked in specific areas of the city. One was a series of homicides featuring women attacked from behind. I won't go into detail—'

'Good.'

'—but, in that investigation, *geography* was a huge factor. The killer selected and murdered women in specific areas.'

'I know the case you're on about. He had a thing for sex workers—'

'He did not. His target was *all* women.'

'What's this got to do with Emma Matheson?'

'Geo-profiling. I've designated Emma Matheson's homicide as a "hotspot" in the general area in which she lived and died. What I'm doing here is examining the wider geographical area surrounding her house to see if there is anything interesting – criminologically speaking—'

'Hang on . . .'

'And, although we are not able to date Emma Matheson's homicide exactly, September 2019 seems to me to be a likely, approximate date, given the post-mortem indication that it occurred up to four years ago, yes?' Not waiting for a response, she continued, 'The concealment of her remains inside number three Forrest Road is, according to my phone calculation, one-point-two-five miles from another homicide which occurred in the area of Forrest Park, the entrance to which is almost directly opposite Emma Matheson's house.'

Sensing the ground moving beneath him, he shook his head. 'I'm not about to extend this investigation on your say-so. Where is your evidence for this "connection"? Our job is—'

He watched her push a file towards him, her bright red index nail tapping it. 'Two years and one month ago, council workmen found female remains whilst mowing areas of grassland in Forrest Park. *This,* Thompson, is geo-profiling. It's about location and its meaning for offenders.' She turned the file towards him.

He looked down at a scene sketch map. 'Hang on. This area you're indicating isn't even part of Forrest Park! I've had a look at that area and I wouldn't even class it as a park. It's an undeveloped area of trees which runs from Forrest Road to Mayville Road, Edgbaston, where it . . .'

Craft was sliding towards him an unfolded section of Ordnance Survey map showing the location of Matheson's house, the entrance to the park, and a direct route through it, indicated by red marker pen. His eyes moved along it to a cross also in red, plus two letters: AF.

'There is often insufficient detail to confirm linkage,' she said, 'but what I am suggesting is that those who are aware of this additional open area would simply assume that it *is* part of Forrest Park.'

Thompson was frowning at the two letters. 'What does "AF" stand for?'

'It identifies where the remains of a young woman named Alicia Franks were found' – she pointed again – 'right here, in what you term is an unrelated area' – she moved her finger along – 'which runs on from the park before joining an additional area of parkland running parallel to, but some distance away from, the main road. Alicia went missing in mid-December 2019 and her remains were discovered at the end of January 2020.'

'It looks to me like you're extending Forrest Park to create a link. There's zero similarity between Matheson's homicide in her home, its concealment, and this Alicia—'

'What I am suggesting is based in logic, DCI Thompson. The homicides of Emma Matheson and Alicia Franks are linked by two factors: *geography* and *time.* Alicia Franks died within weeks of

Emma Matheson. No one made the connection because no one knew that Emma Matheson was dead.' She took a typewritten sheet from the file. 'This is Alicia Franks' post-mortem report: she was thirty-two years old when she disappeared in mid-December 2019 and had been on a night out with female friends in Birmingham city centre, following which she reportedly took a taxi home. Whether she did or not remains unclear. She never arrived. A family member reported her missing, but *this* is what you need to look at.'

Craft pushed a second sheet towards him. It was of a type Thompson had seen in homicide cases, depicting two asexual, stylized outlines of the human body, front and back. His eyes fixed on the significant damage indicated to the frontal aspect of Franks' forehead, extending downwards to the cheekbones and nasal cavity, also a written reference to brain injury. He studied the areas of damage, aware of Craft restlessly pacing, muttered words coming to him at a fast rate, emphasizing whatever points she was making with rapid hand movements.

Thompson eyed her. 'I'm *trying* to *think* here.'

She stopped.

He had had zero involvement in the Franks case but it was ringing bells for him. He walked away from Craft, his eyes fixed on countless alphabetized evidence boxes, his hand running over them. He stopped, lifted one down, brought it to the table and dropped it there. 'Alicia Franks. A young woman with a good job and a life. Not a middle-aged alcoholic—'

'I have something else for you.' He watched Craft head to the shelves, returning with a second box. Removing the lid, she searched papers and placed a similar A4 sheet in front of him. 'Alicia Franks was not the only victim within that location. There was another attack there, but on that occasion, the victim survived.' She pointed to a printed name. 'Penny Bristow. Twenty-seven years old when she was attacked in February 2020, just weeks after Franks. Look at *her* injuries, Thompson.'

He reached for the sheet and studied the damage to the head. He looked up at Craft. 'I'm not seeing anything like the injuries inflicted on Franks.'

Craft placed two high-resolution photographs in front of him. 'Look at these. This is Franks, post-mortem' – he grimaced – 'which shows a direct, savage hit to her forehead. *This* one taken of Bristow in hospital shows bruising plus grazing off-centre to her forehead' – she tracked it – 'and on this side of the head, there's a *second* area of more serious injury within her hairline, see?'

'What I'm not seeing is any similarity between these two cases, nor to that of Emma Matheson. What's your point?'

She took a deep breath. 'Proximity. Leaving Matheson to one side for now, these two attacks *are* similar. It is my opinion that Penny Bristow survived for *one* reason only: she was not on a night out when she was attacked. She was returning from her city centre job at around seven p.m. and had not consumed alcohol.' She looked at Thompson. 'I am saying that Penny Bristow was fully alert. She *saw* that first blow coming and she took avoidant action. It probably saved her life.' She waited for Thompson to consider this, adding, '*Two* women subjected to very similar physical attacks in the general proximity of Emma Matheson's home and within a fairly close timescale.'

'I see your point about the attacks on the two young women, but where's the link to Emma Matheson, a reclusive, middle-aged alcoholic?'

'As I've already said, it's about proximity and time. How many female homicide cases have you dealt with in your career?'

She watched him bristle. 'Around five or six. Your point?'

'How many of those were sexually motivated?'

'One. Which doesn't mean I know nothing about sexual homicide.'

'I am not suggesting it does. My purpose in asking is this: when males attack females in the manner indicated by these two cases, how do they go about it?'

'It all depends.'

She sighed. 'What is the usual *direction* of approach?'

'Generally, from behind—'

'*Exactly*, and for two very good reasons. One, it gives said attacker the element of surprise. Two, he avoids the risk of subsequent identification, should the attack fail for some reason, as it did with Penny Bristow. To attack face on, as she and Franks were, is *very* unusual.'

'I see what you're saying, but—'

'Good. Because this offender *wanted* his victims to *see* him.'

He shook his head. 'No, no, that makes no sense. Why would he put himself at such risk?'

'Because there was something he wanted from them.'

'Like what?'

'Direct eye contact. I believe he wanted to *see*, to *experience* their fear.'

Thompson said nothing, then: 'I still don't get your suggestion that there's some kind of link between these two cases and the murder of Emma Matheson. Both were investigated by West Midlands Police.'

'Who had no idea at that time that Emma Matheson was dead inside the basement of her house. These two homicides are about *geography* and *time*. How many killers would you anticipate operating in a relatively small area such as this at the same time? But that is not the only link I am seeing to Matheson. She was strangled. From *behind*. Consider this, Thompson: strangulation is generally motivated by fury towards a victim, say, an intimate partner, sometimes to women in general. It is a form of extreme, face-to-face retribution for what a killer believes are unforgiveable or unacceptable aspects of women and their behaviour. Matheson's homicide was not of that order, plus she and her killer knew each other.'

'Matheson was a recluse. She scarcely had a life. How does she fit that line of thinking?'

'We are back to *location*. Her home, its proximity to Forrest Park and the proximity of these two attacks – yes, I *know* you do not accept it, but what her location and the way in which Matheson was concealed is telling me is that her killer came to her home and she allowed him inside because she *knew* him.' Arms folded, her eyes fixed on his, she said, 'You have read my notes on her homicide and now, if you are prepared to listen, I'll tell you how I think it happened.'

'Carry on.'

'He went to Matheson's house. He knew she had a problem with alcohol. He very likely brought alcohol with him, so why not the means to strangle her also? Now, here is the interesting bit, theoretically speaking, as to why he *chose* to approach her from behind.'

Thompson was now experiencing the full force of Craft's confidence in what she was saying.

'He wanted to *avoid* eye contact whilst he killed her because they had a shared history of some kind. The difference between these three attacks is that there was a pre-existing relationship of some kind between Matheson and her killer, yet nothing of the kind for either Franks or Bristow. *They* were strangers to him.' Her hands on the table, she looked down at the data. 'I can't rule out the possibility that Matheson and her killer may have wanted something from each other.'

Thompson stared at her. 'You saw the house. She *had* nothing.'

He watched Craft pace. She looked up at him, bright-eyed. 'Maybe it was her silence he wanted? Knowing she was alcoholic, perhaps he had started to doubt her trustworthiness, her reliability.'

'All we actually know is that Matheson was likely needy and vulnerable.'

They locked eyes. In the ensuing silence, Craft said, 'I agree. His arrival with a bottle would have ensured him a welcome.'

'This is all theorizing. Where's the proof?' He raised both hands. 'OK, OK, I hear you, but as SIO I have to work from facts, *evidence*.' He took a few steps from her, turned. 'Your experience of homicides is entirely from case papers, right?'

'Plus, years of academic study of forensic psychology. Do you have a problem with that?'

'It means your involvement in an actual, hands-on homicide investigation is very limited.'

'I'm not about to prove my investigative forensic capabilities to anybody, especially somebody I happen to know has worked just five homicides, all of which were singularly straightforward.'

He stared at her. 'You've checked up on me! Sugar-coat it, why don't you?'

'I do not know how to do that.'

'*That,* I believe.' He gave her an irritated look. 'You've checked my investigative history and—'

'It appears I was right to do so, given your obsession with mine.'

He glared at her, turned away, hands in his pockets. 'My advice is don't apply to join the Diplomatic Corp.'

'Whatever that means, my involvement in six of those cases led directly to a correct identification of each killer.'

'According to Holdsworth, there were seven. What happened on the seventh?'

She sighed, looked towards the ceiling. 'When I first became involved in that seventh case, there was no specific suspect at all. I psychologically evaluated each of the individuals referred to by name in the case documentation. The individual I identified was not under any suspicion at the time but was later arrested *and* convicted. I do not regard that case as a "win" because I failed to convince anyone of my suspicions' – she looked steadily at him – 'and another woman lost her life. You're welcome to check what I just said whilst I pursue my theory of a connection between Emma Matheson's homicide and that of Alicia Franks and the attack on Penny Bristow.' She hesitated, looking suddenly very young. 'About yesterday, my leaving Forrest Road so abruptly . . .' She shook her head, turned from him. 'Forget it.'

He watched her head for the stairs. '*Craft?*'

She turned back to him. He came to her, holding out a newspaper cutting from the previous day.

She took it, read the heading, *Killer On The Loose In Forrest Road Area*, and looked up at him. 'Did you brief them?'

He shook his head. 'Not me. The press already knows about Matheson and we have any number of frustrated builders to thank for that.' He took it from her. 'I'm guessing you'll pursue your idea. Just keep me informed, but – and I mean this – be careful.'

Her neat brows came together. 'Meaning what, exactly?'

He eyed her. 'You make hard work of everything! Ninety-nine per cent of women hearing what I just said and knowing the situation as *you've* just described it would immediately get it. If you are right, this killer has a big problem with women. I'll be briefing the media about the need for caution, advising women not to leave themselves vulnerable in the Forrest Park area until there's an arrest. Which includes *you*.'

'Maybe I am the one per cent.'

He watched her go. He had not made a dent in her theorizing. He could not recall meeting anybody like her. Well-informed. Determined. Wilful. Even if he blocked her, he guessed she would do what she wanted. He looked at the case information on the table, pulled it together and returned it to the folder. Pushing the folder back into its box, he stopped, pulled it out again and took it upstairs with him. He needed to think. He needed strong coffee.

Craft was in deep thought, unaware of Thompson coming into the office. She was preoccupied with two women, one of whom had met her death in Forrest Park, the other attacked there and left for dead. Alicia Franks had been the victim of a brutal murder no more than two-thirds of a mile from Emma Matheson's house. What appeared to be chance meetings of Franks and Bristow with their attacker strongly suggested that they were strangers. He had left their belongings untouched. There was no established link between the two young women in life. The only factual links that Craft had identified so far were the similarities of attack and place. Penny Bristow survived. She saw her attacker. According to what Craft had read, he made some kind of verbal overture to her then struck her once, twice on the head. Craft looked down at all she had written so far. What might she predict about this man at this stage? The coolness and planning of Emma Matheson's murder suggested a mature male, yet the nature of the attacks on Alicia Franks and Penny Bristow had the hallmarks of someone younger, impulsive. Was she wrong in thinking that the man Emma Matheson had allowed into her house was significantly older than his twenties – a mature male, strong on planning and intelligence? If this was the same assailant who had attacked Franks and Bristow, how to explain the seeming age disparity and indications of a sudden descent into fury? It was not the only aspect of those two attacks which were causing her confusion. Neither file indicated forensic evidence of sexual attack. She shook her head. 'And that, for me, makes no sense at all.'

'What doesn't?'

She glanced up at Thompson, a phrase her partner Tom sometimes used forming in her head, thinking how much she was missing him.

'Something and nothing.'

SEVEN

Saturday 19 October, 6.30 a.m.

Thompson was on his phone to Sandhu at Headquarters as he shrugged into his coat, taking the energy bar his wife was holding out to him. 'I'm on my way to Forrest Road.'

'We've got Emma's medical records, and Forensics have phoned to say they've got something for us, sir.'

'Yeah? What?'

'They didn't say. Probably above my paygrade.'

Coming inside Headquarters forty minutes later he got a heads-up from the officer on duty. 'Sir, you're wanted by Forensics!'

'Yeah, I know.' He took the stairs to the department and was let inside by Mike Bass, Head of Forensics.

'I've got a couple of items on your Matheson investigation, Steve.'

Thompson followed him to an examination table, watched Bass's gloved hands reach for a large brown paper bag, unseal it and bring out the colourful pink-to-red item found on Matheson's remains. Unfolding it, he placed it carefully on the examination table. It was a dress, heavily mired in places. He looked up at Thompson. 'It's purge fluid which comes from body orifices roughly two to three weeks after death.'

'Thanks for that.' Thompson pointed at the dress. 'I can't get my head around Emma Matheson owning this. The stuff in her wardrobe, such as it was, suggested a "uniform": one or two unravelling jumpers and some ratty-looking leggings.' He looked up at Bass. 'But you're going to tell me otherwise.'

'The predominant DNA I've recovered from it so far is all Emma Matheson's, but I wanted you to know that this dress is a significant anomaly. It is no off-the-peg item, DCI Thompson. Information you've provided about your victim is that at the time of her death she was living in reduced circumstances, yet *this* was an extremely expensive item of clothing when purchased.'

Thompson frowned at it, thinking how gaudy it was.

Bass said, 'I went online to check it out. According to its label, it is a designer item, a Valentino, circa 1990s to the early 2000s, retailing at the time at around five thousand pounds.'

Thompson's head came up. 'For one *dress*?' He shook his head. 'You're having me on!'

'Given the extremely meagre wardrobe you've described, it suggests a monumental decline in her fortunes during the last two decades or so of her life.' He glanced up at Thompson. 'Possibly it was a gift?'

Thompson was weighing up Bass's words, thinking it would not be easy to establish now. He re-tuned to Bass's voice.

'Matheson was wearing this dress when she was attacked and killed. I'm still in the process of testing it for DNA other than hers and have found nothing so far. What I do have are these.'

Thompson looked down at a small glass slide.

'These are hairs. Dog hairs, to be precise. Reddish-brown. Did the victim own a dog?'

'Not to my knowledge. She could barely look after herself.'

'In that case, there's a possibility that her killer is the owner.'

'Which narrows our search down to thousands. Where did you find them?'

'Inside the plastic bag located with her remains. A tidy killer, DCI Thompson.'

'Were there hairs on the dress?'

Bass shook his head. 'There was a complete absence of any hairs on it. Those dog hairs had adhered to an inside corner of the plastic bag. We still need to examine the ligatures found on the remains which will need very careful handling. If we find anything of interest, I'll let you know. The swabs taken from the remains by the pathologist indicate pollen and seeds which suggests a very speculative time of death to be mid to late summer but that is as far as I'll go on that.'

'Have SOCO reported yet?'

Bass reached for a slim document and passed it to him. 'They're known as crime scene investigators to us. I'm guessing that you will welcome the final paragraph.'

Thinking that acronyms in policing changed more often than the weather, Thompson skimmed his way through the detail:

> . . . multiple fingerprints lifted from the property . . . majority identified as Matheson's own via matches with her prints on file for a minor breach of the peace some five years earlier . . . all others run through IDENT1 for potential matches . . .

He turned to the final short paragraph, read a name, plus the offences attributed to it, thinking that this could be the first useful break they had had.

Back in his office, he went directly to his computer, searched the name and absorbed the related details. Seizing his phone, he sent Craft a text: *DO NOT on any account follow up your Forrest Park angle or any other relating to that area until I see you. I'm at Headquarters. Ring me. There has been a development.*

Craft had left her apartment at precisely eight a.m. and driven to Headquarters. With no sign of Thompson, except for his parked vehicle, she went inside and collected copy documents left for her. Back inside her car she absorbed Russo's confirmation that strangulation had been from behind via the use of a strong, off-white ligature. Craft was now convinced that strangling from that position was relevant to Matheson's murder because it was so unusual. She read on that within the folds of the remains a limited amount of pollen and some seeds suggested that death had possibly occurred during mid-to-late summer of the year Matheson was believed to have been killed.

Leaving Headquarters, she drove to Forrest Road and parked close to the entrance to Forrest Park. Getting out of her car into a chill wind, she tucked her trousers inside her glossy black rubber boots, pulled her scarf around her neck and zipped up her jacket. Emma Matheson's one-time home, crime scene tape fluttering, looked bleak. Uninviting. Reaching inside her car, she brought out a small bunch of flowers and headed for the house. Somewhere here there was an officer, possibly two, on guard. Seeing no one, she went to the front door, leant down, gently placing the flowers to one side of it, then straightened, watching cellophane and yellow and white petals quivering in the stiff breeze.

'Hey, *you*!' She turned to see DC Sullivan coming towards her. 'What do you think you're doing?'

'I *know* what I am doing. My job.' Walking away from him and the house, she went back towards the park. He watched her go. He was not fooled by the heater and the biscuits. He had already decided that she was trouble, too clever for her own good. He took out his phone, tapped it and waited.

'It's Sullivan, sir. I've just come on duty. You asked for a heads-up on anybody seen around number three. Craft has just arrived—'

'That's *Professor* Craft.'

'Yeah, her. She's dropped off some flowers at the house and now she's on her way into the park—'

The call ended on a series of expletives from Thompson. Sullivan moved quickly to the park's entrance, in time to see Craft walking briskly some distance away. He soon lost sight of her within the heavy tree cover. She was a good-looking, snappy bitch with a quick mouth, but she interested him.

Craft's motive in coming to the park was to directly explore its geography, given her theory that this large space and Forrest Road bounding it were connected by violence to three women: Emma Matheson, Alicia Franks and Penny Bristow. She needed to find that connection. Excising all thoughts of Thompson from her mind, she gazed around as she walked, revising her opinion of the area. This was not a park in the cultivated sense. More an undulating area of undeveloped land of heavy tree cover and incidental pathways. She walked quickly on, thinking of its typical users: exercise fanatics; runners; extreme cyclists? No, too many trees. Dog walkers? This was not the kind of terrain for Percy. He was too little. She would never find him. She pressed on, thinking this was an ideal day to be here. Conditions were dry. She glanced down at her muddy boots. Mostly. At least it was not raining. Hands deep into the pockets of her down jacket, she followed the path for several minutes, determined to demonstrate her theory to Thompson that the violence inside number three Forrest Road, and the attacks on two women in this expansive area, were connected. Taking out her phone, ignoring the single, flagged text message from him, she looked again at the map she had studied prior to setting out. It told her that she still had some way to go to reach where she wanted to be. She slid the phone back inside her pocket and walked on in dull October cloud, heart rate increasing along with her body temperature. Removing her scarf, pushing it into her coat pocket, she followed the path's steep incline, realizing that she had not seen anyone here since she had begun her walk. It supported her theory that the attacks on two women were perpetrated by an individual who knew this place well and that it was not frequented by many people. If Emma Matheson had had any interest in her geographical surroundings, it might have taken her to her front windows, seeing the entrance to this place looking back at her.

She walked on, the ground rising again. Pausing halfway up the incline, heart thudding in her ears, she picked up very occasional bird whistles and furtive rustlings of unseen creatures hurrying along tiny runs. Rotating her shoulders, she got out her phone and tapped a number. 'Good morning, Naz. Is DCI Thompson there?'

'Hey, Professor Craft. No, he isn't, but I heard he wants to speak to you.'

'When you see him, tell him—' A sharp twig-snap made her flinch, took her eyes to her left. Gripping her phone, she lowered her voice. 'Tell him I'm following up my Forrest Park theory.' Ending the call, she looked in the direction of the sound, seeing no movement but convinced that someone or something was here. Hearing sudden sounds of branches being displaced, seeing only heavy tree cover around her, she brought her breathing under control. Glancing up at gunmetal cloud now darkening the area, she walked quickly on, shoulders prickling. Cresting the steep incline, she glanced behind her, seeing only a press of trees like sentinels. Ahead was open space, a snaking Bristol Road visible in the distance. Still vigilant, she moved quickly downward towards it. Another few minutes and she would be close to where Alicia Franks' remains had been thrown away.

Reaching the spot, she paused, looked down at the ditch, the sharp wind stirring tiny ripples on the water gathered there. Another cautionary check on her surroundings and she knelt, reaching out her hand to it. Was there water here when Alicia was left? *How cold must she have felt . . .* The prickling sensation ran across her shoulders again. Straightening, breathing fast, she headed for the main road and its traffic, thinking over her responses to this place. She had once been criticized by a lecturer during her training for 'allowing a degree of imagination to interfere with her scientific theorizing'. The criticism had upset and angered her. He had tried to placate her by saying that her capacity for 'thinking outside the box' was a significant plus. She had dismissed this, wondering where or how a damned box was relevant.

She took out her phone again, tapped a number and listened as it rang. 'Hello, yes, a taxi, please, to the junction of Bristol Road and' – she read a distant road name now coming into view – 'Lister Avenue. I'll be waiting. Five minutes? Thank you.'

Ending the call, within sight of people and traffic, she evaluated her involuntary skin creep of a short time before. This investigation was difficult enough without creating false attributions. She shook her head. No. Someone *had* been there, his or her movements furtive . . .

Seeing a taxi swoop into a space on the opposite side of the road, she sped to it and climbed inside. Pushing her hands inside her pockets, she frowned. No scarf. She looked out of the window at the park: a distant, unidentifiable figure moving quickly through the trees. She sat back, heart pounding, her fingers tapping both her thumbs to a litany running inside her head: *Alicia-Franks-Penny-Bristow-Alicia-Franks-Penny-Bristow-Emma-Matheson.*

Coming into Headquarters, Craft took the stairs down to the document store and located the box she had searched through a short time ago. Hefting it on to the table, her fingers walked the files for the one she had left here. It was not here. She checked again, left the box where it was, went upstairs and headed to Thompson's office. Pushing open the door, she found him in discussion with Russo, the pathologist, Bass, the Head of Forensics and officers Ashton and Sandhu. They looked up as she came inside, then down to her muddy boots.

'Where is the file on Franks and Bristow?' she demanded of Thompson. 'I need it. *Now.*'

A nod from Thompson and the others stood and silently left the room. He sat back, looking up at her. 'You've missed a discussion on one or two forensic leads, but I'm assuming you got my email about Emma Matheson and one very expensive frock?'

Her impatience surged. 'Yes. I know about that and the dog hairs.'

'You don't know the latest findings? Too busy to read my text message?'

'I was very focused—'

'It said *not* to follow up the Franks-Bristow-Forrest-Park angle.'

Realizing that Sullivan had probably informed him of her movements, she snapped, 'I was already *there*, and now I want that file!'

'By ignoring an order, you put yourself at potential risk.'

She stared at him, recalling her unease inside that park. She would not admit it to him. It would only confirm his view of what she had done and make him angry. Angrier. Craft did not like other people's anger. 'I was fine and I don't take orders—'

'You do, if you're part of my team!'

'I promise I'll read all future communications.'

He said nothing. He was re-evaluating his impressions of her so far. There was something about her, something . . . not young, exactly, something . . . unfinished. A tendency to take things literally. She was looking at him, clear blue eyes wide.

He said, 'We've got two DNA results from Matheson's dress. One which belonged to Matheson, the other to somebody who's a convicted sex offender.' He glanced at his watch. 'He's in the building and I'm interviewing him in five minutes—'

'I *must* be there!'

'DC Ashton is doing the interview with me.'

'No! I *must* be there!'

He stood, looking down at her.

She held his gaze. 'I am as much a part of this investigation as DC Ashton, so that is neither fair nor reasonable.'

He picked up a file from the table. 'In my experience, life rarely is.'

She watched him move to the door. He opened it, then looked back at her. 'Are you with us or not?'

She stood and came to him.

'Now that's sorted, what's with the flowers at Matheson's house?'

He watched as a faint flush came to her face.

She said, 'Emma Matheson had no one to help or support her when she was alive. There is a need to mark her life now that she has gone.'

'Let's hope you haven't drawn more people to what is still an important forensic scene.' He studied her. 'Come with me.'

She followed him out of the office, along the corridor and upstairs to a room with a nameplate on the door: Interview Room 2. Opening it, seeing her move to follow him, he pointed. 'You'll be in there.' She looked to where he was indicating a nearby door. 'Got something to write with?'

She shook her head.

He held out a pen to her. 'There's usually note-taking stuff in there but take that, just in case.'

Craft took it and went inside the room to find a single chair, a trolley supporting a TV monitor and a table on which was a notepad. After a few seconds, the screen leapt to life, showing the interior of Interview Room 2, the camera positioned somewhat above Thompson, his facial expression serious as he entered the room and sat. Ashton appeared and took the chair next to him, both facing two men across the table.

EIGHT

3.05 p.m.

Craft's eyes were fixed on the monitor screen and the well-kempt fortyish male and the tight-lipped dour man sitting next to him.

Thompson said, 'You are local, Mr Lawson, and you're also very familiar with Forrest Road and Forrest Park.'

'In the sense that I know *of* them, yes.'

'A female resident of Forrest Road whose house is situated directly opposite to an entrance to Forrest Park has been murdered.' He did not elaborate further, except to add, 'Does the name Emma Matheson mean anything to you?'

Craft had only a partial view of Lawson's face but she noted a sudden tightening.

'No. It does not.'

Her eyes narrowed at the falsehood.

Thompson said, 'Are you saying you have *zero* knowledge of Emma Matheson?'

'That is correct, yes.'

'You never met her.'

'Correct.'

Thompson took a printed sheet from Ashton, gazed down at it for some seconds, then at Lawson. 'Mr Lawson, I have a serious problem with what you've just said.'

Lawson's response took its time coming. 'I don't see why.'

'Then I'll tell you. Emma Matheson owned a very expensive dress. We have it here, in this building.'

Lawson's eyes moved from Thompson to Ashton and back. 'I have no knowledge of this woman.'

'That dress was found on her remains.'

Craft saw Lawson send a quick glance to his solicitor.

'It has been forensically tested and yielded two samples of DNA. Her DNA, of course. It was her dress. The other DNA belongs to someone else.'

There was a pause, following which Lawson slowly shook his head. 'I still have no idea what you are talking about. I know nothing about this woman, nor any dress.'

Craft was now close to the screen, absorbing every nuance of Lawson's voice and what was visible on his face. The reference to DNA had shaken him. She watched him fold his arms, his face expressionless.

'And I have nothing more to say about it.'

He has all the confidence of a practiced liar anticipating bad news, yet he believes that when it arrives, he can deal with it.

Thompson leant closer to him, his voice even. 'The other DNA on that dress is *yours*, Mr Lawson. What do you say to that?'

Lawson gave a casual shrug. 'I can only surmise that your forensic testing is at fault, that there's been some contamination—'

'Let's not waste each other's time, Dennis!'

Lawson frowned at the use of his first name.

Craft's eyes moved slowly over him, thinking how easy it would be for Lawson to present as a trusted authority figure: manager, lawyer, police officer. Or the college lecturer he once was, according to the information she had from Thompson. Somebody able to present to any female as reliable. Safe.

Thompson's eyes were fixed on him. 'Dennis, I'll remind you that you are under caution and that you have an offence history: three sexual assaults against female students, all of which occurred on college premises, for which you were given a four-year prison sentence, of which you served two. You were released six months ago—'

The young lawyer intervened. 'My client pleaded not guilty to all three charges and—'

'The jury decided otherwise. Following those offences of which you were convicted and your release from prison, you "branched out" geographically and were arrested for the attempted rape of a woman in Forrest Park.'

Lawson shook his head, his lawyer snapping, '*You* are overstepping, DCI Thompson! My client continues to categorically deny those three earlier charges *and* the allegation of attempted rape which was entirely malicious, as indicated by the fact that it *never* saw the inside of a courtroom.'

'I've read the file. In my opinion, it should have done.' Thompson transferred his attention to Lawson. 'I'm trying to think of one single reason why a thirty-five-year-old woman of good character would approach you, a total stranger, in that park and agree to have sex.'

Lawson sighed, shook his head.

Thompson glanced to Ashton. 'Remind Mr Lawson of his original response to that allegation while I try to keep a straight face.'

'DCI *Thompson*!' The lawyer gave him a furious look.

Ashton said, 'According to your statement, Mr Lawson, the woman in question, quote, "approached me, admired my dog, and volunteered that she was there for a little 'sunbathing', at which she removed her T-shirt—"'

'That is *precisely* what happened!' snapped Lawson.

Thompson stared at him. 'Really? If I accept what you just said, which I don't, it's difficult to see how such a calm exchange was followed by that woman stating that she was overpowered by you and forced into attempted sexual intercourse.'

Lawson murmured something to his lawyer, whose gaze shifted to Thompson. 'If you have all the facts available, DCI Thompson, you are fully aware that that woman had no specific injuries when she was physically examined by a police doctor and that she very soon retracted her allegation.'

Thompson was silently seething. He changed direction. 'Our current focus is the death of Emma Matheson.'

Lawson rolled his eyes. 'As I've already *said*—'

'Even without your DNA, your name would have come up sooner or later because you're a convicted sex offender *and* local.'

Craft's attention was fixed on Lawson, knowing that this was an offender who would deny and deny until hell froze, and then deny some more. His sudden stillness told her that he knew where the interview was heading and was very busy evaluating all possible responses.

Thompson's entire focus was on him. 'The most charitable construction I can place on your DNA being on Emma Matheson's dress is that you persuaded a vulnerable woman to have sex with you—'

'I did not!'

'—and I'm not feeling charitable! Not only does it tell me that you had sexual contact with her, it also strongly suggests that you had some involvement in her death.'

Lawson shook his head. 'You have this all wrong.'

Thompson was confident he had not. He had read all the available information on Lawson, whose mother had never accepted his prior convictions and had the financial resources to support and bail him out wherever and whenever possible. 'Evidence is always wrong, according to people like you, Dennis. What *you* got wrong was leaving that dress behind.'

Craft watched Lawson's face, saw the realization that denials were not going to get him out of this room. There was a brief silence. 'OK. We did have sex at her house, which was *entirely* consensual, I'll have you know.'

'With a woman whom we know had a level of dependency on alcohol.' He glanced at Ashton. 'I can't see that going down well with a jury, can you?'

The door opened. They looked up to see Craft in the doorway, pointing at Lawson. 'Mr Lawson, where was Emma Matheson's dress when you last saw it at her house?'

Thompson was on his feet, taking her by her arm, speaking over his shoulder to Ashton. 'Pause the recording!' He took Craft into the corridor and pulled the door shut, keeping his voice low. 'What the *hell* do you think you're *doing*, interrupting a formal interview!'

'Let *go* of my arm!'

He did.

'Lawson had sex with Emma Matheson but I doubt he killed her—'

'Keep your voice *down*. He is in the frame because he's a convicted rapist!'

'You have no direct evidence of physical coercion towards Emma Matheson. I'm saying that in Emma Matheson's case I doubt you can prove rape.' She waited, aware that he was still seething. 'Thompson, I *know* about men like Lawson. They rely on persuasion and cunning and, yes, alcohol or similar, to achieve what they want. Lawson is a despicable human being but he does not strangle his victims and hide their—'

'That's a questionable distinction you're making, Craft.'

'That distinction does not please me, but, in this instance, it has relevance. Emma Matheson's killer strangled her. He tied her up, pushed her body into a space he had pre-prepared. *He* is a planner. Lawson's approach to all females who "fit" his requirements is that of an opportunist.' Craft ran her fingers through her hair. 'Ask him where sex occurred with Emma Matheson at three Forrest Road. Ask him to describe that dress. Ask him if it was removed in his presence. Lastly, ask him what happened to it.'

He watched her return to the observation room and disappear inside.

He went back to the interview. 'A few more questions, Mr Lawson.'

Lawson sighed. 'The tedium of this whole episode was all too briefly alleviated by the arrival of that extremely striking young woman, but now my legal representative is saying that you either charge or release me.'

Thompson eyed him. 'We've got your DNA on her dress, Dennis. Where in that house did sex occur?'

'I did *not* rape her!'

'You're not listening and I think your solicitor is wanting to say something to you.'

Ignoring Thompson, the solicitor moved closer to Lawson, raising his hand to obscure what was being said. Thompson folded his arms and examined the ceiling.

Lawson nodded, looked directly at him. 'I did go to her house like I said, but that was not the only time we met. Purely by chance I saw her walking along the main road towards Forrest Road in very heavy rain and I stopped to give her a lift to where she lived.'

'Very chivalrous. And following that, you had sex with her.'

'Not that day, no. I felt sorry for her because she seemed lonely – a bit down on her luck. She invited me to her house for a drink a couple of evenings later.'

'When was this?'

'I can't remember the date.'

'The month and year will do,' said Thompson, recalling that seeds and pollen had been present on Matheson's remains and the possibility that these had been left on her body around summertime.

Lawson shrugged. 'I'm not certain of the year but I'd say it was around late August or so.'

'You acknowledge that you went to her house and sex occurred between you and Emma Matheson?'

Lawson glanced at his solicitor then nodded. 'I immediately regretted it. Regretted the whole thing. When I arrived, it was obvious she had already had a few drinks and' – he shook his head – 'she had made some effort with herself, done her hair, dressed up, but to be frank she looked pathetic.'

Thompson's dislike of Lawson soared. 'What was she wearing when you arrived?'

Lawson shrugged. 'A short thing which did her no favours, I can tell you.'

'Describe this *thing*, its colour.'

Lawson shrugged again. 'It was a dress. Red is all I remember. Sparkly.'

'Was that item of clothing removed during the time you were there?'

Lawson smirked. 'Mercifully, no. I don't wish to sound unchivalrous about the woman, but you've heard what I've said about her. She was dressed throughout the entire time I was with her. She gave me a couple of drinks, a very nice brandy as far as I recall, and it was all done and dusted within fifteen minutes.'

'Where did sex occur?'

'Downstairs in what looked like a living room. On a sofa. There wasn't much else in there.'

'And you left as soon as you could?'

'Too right, I did. Once I was inside that house it suddenly occurred to me that she had serious financial problems and I didn't want to get involved with that.'

Thompson regarded him with deep dislike. 'I don't suppose you did. Where was this red sparkly dress she was wearing at the time you left the house?'

'As I already said, she was still wearing it.'

'Where was she?'

'Meaning?'

'*Meaning* where was she in the house as you left?'

Lawson shrugged. 'She was in the living room I just told you about. On the sofa. *Alive.*'

Thompson had a sudden thought. 'You owned a dog.'

'What?'

'You said earlier that the woman in Forrest Park admired your dog.'

'So?'

'What is it?'

Lawson eye-rolled to his solicitor. 'It died.'

'When?'

Lawson gave another shrug. 'A few weeks ago.'

'What was it?'

'What do you mean?'

'The breed!' snapped Thompson, seeing the solicitor get to his feet.

'A standard poodle. It was actually my mother's.'

They were back in the office. Craft said, 'Dennis Lawson did not kill Emma Matteson.'

'Because of his gift for spinning a tale? I'm not ready to rule him out.' He looked at her. 'How do you know he didn't?'

'Because I watched and listened to him. Lawson is the type of offender who operates by being initially conversational with his victims, in some cases, for example, with his young students, relying on the subtlety of the grooming process. Lawson is a deplorable individual but he is not psychopathic. Most serial killers are. The individual who killed Matheson also killed Alicia Franks and struck Penny Bristow on her upper face and head.'

He sat upright on his chair. 'We've got nothing so far to connect Lawson to either of those attacks, and forget the "serial" bit because we're talking of just *two* murders.'

She shrugged. 'If that makes you feel better, but you're wrong.'

'I want to talk to Bristow before I make up my mind.'

'I cannot believe that you are *still* doubting that you have a serial offender operating here.'

He looked irritated. 'All I know for certain is that since you got involved in this investigation, I've suddenly got *two* homicides, one serious attack and no clue as to who's responsible.'

Craft shook her head. 'You're telling yourself that the nature of the deaths of Matheson and Franks and the attack on Bristow are all figments of my imagination?'

He gave her a sideways glance. 'Ah! So, you do "do" sarcasm! Just so you know, I've been to see Holdsworth about extra officers I keep requesting on the basis of the number of victims we now have.'

'How many are we getting?'

'None, right now. It's a budgeting problem.'

'So, when?'

'When he decides it's possible.'

Craft stood. 'He does not fully comprehend the situation we have here. I shall inform him that we're dealing with a massive and continuing risk to women posed by this offender—'

'No, you don't! In case it's slipped your mind who the SIO is on this investigation, it's me. *I* deal with Holdsworth and I influence the decisions he makes. I look for evidence. I follow it up. What I don't do is look for complications.'

She pointed at him. 'You already *have* complications! This whole investigation is one massive complication. If you do not understand or accept that, you are going to fail!'

'In that case, *show* me there's a serial killer at work here,' he demanded.

She came back to the table. 'I have given you all the theory that relates to these homicides and the attack on Penny so you know what you are up against here. I *know* the nature of this killer from many prison visits I made when I was training, whereas you seem to think you would simply recognize him for what he is. Forget it, Thompson. This killer has a face he presents to the world which is, in all likelihood, genial, engaging. In reality he is calculating, cold and he could be just about anybody you might come across if you do not know what you are really seeing.'

'Ha! When I'm under pressure on an investigation, the one thing I look forward to is a bit of psychological theory.'

'You never said . . . Oh. I get it.' She turned from him. 'I am leaving.'

He batted his hands. 'I want to hear whatever you've got to say, just keep the psycho-speak to a minimum.'

The door opened and Sandhu cane inside. She halted. 'If this is a private discussion—'

Thompson said, 'Strictly business. Have a seat. Professor Craft is about to give us some psychological theory on serial killers.'

The young officer's face brightening, she took a seat, pulled a notebook from her bag and was now regarding Craft with keen anticipation.

Craft took a few paces then turned to them. 'Serial killers tend to present as cool and unemotional. They also have the capacity to charm as and when required. They are adept at doing what they do. They do not attract attention to themselves. They are very difficult to identify from their daily lives. We know them only by their actions. They are hunters. They seek out the vulnerable and await their opportunity. Along with their perception of vulnerability goes desirability. Attractiveness is, of course, subjective. It depends on what the killer looks for in a victim in terms of age, ethnicity, or some other characteristic known only to him which he values. The two attacks inside Forrest Park suggest it is attractive adult females that interest him. It tells us that he has confidence in his ability to ensnare women who have experience of life. Blonde-haired women in their mid-to-late-twenties are his victims of choice, yet those are not all he looks for.' She went to the whiteboard. 'Serial killers have a significant need to be in control of females. Lack of control means risk – of humiliation and/or rejection. A significant proportion of them do what they do because the identification of a would-be victim, the ensnaring, are significant sources of pleasure.'

PC Sandhu wrote quickly as Craft continued.

'His key interests involve humiliating and punishing females via the use of anger, power-assertiveness and sadistic behaviours. We do not have any direct evidence of a sexual attack on Alicia Franks but we know he caused significant damage to her face, and may have immersed her in water. It is very likely that latter action was his attempt to neutralize any DNA evidence.'

The office door opened and Ashton and Sullivan entered.

Thompson said, 'You're saying you think he struck her, then sexually attacked her?'

'I think it is highly possible. We have a similar situation for Penny Bristow. She survived but made no reference to being sexually attacked. Later, at the hospital and still in a confused state of mind, she referred only to having fallen and hurt herself. Busy hospital staff took her at her word and did not test for evidence of sexual assault.'

Arms folded, Sullivan stared at Sandhu quickly notetaking, then back to Craft.

'The absence of physical or other evidence is not enough to rule out sexual attack. Both women were alone in the evening and within a dark, wooded area so it is very likely that they endured similar attacks. It is extremely likely that in Bristow's case something happened to interrupt the destruction he had previously inflicted on Franks.' She returned to the table. 'Cool, unemotional in relation to his victims, he is also intelligent, in control of himself and physically presentable. We might assume this on the basis that there is no evidence that either woman attempted to flee or were pursued by him. He is also devoid of empathy, unable to feel pity for the young women he attacks or anyone else. He does not care. During one visit to a secure hospital, I met someone exactly like that. He was a power/control killer, extremely brutal towards his victims yet indifferent to his own actions. The killer in our investigation is an ace manipulator, capable of showing charm yet any emotion he demonstrates is extremely shallow. He knows the words which need to be said but does not feel any of the emotions his words might appear to express.' She paused. 'What might seem to be a complication in this killing of Emma Matheson is, in fact, not necessarily so. I have already stated my opinion that she was killed because her killer viewed her death as *expedient* for himself. He wanted her dead for a reason he alone knows.'

The office was silent for some time after Craft left the room. It was broken by Sullivan. 'I don't buy it.' He looked at his fellow officers. 'Sex. These academic types are all the same – obsessed with it.'

Thompson stood. 'What have you two been doing? Anything to report?'

'Questioning the neighbours at the other end of Forrest Road, sir,' said Ashton. 'I spoke to a woman at number ten, but she was a waste of time. She didn't seem to realize there were builders at number three!'

Sullivan said, 'Numbers fourteen and fifteen were also dead losses in terms of knowing anything, but a woman at number twelve was very pleasant and keen to help. She said she would think about it and contact us if she remembered anything, so I gave her my number.' He winked at Sandhu.

Disliking Sullivan's attitude, Thompson said, '*Hey!* You give *Headquarters*' number only, and I don't want to hear your personal observations about potential witnesses, got it!'

Sullivan smirked. 'Just a bit of banter, sir.'

'I don't care what you call it! Cut it out! Whatever usually passes for humour here, one more comment like that and you'll regret it.' He looked at Sullivan and Ashton. 'Is that clear?'

'Sir,' responded both officers.

Thompson stood, gathering his notes. 'I want Professor Craft's case advice on the board typed up—'

'I've made some notes so I'll do it, sir!' Sandhu went quickly to the computer and sat with her back to Sullivan. Thompson placed his own notes beside hers on the desk, shrugged into his coat and left the office.

Sullivan watched the door close on him then nudged Ashton, his voice now a falsetto. 'I'll do it, *sir*, and while I'm about it, if I come and sit on your lap, is there any chance of a—'

'You two are *disgusting*,' snapped Sandhu.

Ashton protested. 'I didn't say anything!'

'You're as bad. You laugh at anything he says!'

She got a chorus of, '*Ooh-er!*' Sensing that Sullivan was approaching her from behind, she flinched as he placed his big hands either side of the computer and whispered into her hair.

'I think you need a little reminder, Naz. We both outrank you, so' – he brought his face closer to her ear – 'keep your mouth *shut*.'

Ashton and Sullivan were long gone as Sandhu went to the printer to collect copies of Craft's investigative advice and placed them inside DCI Thompson's basket, running her fingers over them, thinking, *This is real police work.* Returning to the computer, she saw an email for Professor Craft's attention with a cryptic heading: 'Harrison Marsh', and redirected it to her. Sandhu liked Craft. She was impressed by her knowledge of offenders who committed serious crimes and was keen to be part of this investigation, whereas all Ashton and Sullivan ever did was sneer and make crude jokes.

NINE

5.05 p.m.

Inside her apartment, the email in front of her, Craft dialled the London number, almost immediately ending the call. Unobtainable. She got out her phone, keyed in a search of 'Harrison Marsh Investments, current location' and got a response, including a Birmingham address and phone number. With a quick glance at the time, hoping that this ex-London firm might work on Saturdays, she tapped the number and waited out several rings. Her call was picked up, a female voice delivering a well-practised response. 'Harrison-Marsh-Investments-Executive-Property-Management-how-may-I-help-you?'

Craft gave her name and explained that she was calling on behalf of Detective Chief Inspector Thompson of West Midlands Police. 'My reason for phoning relates to the time Harrison Marsh operated its business in London. DCI Thompson requires a list of your employees during the last ten years, including dates.'

The voice came again, cool now. 'I'm sure you understand that we need to be a little circumspect about responding to requests for company information via the phone.' She continued by stating that upon receipt of a formal request from DCI Thompson, explaining the purpose of his inquiry, the historic information he required would be sent to him. The call ended abruptly. Craft sat, frustrated, wondering why people made everything so complicated. Minutes later she was reading through Harrison Marsh's website information: the highly successful property management company had relocated from London, bringing their years of property letting expertise to Birmingham, 'the UK's second major city'. She tutted, thinking of her partner: 'This is what Tom calls "fluff".' There were brief references to a Richard Harrison and a Phillip Marsh and that was it, apart from a city centre address. Doubting that the woman who had taken her phone call had noted it and, in any event, Craft had not supplied her own name, she now wanted a face-to-face meeting with someone at this company to understand what was happening inside it when it was based in London and Emma Matheson still had a job and a life.

Reaching for her phone again, she tapped the company's number and waited for a response, ended the call when she realized how late it was and of course it was a Saturday after all. She would ring first thing on Monday morning. She spent the next hour and a half making investigative notes on her laptop. An hour later, Craft started awake on the sofa, disorientated, to the sound of the power shower. Sitting up, she saw the silver-coloured suitcase in the hall, heard the shower being turned off and its large, curved door slide smoothly open. '*Tom?*' A tall man appeared from the direction of the bathroom, his hair damp, a towel wrapped around his waist. He raised his hand to her, disappeared into the bedroom, returning almost immediately wearing a towelling robe.

'My flight from Brussels was delayed.' He came to her and held her. She closed her eyes, relishing Tom's warmth, his safety. He whispered, 'I'm glad to be home, Tig. I've missed you. Where's Percy?'

'My mother has him.'

An hour later, she was lying next to Tom in their bed, her head on his chest, his voice thrumming in her ear. 'How's it going, helping police with their inquires?'

She raised her head, looked at him. 'That's a kind of joke, isn't it?' He grinned and she stroked his chest. 'It's going OK. Very busy. It's a big investigation – although I'm not sure DCI Thompson sees it like that, yet.'

'I knew you'd be fine.'

'You always say that, Tom.'

'And I'm invariably right, because I know you, maybe better than you know yourself.' He fell silent, then: 'I've requested a change to my working week and I'm now waiting to see what Paul comes up with.' Paul was Tom's boss. 'I don't want to be away so often.'

'Why not?' She looked up, saw him smile, shake his head.

'Because I want to be with *you*.'

'Really?'

'Yes,' he whispered. 'We're Tig 'n' Tom.'

She sighed. 'That sounds really . . . weird.'

He laughed. 'Sounds great to me.'

'What about your job?'

'I'll transfer to the London office to cut down on the travelling and probably set up a home office in the spare bedroom. I'll still be away but not so often and for less time. What do you think of that?'

'OK.'

'It changes our relationship, Tig.'

'Does it? Why?'

'Because it's time it changed.'

'I do *not* like change. The way things are is . . . exactly how I like them.'

'Most situations change with time, you know.' His voice softened. 'And I think our relationship needs to do that. I want it to, Tig. I want us to be together, living an everyday kind of life. How do you feel about that?'

She sat up, fingers, hands restless. 'I don't see *why*. Everyone knows we are together, even Percy. They *see* us together.' Her words sped up. 'I don't understand this need for change. *Why* is change always good? *I* don't think change *is* good. I don't like it . . .' Breathless, she watched him slide his hand under the pillow and bring out the small box she had seen before – once? twice?

She shook her head. 'Don't open it, Tom! If we don't look at it, everything stays the same and—'

He opened it. She gazed down at the intense blue sapphires flanked by diamonds.

'No, Tom.'

'We've been together a long time. We love each other. We know each other's ways and . . . I understand you, Tig. I want us to get married.'

She drew her knees to her chest and laid her head on them. 'I told you before, it won't work.'

'It's already working.'

'You always see things as easy, Tom. Things are not easy. If we spend more time together, you will see that I am right.'

'I want more time with you, quirky girl.'

She shook her head. 'Think about it, Tom. What about when I

lose it? You know, my "Vesuviuses"?' She listened to his low laugh.

'I don't think you can make that a plural, Tig. It's just "Vesuvius".' He gently placed his hands either side of her face. 'It's just "stuff". Remember when I couldn't find my keys the last time I was here, in a rush and I was going crazy?'

She looked up at him. 'You know that that is different.'

'Yes, it is, but it's not a reason to stop us being together and happy, just as we are now.'

She lay down, looked up at him as he stroked her face.

'We know each other, Tig, and we've loved each other for a long time. We understand each other and we're great together.'

'I don't want children, Tom.'

'I know. You've said.'

'I *won't* change my mind.'

The out-loud words silenced them both.

She looked steadily up at him. 'I mean it.'

He nodded. More silence. 'I can live with that. How about we get "creative" in other ways? Take up some new interests?'

'Like, what?'

'I'm thinking about it. What's your attitude to wild goat herding? *Or* how about nude knitting on skis?' He grinned at her startled look, followed by the sound, the feel of her laughing against his chest.

TEN

Monday 21 October, 7.43 a.m.

Thompson was pacing his office. Following Saturday's interview of Lawson, he knew he could not charge him with Emma Matheson's murder because he had no reliable indication as to when, exactly, she had died. And what else did he have? Nothing. He sat, his attention on two slim files of information on the attacks at Forrest Park. He could see that the Franks-Bristow attacks were connected, yet Craft was insisting on some kind of connection to Matheson's death. That was the bit Thompson did not like. It was a complication he did not want. And, unless new information indicated otherwise, Lawson as a suspect for Matheson was nowhere, due to his claim that sex was consensual. Matheson was now unavailable to refute it and the CPS would not proceed on historical DNA evidence alone. Yes, Craft was hot on theory but what he needed right now was evidence-based leads. He put his head in his hands, already tired, the day hardly started. *She is irritating me. Getting on my nerves with her certainties, her restlessness.* He came up with another word for her: unknowable. He shook his head. That was not right either. She probably had an IQ off the scale but that would not account for why, after several days, he still had no real handle on her. She rarely talked about herself but had referred to a mother. No mention of a father, brothers or sisters. No reference to a private life. He clicked his fingers. He had it. Craft was a clever, spoiled, only child, now adult, with a bad case of her-way-or-no-way.

He opened the files, soon immersed in the details of what had happened to Franks and Bristow. After several minutes' reading he got what Craft had said about proximity. It had solved many a homicide. He looked for the details of Alicia Franks' death, pulled the post-mortem photographs from their envelope, wincing at the damage to the young woman's forehead and lower face. She had stood no chance. Returning the photographs to the envelope, he turned to the information on Penny Bristow, searching it, looking for something specific which had to be here. He stopped, his heart dropping inside his chest. He searched again, still not finding it. Quickly turning to the first page of each file, he checked the names of the SIO for both investigations: Detective Chief Inspector Don Williams. Thompson knew Williams only by reputation. A long-serving officer who had had health problems during his time here at Headquarters. Gossip at the time had it that he was unsympathetic towards female victims of sex crimes and would not go that extra investigative mile where they were concerned. Williams was now dead.

Leaving the table, Thompson made himself hot, strong coffee with plenty of sugar. Did Williams' health problems and his general attitude to sex crimes go some way to explain the glaring omission he had just noted in the Bristow file? He shook his head, still struggling to comprehend such a fundamental absence: Penny Bristow had never been formally interviewed about the attack on her. She had been spoken to very briefly by Williams shortly after her arrival at hospital and a second time prior to her leaving it to return home.

Thompson re-read the brief accounts of both. On that first occasion Bristow had been in and out of consciousness and hospital staff had encouraged Williams to delay his talk with her. Williams' own notes of his second hospital visit indicated that it had taken place thirty minutes prior to Bristow being discharged. Thompson read on. Williams had asked her if she recalled any detail of the attack, to which Bristow had replied, 'Not much. It's mixed up . . . confusing . . . it hurt. He hurt me.' According to Williams, he had then informed Bristow that he would see her again once she was home. Thompson searched for that third time, not finding confirmation that it had ever happened. Nor was it shown in the list of case documents. There was a note that Bristow had come to Headquarters a week after her return home, but had been turned away as no one was available to speak to her.

He felt a sudden rush of anger at Williams' neglect to officially interview Bristow at all. He was obviously not up to the job back then health-wise, nor in terms of his attitude to victims and should not have been SIO on this type of investigation. He pushed the files away, staring at them, drumming his fingers on the table. Reaching for them again, he went through them until he found contact details for Bristow. He checked his watch, frustrated that it was too early for a phone call.

9.58 a.m.

Craft navigated her way around a traffic island, anxieties blossoming inside her head regarding Thompson. She wanted to prove to herself and to him that she could be part of this ongoing investigation, yet was very much aware of the disconnect between them. She had the psychological theory. He was totally focused on physical proof. She braked as an opportunistic van suddenly pushed its way in front of her. Heart now racing, she continued along the busy main road. She had to become more involved in investigative work. Show Thompson and everyone else at Headquarters that she could do it, rather than continue to do solitary paper evaluations. This was make-or-break time. She had to step up and prove herself. Be part of the team. Her anxiety soared. It was not just about the disparity with which each of them approached crime investigation. It was more fundamental than that. It was about being herself. Taking ownership of who, what she was . . . A voice inside her head said, '*See? You can't do it. Don't even try.*' She accelerated past the now-slow-moving van. 'Shut up!'

Craft came inside the city centre offices' modern reception area, across the wall behind the desk the name 'Harrison Marsh Investments' in large gilt letters on a pale grey background. The receptionist looked up, gave her a brief glance, then a double-take at the striking blonde hair and shiny red lips. Producing a professional smile, she said, 'Good *morning.* Can I help you?'

'I am Professor Teigan Craft and I need to speak to Ms Helen Drew. I intended arriving at nine a.m. I apologize for my lateness.'

The receptionist smiled. 'Given the state of traffic and roadworks around the city centre, I'm surprised you're here now.'

'Are you?'

Craft saw her smile again, watched her check her desk diary. 'I don't have any record of an appointment for you with Helen this morning.'

'That is because I don't have one. I obtained Helen Drew's name from your company website.'

The receptionist gave Craft a studied look then, 'Just a moment, please.' She reached for the phone, spoke very quietly into it. Craft waited. She had gone back to the company's website at six a.m. to look at personnel photographs and details. Just one employee fitted her need: Helen Drew was in her late forties.

The receptionist put down the phone. 'If you'd like to take a seat, Professor Craft, Helen won't keep you long.'

Craft headed for one of several bright orange chairs and sat, reaching for one of several glossy, buy-to-rent properties, the purchase prices astronomical to Craft. Focusing on her breathing, fingers tapping, she was thinking how best to manage this imminent meeting and get what she wanted: *How old were you when you started working for Harrison Marsh, Ms Drew? Too direct. Too personal.* She had learned from experience that many women did not like questions about age. Which was idiotic and—

'Professor Craft?' She looked up at a pleasant woman in her late forties or thereabouts who was holding out her hand. Craft stood and took it in hers. 'I'm Helen Drew. Would you like to come with me?'

'Yes, I would.' Craft followed her out of the reception area, the receptionist watching her go, then along a corridor and into a pleasant office of bright, modern furniture and flourishing plants.

Drew said, 'Please, sit down,' indicating a turquoise sofa.

Craft sank on to it. 'Thank you for agreeing to see me.'

Drew smiled. 'I'm just catching up on things this morning before my meetings later. It made sense to see you straightaway. How can I help?'

On a surge of anxiety, Craft took a deep breath and went with her rehearsed story, feeling Drew's eyes on her. 'So, after living in London for a number of years I have recently relocated here and I am interested in an investment opportunity in a worthwhile rental property. In the Forrest Park area of the city.' She stopped, feeling the usual hint of dizziness lying gave her.

Drew smiled, reaching for one of several ring binders on the low table between them. 'I can show you properties which might interest you in the general area of Forrest Park if you can give me an idea of the kind of financial commitment you are considering making. It could narrow our search.'

Flummoxed by a question she had not anticipated, Craft said, 'Yes . . . well, I was thinking . . . I suppose, a few thousand or so – or maybe even . . . many thousands? I'm not too sure . . .'

She watched as Drew closed the binder, her voice cooling now. 'Professor Craft, why are you here?'

Craft felt her anxiety drain away. In her dealings with other people, she was invariably direct, spoke her mind, finding pretence uncomfortable and difficult to do. On a quick surge of relief, she reached for her bag and took out her Headquarters ID. 'I need information about Harrison Marsh when it was based in London.'

'For what purpose?' asked Drew, frowning at the ID.

Craft sat forward, her eyes fixed on the woman opposite her. 'Ms Drew, I'm a forensic psychologist and I'm currently working with the police.'

She saw Drew's eyes widen.

'I apologize for not being direct—'

'My advice, Professor Craft, is not to dissemble. To be frank, you are not very good at it.'

'I know, but if you could give me thirty minutes—'

'Am I also right in thinking that you want information about someone or something connected with this company?'

'Yes.' She looked up as Drew stood.

'The accepted way for making inquiries of any company, including this one, is to explain in writing precisely what is wanted and why. I am not about to divulge *any* information to you without that and I want you to leave. *Now*.'

'*No*. I must talk to you. I shall not leave until I do.'

'In that case, I'm ringing Security.'

Seeing Drew move quickly to her desk and reach for the phone, Craft leapt to her feet.

'*Wait*. The time I'm interested in is many years ago. I need to know about a woman named Emma Matheson.'

Heart pounding, she waited. The phone went down. Drew slowly turned to her.

'Tell me exactly what you want to know and why and I'll decide if I can help you.'

'I'm part of a homicide investigation in relation to Emma Matheson.'

Shock registered on Drew's face; she was evidently unaware of recent media reports. '*Homicide?* What happened to Emma?'

'I'm sorry, I can't divulge specific details beyond Ms Matheson having died a few years ago. Please, I need to know anything you recall about her.'

She watched Drew hesitate. 'What you are asking . . . it was a long time ago when I knew Emma. I need time to think.'

Craft nodded, waited. After a pause of several seconds, Drew motioned Craft to sit and did the same.

'I started working for Harrison Marsh at their London office more than twenty years ago. Prior to joining it, I was keeping myself just about solvent with a lot of temporary work. As soon as I joined the company, I just loved it. The work itself, the people there. I suppose I wasn't very worldly and for me it had an exciting vibe. Buy-to-rent property was in demand and we were all ambitious.' Her smile disappeared. She shook her head. 'I'm guessing that Emma was in her forties when she died?'

Craft said nothing.

Drew sighed. 'It's fortunate we don't know what lies ahead for us. Whatever you think you know about Emma Matheson, when I knew her she was an attractive young woman, good at her job, with a brilliant knack for summing up clients' wants and matching them to properties which suited their requirements. Not only that, she did it in a way that made them think she really cared about their needs rather than her commission. Many of them came back to her over time to buy more properties to add to their portfolios. She was a real force.'

Craft was thinking of her own knowledge of Emma Matheson. The way she had been living at Forrest Road, the way she had died.

Drew was speaking again. 'The problem was the entertaining done with prospective clients. You know, the drinking culture back then. After I'd been at the firm for a couple of years I stayed away from it, but by the time I left I realized that Emma was well into it. We didn't keep in touch. I would have liked to but I knew she wouldn't have been interested. She was a very "of-the-moment" person, you know?'

What Craft was hearing was giving her a new and vital perspective on Matheson. 'To your knowledge, did Emma form relationships? With work colleagues, I mean.'

'I know what you mean, Professor Craft. Yes, she did.' Drew shrugged. 'It's all so long ago, what does it matter? That's where Phillip Marsh comes into the picture. She and Phillip were in a relationship. Neither of them was married and he was quite a few years older than her.'

'Did it continue for long?'

'As far as I know, around two years, which was a long time for Emma.'

'Did she have relationships with other colleagues?'

'I can't answer because I don't know, but it's very possible.'

'Do you know why the relationship with Phillip Marsh ended?'

'Phillip was killed.'

Craft's head came up, her eyes fixing on Drew.

'He left the office one evening at about six p.m., which was unusual for him. He tended to work late and avoid the crush on the Underground. On that specific evening, he changed his routine, headed early to the station which would have been packed at that time, and . . . he fell from the platform into the path of one of the trains.'

Not registering any impact on her face, Craft quickly absorbed Drew's words. She stuck with facts. 'Which station was this?'

'Bank. Our office was a short distance from it.'

'There would have been an investigation?'

'The transport police got involved. Their conclusion was that it was an accident. There was an inquest because Phillip had high blood pressure and it was thought that that might have contributed to what happened to him. The inquest took it into consideration.' She shook her head. 'He was such a kind, generous man. Where is the sense in that?'

Craft was at a loss to know what to say.

Drew continued, 'I look back on it as a great time when I felt really grown-up and successful from just being there.'

By the time Craft left Harrison Marsh, she was thinking of tragedies. Two of them.

ELEVEN

11.40 a.m.

Thompson was inside his office demanding information from Ashton, Sullivan and Sandhu. 'Whatever else you've managed to get from Forrest Road residents, make it worth listening to.' He looked up as the door opened and Craft came inside. He glanced at his watch. '*Evening*.'

Uncertain, she picked up a nudge from Sullivan to Ashton.

Thompson continued. 'This meeting started over half an hour ago. I'm getting an update on the current situation from everybody.' He eyed them. 'Come *on*! Forrest Road residents! What else have you found out? Sandhu?'

She shook her head. 'Nothing useful, sir. Those I spoke to at the far end of the road were mostly unaware that number three was even occupied. There are a lot of trees around those houses.'

'They're aware of it *now*,' snapped Thompson, his eyes sweeping over them. 'They must know from the news that something bad happened inside that house.' He looked to Sandhu again. 'You questioned them, rather than just asking if they knew anything?'

'Yes, sir.' She consulted her notebook. 'I asked several, specific questions I thought might get results – like, had they seen any strangers hanging around the road? Had they experienced any unknown persons knocking on their doors and making inquiries about number three, that kind of thing, but it's a long time ago, sir. I got nothing. It's like Matheson never existed while she lived there.'

He transferred his attention to Sullivan, who was lounging, legs spread. 'Anything?'

'Not a thing. Complete waste of time.' He felt Thompson's eyes on him. 'Sir.'

Thompson's attention settled on Ashton. 'Any residents left to question?'

'No, sir. All spoken to.'

Thompson made a quick note. This was worse than he had anticipated. The door suddenly opened and a tall, heavy-set, mid-thirties man came inside to sudden cheers from Ashton and Sullivan.

'Look who it is!' shouted Sullivan.

The loud welcome caught Craft off-guard. She started as Ashton shouted, 'Data Dave! Bloody hell, where've you been hiding yourself? Cavorting on a beach, somewhere?'

The newcomer grinned. 'What happens on beaches stays on beaches. Hi, Naz.'

Craft absorbed the newcomer's friendliness, the unexpectedly soft voice for such a big man, watched as he headed for a desk in the corner of the room supporting a computer, a printer sitting on a small table to one side. Thompson gestured for Craft to follow as he headed to him and held out his hand.

'DCI Steve Thompson, SIO for the Emma Matheson homicide. I was told to expect you.'

The newcomer took the proffered hand. 'David Brown, data analyst. I've seen the media reports. It sounds complex.'

His eyes straying to Craft, Thompson said, 'This is Professor Teigan Craft who is already assisting us. Leads are thin on the ground, but now you're here' – he gestured to the room – 'welcome to the nerve centre.'

Brown gave him a doubtful look. 'I think there must be some confusion as to why I'm here. I've been brought in to analyse volume crime – burglaries and so forth, for West Midlands Police.'

Thompson looked vexed. 'I assumed . . . Whose idea was that?'

'The chief constable's. Volume crime costs a lot in terms of investigative time, often with poor results. No offence.' Brown pointed to the computer. 'The chief constable's brief is likely to take up most of the time I'm here, but if there is any to spare, I could give you a hand. I studied criminology as part of my degree. I was just about to move this hardware to an upstairs office I've been allocated, but if it's OK with you, I could work from here. I prefer being where the action is.'

'You might regret that offer,' said Thompson.

Brown grinned. 'If I've got the time, it's no problem.'

'Given your criminology background, you could be a big help to us, Mr Brown.'

'It's David. I'll do whatever I can to assist while I'm here.'

About to follow Thompson, Craft said, 'David, I would really appreciate discussing our current homicide investigation with you at some point.' Leaving him to settle in, she went to Thompson and talked through the information she had gathered from her visit to Harrison Marsh.

After listening to her, Thompson slow hand-clapped over Ashton's and Sullivan's voices. 'Listen up! So far, we've focused on the last four years of Emma Matheson's life, which due to her lifestyle, has got us precisely nowhere. That's changed, as of now, to an exploration of Matheson's life when she arrived at three Forrest Road. Professor Craft is about to tell you what she's found out.'

'Hey, Dave!' called Sullivan. 'You'll get a lot from our psychologist to keep you busy, you *lucky* man!'

Thompson gave him a look, then turned to her. 'OK, Craft. Let's have it.'

She looked at each of them. 'Harrison Marsh, the firm Emma Matheson joined in the late nineties, relocated around four years ago from London to a city centre office here in Birmingham. I went there this morning to talk with a Helen Drew who started at the company over twenty years ago. She specifically recalls Emma Matheson from that time, also Phillip Marsh, one of the founding partners of the firm. Both Harrison and Marsh are now deceased, Harrison from natural causes at age eighty-one, and Marsh very suddenly and tragically during the time Drew and Matheson worked at the London office.'

Thompson asked, 'Any more details on that?'

'He fell in front of a Tube train.'

There was a short silence.

Thompson asked, 'How did that come about?'

'He went early to the Tube station which was extremely crowded, a departure from his usual routine, and fell into the path of one of the trains. The incident was investigated by the transport police. There was an inquest. Phillip Marsh was known to have high blood pressure. From what I was told, the consensus was that he passed out on the station platform.'

Thompson turned to Ashton. 'Get on to British Transport Police. I want everything they have on that incident.'

'Long time ago, sir.'

'They should still have records so get moving on it.' He looked to Sullivan. 'Get a copy of Marsh's inquest report from the London Coroner's office.'

'There is something else,' said Craft. 'According to what Drew told me, Phillip Marsh and Emma Matheson were in a relationship at that time. Drew described him as a kind, generous man, which might explain how Matheson came to—'

'—own a frock with a price tag of five grand!' said Thompson. 'Go back to Harrison Marsh. See if you can get anything else out of them.'

Craft shook her head. 'Helen Drew is the only current employee who also worked there at that time.'

Thompson thought about it. 'I still want the other employees questioned. Sandhu? Get the contact details from Professor Craft, then go and have a chat with them. People in offices talk. If the gossip is worth attention, such as Marsh's relationship with Matheson or his death, it could have remained a talking point over the years. They might have information without realizing it.' He looked down at his notes, then up at Sullivan. 'How's it going with questioning the local outlets nearest to Forrest Road?'

'All done. Nothing of interest.'

'Go back there. A follow-up visit often improves people's recall. If you still get nothing, identify retail outlets in the next closest area and do the same there. Yes, Sandhu?'

'You wanted me on the Bristow visit, sir!'

'Change of plan. Professor Craft is on that with me.'

Craft looked at him, then at Sandhu, who glanced away, her face closed.

Thompson was clearly irritated. 'According to what Craft has found out and which is confirmed by my reading of the file, such as it is, Bristow was never properly interviewed at the time of her attack.' He saw glances being exchanged. 'I've contacted Bristow and Craft and I are about to put that right. Sandhu, phone Harrison Marsh, speak to this Helen Drew. Try to get whatever you can out of her.'

* * *

Craft was inside Thompson's vehicle. 'Officer Sandhu is not pleased with your change of plan.'

'I'm not here to please people,' he muttered. 'She'll get over it.' Nothing else was said during most of the journey, which Craft was following on the satnav screen. 'We're almost at Bristow's address and' – she pointed – 'a short distance in that direction is Forrest Park. I'm wondering whether whoever killed Franks and attacked Bristow is local.'

'If he is and he was offending on his own doorstep, he's not the sharpest knife, is he?'

She frowned. 'I've already *told* you that he's intelligent!'

'What's eating you?'

'Officer Sandhu was very keen to do this visit to Bristow and she's upset because you chose me to do it.'

'For the simple reason I want the interviewing expertise you'll have developed as part of your job to obtain sensitive witness information from Bristow.' He pulled quickly into the kerb and pointed. 'That's the house. The one with the yellow front door. We need all we can get from her, meaning anything and everything. The SIO leading the case back then messed up, big time. Having never properly interviewed her, if he wasn't dead, I'd be advising Holdsworth to lodge a formal complaint against him, no matter how long ago it was. But as things stand it's why we're here now. To get that information from her.' He waited. 'What's with the face?'

Craft opened the passenger door. 'It might not be as simple as you appear to think.'

They left the vehicle and walked the path to the bright front door. He rang the bell and they waited. About to ring again, Craft's sudden headshake stopped him. Subtle sounds were now audible from within the house. The door opened a narrow distance, limited by a length of sturdy chain. Thompson held up his ID. 'Miss Bristow? I'm Detective Chief Inspector Steve Thompson.' The gap between door and jamb slowly narrowed, the chain was released and the door opened fully.

Bristow whispered, 'Come in,' and walked from the door.

Exchanging a quick glance with Craft, Thompson led the way inside. It was warm. Very warm. Moving in the direction Bristow had gone, they came into a small sitting room where a gas fire was blazing. Bristow turned to them and Craft saw how pale she was.

Not a vestige of colour. Thompson said, 'Miss Bristow, this is my colleague Professor Teigan Craft. She is a forensic psychologist.'

Bristow did not respond, beyond her eyes moving to Craft.

'Like I said to you on the phone, I'm the senior investigative officer in relation to offences committed within the Forrest Park area, including your experience. We are very grateful to you for agreeing this visit—'

'I told you already – I can't help you,' she whispered.

Thompson nodded. 'Let's see how we go, shall we?'

She turned from them, heading to a door on the other side of the room. 'I'll make some tea.'

Seeing Thompson about to decline, Craft shook her head, whispered, 'Let her do it.'

They sat, Thompson frowning at the fire, unzipping his heavy jacket.

Craft's eyes moved over vigorous indoor plants, then on to the floor and several books lying there, gathering a sense of the woman who lived in this hot, silent house. She inclined her head to read a title: *The Probation Service. Social Science for Probation Officers.* She straightened as Bristow returned with a laden tray.

Thompson went to her, took it from her and carried it to a low table between the two sofas.

She said, 'Thank you,' her voice barely audible.

He regained his seat next to Craft. 'Nice weather we're having today. Quite warm for the time of year.'

Bristow said, 'Is it? I don't go out much.' She handed mugs to them, a slight tremor in her hands.

They sat in silence. Thompson sipped tea, smiled, nodded. 'Very nice. Professor Craft here will tell you I'm picky about my tea.'

This was news to Craft.

Bristow nodded. No smile.

'I explained on the phone why we wanted to talk to you, Miss Bristow. We need you to give us details about what happened at Forrest Park.'

'I'm sorry, but you've had a wasted journey.'

'You were doubtful on the phone but we thought it was worth a visit, a chance to talk to you face-to—'

'I can't help you.' Bristow gazed at him, then away.

Thompson sent Craft a meaningful look.

She said, 'Ms Bristow, we have familiarized ourselves with your situation around three years ago. You worked for the probation service . . .'

'I still do, sort of. I work mostly from here.'

'And you were returning home from work that evening.'

Bristow's eyes were now fixed on Craft.

'You were walking along the road skirting the park. At some point you entered the park.'

Bristow was on her feet, unsteady, one hand at her chest, her face slick with perspiration. 'No, *please*—'

Thompson shot up.

Craft whispered, 'Do *not* touch her. Sit. Be quiet.'

He watched her get up and move slowly, closer to Bristow, her voice low. 'May I call you Penny? . . . You're safe, Penny. Breathe slowly . . . slowly . . . that's good . . . really good.'

Bristow clutched Craft's outstretched hand.

'I want you to listen to my voice and breathe as I count . . . one . . . two . . . three . . . four . . . five . . . six . . . That's really good. Well done.'

Thompson watched as Craft led her back to the sofa where she sat, her face paler than when they arrived, dark shadows now visible beneath her eyes.

Craft kept her voice low, knowing from her training but also from direct personal experience what was happening to this woman. 'How long have you been having panic attacks, Penny?'

Bristow swallowed, pushed her hair from around her face. 'It started soon after . . . what happened . . . in that place,' she whispered.

'That's understandable, yet still a long time ago.'

Bristow nodded. 'I was referred to someone about it ages ago. He talked to me and suggested hypnosis. I didn't want to do it, but I thought it might help me . . . but it was no good. He said I was "resistant".' Her eyes filled. 'I don't want to live my life like *this.* I really tried, but I just could not let go.'

'I understand,' said Craft quietly. 'Letting go feels like losing control, which in itself is frightening.'

Bristow looked at her and whispered, 'That's exactly what it felt like. I think he was annoyed that I was wasting his time, but I just could not do it.'

'And you've been having panic attacks fairly often ever since?'

Bristow nodded, bowed her head and sobbed.

Craft's eyes went to Thompson, giving him a direct look.

He nodded. 'Miss Bristow? Penny, I can see you are probably not up to this meeting right now. How about I phone you in a day or so to arrange to see you again and—?'

'It's no good! I can't tell you anything about what happened. It's all, just . . . gone and . . . I don't know which is worse – remembering or not remembering. All I know is I can't do it!'

Craft stood, held out her hand. 'It's OK, Penny. We hear you.'

Bristow took Craft's hand in hers. 'All I can tell you is that I was on the road which runs alongside that place and it was a really quiet evening and I just carried on walking, my mind on work and' – she shook her head – 'it's like a curtain suddenly drops and . . . I can't recall anything else. I just don't have the memory . . . the words.'

They left the house and were sitting inside Thompson's vehicle. He said, 'That was awful to hear. Good job you were there. I wouldn't have had a clue what to say to her.' He looked across at Craft. 'Our only living witness is of no use.' He rubbed his eyes, blinked. 'Whoever attacked her, I'd like to punch out his lights. I'm also starting to think there's not a hope of us finding him.'

Craft turned to him. 'We don't give up on Penny Bristow. She is a key witness. I have an idea.'

'You're saying you're going to get her talking?'

'We both know I can't do that. I'm too involved in this investigation. If it ever gets as far as a court hearing, I run the risk of being accused of witness interference.'

Thompson waited. 'Too right. So, where do we go from here?'

'I think I know someone who might be able to help us.'

'You heard her. She doesn't want to know.'

'I also heard that she is extremely unhappy about how she is currently living. It sounds to me like no life, which is something she does not deserve.'

They were back at Headquarters. Craft dropped her bag on the table. 'From what you've told me, the officer who headed the Bristow investigation was seriously incompetent.'

'He was ill—'

'I don't care what construction is put on it, he had a job to do and he did not do it. If he knew he was not up to the job, he should have admitted it and let the investigation go to someone else.'

Thompson leant against the table, his focus on the floor. 'Craft, I get the impression that everything in your world is simple, explainable, right or wrong, but people aren't always that straightforward.'

Craft eyed him, thinking, *Yes, I know that.* She watched as he reached for a file, a sudden thought occurring to her: had this Don Williams been a friend of Thompson's? If that was the case, he still needed to hear what she had to say. 'If Penny Bristow had been properly and sensitively interviewed at that time, it's very possible she would have been able to divulge at least some of her experience and this whole case might have been resolved.'

'You don't know that for certain.'

'It's a professional guess.'

Leafing through the file, Thompson stopped at two photographs of Bristow. He tapped them. 'We know what was done to her. The first blow was intended as a strike at her forehead, but it glanced off and' – he pointed to lines of text – 'according to the medic who examined her at the hospital, in his opinion the second blow to her temple was a fast, hefty backhander.' He shook his head. 'I'm thinking brain damage here and no amount of talking to Bristow is going to help us if that's the case.'

Craft's thinking was focused on how Penny Bristow became a victim of the attack. If there had been some kind of verbal engagement between her and her attacker, it might yield leads, yet only Penny knew what had occurred. Craft said, 'What would your response be if you were out one evening and made some innocuous verbal overture to a female and—?'

'It wouldn't happen. I've got teenage daughters and I don't go around making "overtures" to women.'

She nodded. 'I'm thinking that if he spoke to Penny Bristow as a first attempt at engagement, it's highly likely she would have rebuffed him in some way. So, what does he do? Does he walk away? No. Why not?' She turned to Thompson. 'I suspect that *any* refusal by a female to an overture from him, no matter the words or how they were said, would be construed by him as female judgement and rejection. It is *that* which infuriates him. Whoever he is, he is a timebomb where women are concerned.'

Thompson could not think of anything constructive to say. 'Coffee?'

'Please.'

He began organizing it, watching her with her phone, thumbs

moving fast. Craft knew him well enough now to understand that he was not always entirely welcoming of direct statements of psychological theory.

His own phone pinged. He took it out of his pocket, read the few words: *This is a man quick to perceive female rejection. When he does, no matter how it is expressed, even by so much as a look, he erupts in a frenzy of rage and physical violence.*

She saw him read it, then bring coffee to the table.

'Anything to add?' he asked.

'Yes. He had zero empathy for Bristow. His focus was entirely on his own response, his fury at what he saw as her dismissal of him. I read a simple, chilling statement once, I don't recall its origin, but it sums up Alicia's and Penny's situation at the time: "Offend a psychopath and you unleash his potential to destroy the world".'

'How does that fit with Emma Matheson's murder?'

'It does not.'

'You're now saying they're not connected?'

'No. I'm repeating what I've said all along: Emma Matheson had an entirely different meaning for whoever killed her.'

'Where does that get us?'

'Nowhere, until we know the nature of his relationship with Matheson. Which is making me reconsider his age now. If he knew Matheson, if they shared a history, he could be into his late forties now.'

Thompson sighed. 'I've got this feeling that we're on a fast journey to nowhere.'

'No, no, you are wrong. We are learning about him through small, incremental details.'

'We'd better get a shift on, then.' He gave her a direct look. 'I don't think you get it, Craft. For me, Matheson is no theoretical exercise. The minute her remains were found, she became *my* responsibility. If *I* don't get answers, I can see this investigation going stone cold and all three cases ending up in the basement here.'

After a short silence, she shook her head. 'Psychology will save us.'

He looked at her, losing the slight smile when he realized she was deadly serious. 'Any *actual* ideas as to what we do so that happens?'

'I'll give it some consideration.'

He sighed, shook his head. 'Yeah, you do that, and make it quick because I'm already finding this case stressful and exhausting.'

'How odd,' she said quietly. 'I find complex homicide an interesting distraction. At times a de-stressor.'

He stared at her. 'Somehow, that doesn't surprise me.' After a brief hesitation, he asked, 'What do you do when you're not working, Craft?'

'I read current psychological research papers, textbooks and accounts of police homicide investigations because it is important to stay updated. It is also my fascination.'

'I should have guessed.' He reached for his lunch in a grease-stained paper bag, then looked at Craft, a sandwich on a paper towel in front of her. 'What've you got today?'

'Feta cheese and gherkin.'

'You always have that.'

'Only on three days of the week.'

'What about the other two?'

'Smoked salmon.'

She watched him open the bag, remove a golden-brown square of flaky pastry and bite into it, a meaty smell drifting over to her.

Wiping his fingers on a paper towel, he watched her with her phone. 'Who are you calling?'

'Someone I know who might be able to assist us with Penny Bristow's difficulties of recall. *Damn!* I *hate* answering machines.'

At home that evening, Craft was on the phone, finally talking to the professional she considered ideal to work with Penny Bristow. 'Lydia, if you can help us, she sustained blows to the forehead and right temple in an attack, but I'm hopeful that in the right environment, she could recall at least some details of what happened to her. If you agree to help, and she reveals something relevant to our investigation, we have a chance of stopping this killer before there are further victims.' She paused. 'Which I am sure there will be.'

Craft listened to the voice in her ear and frowned. 'You're saying you can't help us?'

Tom leant into the room, pointing at his watch. She nodded to him.

'Lydia, I heard what you just said, but I have witnessed zero indication of brain damage. The DCI and I spent over an hour with her and I observed nothing which even suggested it. She attended well and there was no indication of difficulties focusing on or processing our conversation. She also made us nice tea . . .' Craft paused. 'I know I'm straying into your area of expertise, Lydia, but my opinion of what I heard and observed is psychological resistance to trauma. *Please* agree to see her. She is our best – currently our only – chance of identifying this monster.' She listened. 'You'll think about it? Oh, Lydia, that's great! I would do it myself but that would risk accusations of witness influence.' She nodded. 'I'll let you know as soon as I can if she'd be interested in meeting with you. Thank you so much.'

TWELVE

Tuesday 22 October, 8.30 a.m.

The first image Craft got as she came into the office was Sullivan sitting on the edge of the table, his legs spread, facing Sandhu. Maintaining his position, he glanced up at Craft. She felt an instant rush of anger. *Any male with one iota of self- and other- awareness does not do that.* Ignoring him, she asked Sandhu if Thompson had arrived.

'Pass,' said Sullivan, his eyes fixed on Sandhu. Craft headed for the kettle. Filling it, she heard him say, 'Mine's a heaped instant with three sugars!' Hearing movement, Craft turned to see Sandhu coming towards her looking flustered.

'I'll make myself a coffee when you're done.'

'No problem. How do you take it?' Craft added instant coffee to a mug, glancing to Sullivan then back to the young officer. 'Are you OK?' she said to Sandhu.

'Yeah. No problem.'

The door opened and Thompson came into the office, followed by Ashton in full flow. 'And if you ask me, it's money straight down the drain for some waste-of-space alco.'

'Zip it!' snapped Thompson, several slim bunches of flowers in his hands. Craft recognizing hers among them. He dropped them on to the table. 'Anybody want these?' Not waiting for a response, he said, 'Sullivan! Make yourself useful and take this lot to the squad room. See if anybody there wants them.' To Craft, he added, 'You started a trend at Forrest Road. We've now got the residents leaving floral tributes for a woman few of them bothered about when she was alive, plus people who don't even live in that road bringing them.'

'I am glad but also surprised that it has happened.'

'They probably feel guilty about ignoring Matheson while she was alive, *or* they know there's a chance of being on the telly. I had one of the uniforms take the rest of the flowers to the nearest hospital. We can do without number three being flagged a crime scene.' He headed for the kettle. 'I'm gasping for a coffee.' He selected a mug, rinsed it in the sink. 'The press is now well on to this investigation. I've got officers confining them to the end of Forrest Road behind a barrier so you keep it zipped whenever you're anywhere near there, got it?'

There were murmurs of 'sir'.

'And that applies when you're anywhere outside this building.' He began issuing specific orders to them.

Craft listened to what she recognized as by-the-book, basic investigative moves, her mood lightening as the door opened and David Brown came inside. She raised her hand to him and he came to her. She kept her voice low. 'David? I need to talk to you if you have time?'

He put down his bag. 'Not a problem.'

'Actually, I need to make a phone call first. It won't take long.' Taking out her phone, she tapped the number and waited. 'Penny? This is Dr Teigan Craft. We met . . . yes, that's right. I want you to know that I have contacted a colleague of mine who is a clinical psychologist. Her name is Dr Lydia Wadham. She is very knowledgeable about memory disturbance and she might be able to meet with you to see if she can help.' Craft nodded. 'I know Lydia well. She is patient, she does not judge and she is also understanding and very experienced. How do you feel about seeing her?' She smiled, nodded. 'I appreciate you're agreeing. No. Lydia would not ask you directly about what happened. What she would do is show you how to relax, give yourself a chance to recall in your own time.' Craft listened, then shook her head. 'No, Penny, there are no expectations on you from us at Headquarters, nor from Lydia. It is a "Let's try this and see how we go" situation.' She paused, then added, 'It might help you to get your life back on track. Do you know the location of the clinic – it's on the same site as the main hospital.' Craft paused, listened. 'Penny, I would be happy to be with you but given my current involvement in the police investigation it's best I don't do that. Do you have someone who might go with you?' A quick nod. 'Your sister would be fine. I'll let Dr Wadham know.' She ended the call, looked up to see David Brown's eyes on her. 'Apologies for keeping you waiting. I needed to make that call.'

'No problem.'

She went to where he was now sitting. 'If the young woman I just spoke to is able to talk about the attack on her in Forrest Park, we may yet get a quick resolution of this investigation.'

'That's really good news. I can see how hard you are all working.'

She ran her fingers through her hair, seeing Sullivan coming back through the door. 'Yes, and if she remains resistant to recall—'

'Still more hard work?'

'My fear is that we'll have more victims.'

He sighed. 'I get what you're saying. The physical destruction of people is appalling. What else do you want to talk to me about?'

'Stopping him. The killer. My difficulty is deciding on the best approach. Do you know anything about rational choice theory relating to decision-making?'

'A little, but are you sure he *is* rational?'

She thought how light and pleasant his voice was for a large man. 'I am sure. His behaviour indicates so. The crime scenes show that he is an individual fully in control and extremely capable of weighing up potential consequences for himself. I'm considering his approach to a potential victim to be "How easy or difficult for *me* is an attack on *her* in *this* place?". He wants it to be easy, plus safe and rewarding for himself, so he does what is effectively a cost-benefit analysis.'

Brown's eyebrows rose. 'He sounds like every police officer's nightmare. So calculating. I assume that there must be some serious pathology within him.'

Craft nodded. 'And he is still fully rational according to his own needs. That area of parkland provides him with the very targets he seeks – young, lone women seeking a shortcut. He is there, watching them, waiting and then, he strikes – *B-dum!*'

Brown looked startled.

Craft said, 'You must recognize that sound . . . from a much-loved TV subscription service?'

Listening, Thompson rolled his eyes.

She said, 'Could you give us some analytical assistance, David?'

He looked doubtful. 'My brief here is very specific: analyse burglaries and street robberies and advise on ways to reduce them without causing tensions in local areas. Once that's finished, I'm gone.'

Downcast, Craft nodded. 'I understand.'

'But what I could do, if it's any use, is listen to how the investigation is shaping up, the kind of data that you and the DCI consider relevant, discuss any theories and make some general observations?'

She smiled, held out her hand.

He grinned and took it in his, saying, 'Deal! Keep me informed how it's going. I've got an office upstairs I'm not using. It's probably quieter up there.'

Thompson glanced at them. *Bloody academics. They need a discussion to decide the best place to talk.*

Craft's next words followed him out of the room. 'What really interests me in this investigation, David, is whether this killer engaged with his victims sufficiently to speak to them.'

'As it's a homicide investigation, it seems to me that that's unknowable.'

'We have a victim who survived.'

'Really? Well – that changes the situation somewhat.'

'We're hoping she might be able to tell us of any verbal exchanges which occurred between her and her attacker.'

He glanced at his watch. 'Sorry, I need to get started, but, like I said, I'm up for discussing any theories.' He paused. 'Here is a question for you. Given your forensic knowledge and my degree background in criminology, how long do you think it will take for us to disagree and not be on speaking terms?'

Seeing her startled facial expression, he grinned again. 'That was a joke. Not a very good one.'

She looked confused. 'Oh . . . OK.'

'Working with the police on homicide investigations must be very challenging and stressful.'

'It is, but I have every confidence we'll bring this investigation to a satisfactory conclusion.'

'Are you always so positive?'

'I'm confident that the rational choice theory I mentioned earlier might be helpful because I suspect that both geography and proximity are very relevant to the homicides and the attack which left a woman damaged.' She saw him hesitate.

He said, 'I have to say that in my experience, geography and proximity often do co-occur without any significance at all.'

Craft gave this some thought. 'I hear what you're saying, but I'm talking about geographical profiling as a way of understanding the offender, by establishing the *meaning* of geography and proximity for him personally.'

'I'm still struggling to see a single common theme.'

Craft's brows rose. 'How about the victims are all women?'

He sighed. 'Now you know the low theoretical point I'm coming from.'

'I'm also very interested in victim type. What is it about a victim which grabs this killer's attention? Matheson was some years older, reclusive, alcoholic, not in the best of health. The other two victims were worlds away: young, healthy, employed, with families and all the social involvement typical of their age.'

He shook his head. 'From my admittedly limited perspective on what I've heard so far, I have to say that I doubt a link.'

Craft looked away. 'I understand, but I see "difference" more in terms of the victims' relevance, their meaning for him. Geography is *fact*. Crime scenes are *fact*. The differences in the Forrest Park attacks and that at the Forrest Road house is telling me that this killer *knew* Emma Matheson, possibly for some years prior to her becoming alcohol-dependent and socially isolated.'

There was a short silence. Brown chose his words. 'Any ideas as to his motive?'

She gave it some thought. 'It's possible Emma Matheson knew something about him and he had to silence her, but . . . I could be wrong.'

He laughed. 'Now *that's* refreshing! My observations of psychological profilers from the courses at various headquarters I've worked at suggests most have a modesty by-pass.'

The office door flew open and Thompson leant inside, pointing at Craft. 'Car park! *Now.*'

Sullivan watched her go then turned his attention to Brown. 'You might do well to reconsider hooking up with that one and giving her help.'

'Oh? Why is that?'

'She's trouble.'

'She seems very pleasant to me.'

Sullivan eyed him. 'I'm telling you, get involved with her and you'll regret it. She's hard work and if you do come up with good ideas, she'll take the credit.' His eyes fixed on Sullivan, Brown stood, reached for his backpack, lifted it on to his worktable. 'Thanks, but I prefer to make my own judgements.'

Sullivan shrugged. 'Your decision, your funeral, mate.'

THIRTEEN

Outside in the car park, Craft sent Thompson an irritated glance. 'I was discussing the investigation with David Brown, and I *hate* being interrupted and having my focus broken because it causes me significant discomfort – and *why* is Sullivan not censured for his attitude to—?'

'There's been a development.' They got into Thompson's vehicle. 'Some bloke out jogging this lunchtime has reported finding something. Russo is already there.' He prodded audio system buttons. 'That's all I can tell you. What I want right now is musical distraction and zero chat.' Loud music erupted, striking hard surfaces.

Craft recoiled. 'What the *hell* is this? Turn it *down*!'

He did, slightly. 'It's New Orleans jazz and it works for *me*.' He reversed at speed and they headed out of the car park, but were soon stopped by heavy traffic.

Craft stared out of the window. 'Why am *I* being subjected to this – *noise*?'

He reached for the sound control. 'Don't go moody on me. According to the extreme runner bloke who found it, it's a human bone—'

'I find noise extremely challeng— A *bone*?'

'His job as an ambulance worker says he knows what he was looking at.'

'Where did he see this one?'

'It was only partially covered by soil and grass. Probably the work of a fox or a dog. As to where . . .'

She looked at the route they were now taking, recognition dawning.

He nodded. 'You've got it.'

Finding a parking space in a long line of vehicles on the main road by the entrance to Forrest Park, they got out, Craft gazing up at the October-green-yellow leaf canopy, recalling her unease when she was here alone. Thompson was already on the move. She quickly followed him along a pathway, flanked by two uniformed officers.

'Straight ahead, sir!' called one.

They came to a scene of quiet, orderly activity, SOCOs working behind taut lengths of blue and white tape, Russo and Flood on higher ground, she bent from the waist, pointing as Flood, on his haunches, carefully trowelled a small area. Straightening, her face flushed despite the chill, she raised her thumb to them. By-passing Thompson, ignoring his 'Where's the fire?', Craft quickly covered the small distance to stare down at the area of dark earth the pathologist was indicating.

Thompson arrived as Russo was pointing out a stained brown-to-off-white item with a pale yellowish attachment. 'It's a skull and mandible. Examination of the sagittal suture of the skull and dentition' – Craft felt suddenly odd, unwell, the pathologist's voice wavering towards her – 'gives me an age guestimate of around the late teens— *Thompson*, catch hold of your assistant!'

Thompson turned as Craft fell against him, her eyes unfocused. 'What the—! *OK, OK* . . . steady . . . you're all right. I've got you.'

She hung on to his arm as he lowered her, still spacey, to the ground. Her facial expression slowly normalizing, she swatted away his hands, managed to stand, still unsteady, trying to brush vegetation and soil from her parka, Russo's words drifting towards her on the cold air. 'Take a moment.'

'No. I'm . . . fine. Continue, please.'

Russo gave her a curious look then turned back to the remains. She pointed downwards to where loamy soil still held more bones. 'I'll confirm these details later, but as of now we have female remains, very approximate age late teens, plus a broken hyoid bone highly indicative of strangulation.'

On one knee, Thompson's eyes were fixed on what he could make out within the rich, dark soil. He whispered, 'I don't believe it,' his eyes moving over sloping land, trees and more trees. 'This place is a bloody *graveyard*.'

He got to his feet, brushing dead leaves from his trouser leg and glancing at Craft, whose facial colour had not improved but who seemed otherwise recovered, eyes moving slowly over trees.

Craft said, 'He must feel very at home here to keep revisiting it. This whole area needs excavation.'

Thompson was on his phone, pacing. 'Sir, in my experience ground penetrating radar is probably the speedier option for terrain like this, which means more officers . . .' He absorbed Holdsworth's words. 'Yeah, if that's the maximum available . . .' He frowned as the call ended. 'Holdsworth's under pressure – he's said yes to the radar but only four extra officers.'

Craft was contemplating the ground as Russo came closer, giving her a quick, evaluative glance. 'How are you feeling?'

'Fine.' Craft moved away, the pathologist's words following her on the cold air.

'Low blood sugar! Young women don't eat enough! Get yourself some glucose sweets. Better still, start the day on a fried breakfast!'

Fighting a sudden wave of queasiness, Craft walked slowly to Thompson, his eyes fixed on the press of trees around them.

'This place gives me claustrophobia. It must be more than you bargained for, Craft. It is for me.'

She gazed in the same direction. 'It is shocking, but you're not giving up on it?'

He turned to her, brows climbing. 'If you think I have that luxury, think again. This is *my* investigation. It's my job to find whoever's responsible for this.' He looked at her. 'But you don't have to stick with it.'

'Yes, I do. I want answers.'

'In which case, we had better start finding them, and *quick*.' They walked together, Craft distracted, downbeat. He gave her a quick, sideways glance. 'You OK now?'

'Perfectly fine,' she snapped.

'Then cheer up.'

She closed her eyes. 'I cannot tell you how much I dislike those two words, paired.'

He gave her another once-over, trying to work out her mood. Getting nothing, he went for a positive stance. 'How about this: you and me, we're the dream team. Whoever this killer is, there's no hiding place for him.'

'That sounds like you've been on some kind of incentivization course.'

'Three weeks ago. I've only just remembered it.'

'What happens now?'

'I go home and so do you.'

'Tell Russo when you next see her that *I* am *nobody's assistant*.'

'Tell her yourself. I like living.' They reached his vehicle. 'Know what I think? All this talking in italics you do is wearing you out. I'll drop you at Headquarters and you're free to do whatever you want – like, marching over Poland to two hundred decibels of Wagner.'

She eyed him, grass- and mud-stained, her blonde hair in spikes. 'I have *no* idea what you are talking about.'

He said nothing. He was beginning to get a handle on her: she might have little interest in recent world history, little experience of hands-on investigation, but she missed nothing.

Craft let herself into the apartment. It was silent. Cold. She tapped the hall thermostat, headed for the kitchen, switched on the kettle and stared at water starting to bubble. Flicking the off switch, reaching for a mug, she was stopped by a note propped against it: *Hope your day was good. Look under your pillow. Think 'wedding day'*. She walked slowly to the bedroom, lifted the pillow, the last low winter rays finding the spot. Taking off her engagement ring, she reached for the smooth, white-gold wedding band, slid it on to her finger, feeling the pressure of Tom's need for them to get married, her whole day suddenly crashing her head. She leapt as the apartment phone shrilled. Her mother. The only person who used the landline. Going to the sitting room, she lifted it without speaking.

'It's me, Tig. Is everything OK?'

'Yes.'

'How was your day?'

'Fine.'

'I've got a delivery for you. I'm guessing it's books. It usually is.'

'OK.'

'Shall I come—'

'Tom is impatient for us to get married.'

'I know. You've been together a long time, so I don't understand your reluctance.'

'He wants children, Ma.'

'I imagine he does. I don't see a problem—'

'You should! I see *plenty*.' Ending the call, she returned to the kitchen to make coffee, gave the boiling water tap a push-turn, the childproof light showing, steaming water running from it. Her head was chaotic, full of potential risk, her mind racing. Her life as it was now would change. Thoughts of Tom, the responsibility that went with starting a family with him caused her to swallow hard, a sob pushing its way out of her mouth. *I can't do it! It's too much. I won't be able to do the job I have . . .*

An hour later, her mother let herself into the apartment, calling, 'Tig?'

The little French bulldog ran ahead to Craft sitting cross-legged on the floor, putting his front paws on her knee, his little tail wagging. She lifted him on to her lap, kissed the top of his head. Her mother came into the siting room, giving Craft a second look. 'Are you all right? You look unwell.'

'Don't *fuss*. I'm fine.' She watched her mother draw blinds, then go to the kitchen, returning with mugs of tea. After a few quiet minutes, her mother asked, 'How was your day?'

'I discussed some investigative ideas with a colleague, then went on a scene visit to look at human remains which hopefully will give us more ideas—'

'I get it. What you've just described would stress and agitate most people.'

'I am not stressed. I am not agitated and I am not "most people". You *know* that!'

Her mother gazed at her. 'Yes. You're *you* and you know how to manage your life, which wasn't always the case—'

'I don't want to hear it, Ma.'

'You need to acknowledge how far you've come, Tig. What you've achieved.' There was a short silence. She pointed. 'They're lovely rings and you've got nice hands which show them off.'

Craft straightened her left hand, looked down at the rings. 'They're all part of the problem.'

'Only if you make them one. Don't allow yourself to be a prey to self-doubt. Welcome this as a new phase in your life. Like all the other phases you've coped with.'

Craft thought, *I'm happy with this phase, Ma.* She said, 'You know more than anyone how I hate things to change.'

FOURTEEN

Wednesday 23 October, 8.45 a.m.

The two female officers on desk duty looked up as Craft came into Headquarters. 'Morning, Professor Craft!' said one. Craft tensed, nodded, continuing in the direction of the office. '*Professor?*'

She stopped, slowly turned.

'DCI Thompson has left a message for you to meet him at Forrest Park at around ten o'clock, when he expects Dr Russo to have finished her site examination.' The officer smiled, pointing at Craft. 'I just *love* that coat!'

'I'll go to the park now—'

'Come *on*, give us a quick twirl!'

Momentarily fazed, recalling a university colleague in a similar situation, she slowly turned, arms held wide to show off the black, quilted down coat and toffee-brown faux fur- trimmed hood. 'That's enough. I'll check if DCI Thompson has left me any information, then go to Forrest Park.'

'He said to tell you to approach the park via Green Road where there's a narrow footpath that goes directly into it. The press has the main pathway staked out.'

They watched as she left reception, one of them lowering her voice. 'I thought she was really stand-offish when she first arrived here, but now I know her better, she's all right, isn't she?'

Her colleague said, 'She is, but according to Sullivan, she's a geeky weirdo, too clever for her own good.'

'Ha! Sullivan's got as much use for a clever woman as a rat has for a trap.' They both laughed. 'You saw it?'

'The engagement ring? Would I miss a detail like that?' A short silence fell between them. 'If you want my advice, don't spend too much time talking to Sullivan. He's trouble.'

* * *

Craft checked the wire basket in Thompson's office, finding two items with her name on them. She quickly read the uppermost item: an update on the Forrest Park scene following on from yesterday. The second was a copy of David Brown's brief notes from their discussion the previous day, a Post-it attached: *My version of what we agreed. Good luck with the investigation.*

She drove to the scene and followed Thompson's instructions, leaving her car on Green Road, and heading for the narrow footpath flanked by two officers who allowed her inside. Going directly to the location where they had been the previous day, she found it extensively taped off, officers she did not recognize moving around, one of them prodding the ground using a radar device, others shoulder-to-shoulder on their knees. An officer she did not recognize appeared, barring her way. 'Stop right there, miss! This is a police-protected area!'

She held up her ID. 'Where is DCI Thompson?' She looked to where he was pointing at Thompson some distance away, in what looked to be deep discussion with Russo. She headed for them.

Thompson looked up as she came closer. 'All right?'

'I am.'

'Good. Got an update for you.' He pointed to several distant, numbered red flags. 'See them? Each one is a marker for a buried body part.'

'What?'

'Follow me.' He turned away, then back to her. '*Craft!*'

She followed, now aware of the subdued mood throughout the scene. Reaching the nearest flag, she looked down at a narrow rectangle of dark, newly turned earth, her heart banging in her chest.

Thompson pointed downwards. 'This is what I know from Russo: left leg recovered from here and' – he led the way to the next flag – 'this is where the right leg was concealed. Both were disarticulated through the knee, then bound for ease of burial.'

Craft felt perspiration ooze on to her forehead.

He pointed up the sloping land. 'Flag three way up there on the left is where the left arm, also disarticulated, is being freed and' – his finger moved on – 'ditto for flag four over there – right arm.'

Craft was now hyper-aware of the tension within the whole scene. She glanced at Thompson, his eyes fixed on the flags. 'Whoever he is, he took a risk, choosing accessible land to do this.' She found her voice. 'Quicker and less risky than moving a complete body and burying it.' She looked slowly around the area. 'Dismemberment had to have been done at his leisure, somewhere covert, possibly domestic, after which he prepared each of the deposition places prior to bringing the body parts here separately in darkness to minimize the risk of being observed.'

Thompson's eyes were fixed on the ground. 'Put like that, it sounds simple. To me, it's a bloody nightmare.' He took a few steps away from her. 'All we need to do is locate a house with a bath – oh, and a large freezer.'

'That is self-evident.'

Guessing his words had required no comment, she asked, 'Are we agreed that a reasonably fit male would find walking this steep ground manageable, carrying said packages of body parts?'

'Yeah, and he must know this whole area really well.'

Craft thought of her lost scarf lying somewhere here, of Emma Matheson's remains, once captive in her cold, comfortless house. Seeing Thompson approaching the flags, she followed. As she neared, he said, 'Each part was wrapped in thick paper, except for the skull, which suggests that it was the first item he buried here, following which he refined the process as he continued. All I want is for those wrappings to include some newspaper with a house number and road name written on them.'

She stared at him. 'You really think . . .?'

'No, I don't. Let's hear what Russo's got to tell us.' They headed to the pathologist, who was in conversation with Mike Bass. 'It looks like we might be about to learn something.'

Reaching the trestle table where Russo and Bass were standing, Thompson introduced Craft to Bass, who said, 'We've already met.'

Craft avoiding Bass's direct gaze, they all looked down at what was on the table, Russo saying, 'The actual body parts have gone to the pathology suite to be logged and refrigerated. I can confirm young, white and female.' She pointed her gloved hand to items of thick paper, each one labelled with a number denoting the order of recovery and details of geographical position. Craft and Thompson eyed the stained items. 'You'll probably have no trouble identifying these as items of wallpaper, heavily embossed, ideal for soaking up body fluids.'

Craft got a quick wave of nausea.

'And these' – Russo held up what looked like dark, narrow strips of something – 'are what were used as ties.' Craft and Thompson exchanged quick glances. 'Exactly,' said Russo. '*Very* similar to the ties used to secure Emma Matheson's arms and legs.'

Thompson glanced at the paper items, each retaining much of the shape of what they had once held. Craft's eyes fixed on them as Russo said, 'This is old wallpaper, circa the Seventies at a guess. Probably lying in someone's loft or garage for years.'

Bass shrugged. 'We'll do all we can, but if they're all this old, don't hold out any serious hopes of identifying retail outlets. When I get them all I'll test them for anything useful then send my report to you, Steve, with copies to Lucia and Professor Craft.' He nodded to them and headed down the sloping site.

Russo looked directly at them. '*Please* do not assume that this is a killer with medical knowledge. It's lazy thinking and *very* irritating. All this killer needed was rudimentary anatomical awareness and suitable facilities in which to dismember. My preliminary view is that he used a hacksaw – oh, and do not assume prints on the wrappings. Very unlikely from my initial examination of them.' She squinted up at a now leaden sky. 'I need to finish up here. A guestimate at this stage is that the remains were left here within the last eighteen months, and I can confirm from my brief examination of the body parts that she was younger than your other victims.'

Thompson waited. 'How much younger?'

'Late teenage years.'

Thompson and Craft went down the incline, Craft breaking the silence. 'Has anything else been recovered?'

'Like, what?'

'A long scarf with a leopard pattern in browns and golds.'

He stopped. 'That's very specific.'

She shrugged. 'I lost it when I recently walked from Forrest Road over most of this area. I'm now considering the possibility that it was picked up by somebody, possibly the killer.'

Thompson took out his phone. 'Ashton? Circulate a BOLO for one long scarf, leopard print in browns and golds – yeah.' He ended the call.

Craft said, 'Good retention of detail, Thompson.'

'With a wife and two daughters who expect detailed comments on how they look, it goes with the territory – if you want to stay out of trouble.' They walked from the park on to Green Lane, Thompson preoccupied with thoughts of risk and his two teenage daughters.

'Where are we going?' asked Craft.

'To Headquarters and a heavy-duty "missing persons" search. I'm expecting a DNA result sometime but we need to know, soon as, who this young woman was.'

FIFTEEN

The office would have been silent if it were not for Sandhu's relentless pen clicks, plus the tapping of Thompson's missing persons computer search. Craft's sensitivity to repetitive sounds prompted a quick search of her bag for a small black box containing high-fidelity earplugs. Positioning them inside her ears, looping the lanyard over her head, she began processing swift notes on her iPad of all the theory she knew relating to homicides involving dismemberment and those who indulged in the practice. An hour later Thompson's phone rang and she was aware of him leaving the room. Within a couple of minutes he was back, carrying a large cardboard box. She watched as he took out High Street coffees, placing a cappuccino-to-go in front of Sandhu and the same for Craft.

She looked up. 'Thanks.'

Pointing to his ear, finger to his lips, he took one himself and a muffin from several in the box. 'My treat.' The muffins were quickly taken.

Thompson sipped his black Americano. 'In this line of work there's times when treats aren't treats. They're a necessity.'

Eyeing him across her paper cup, Craft was intuiting his stress level. Medium-high, she decided. Not for the first time, she wondered why Thompson had chosen policing as a career and homicide specifically. Probably not a choice. More a steady progression through cases and ranks. She sent him another glance. Now was as good a time as any for him to hear what she had to say. 'I'm ready to share my knowledge of dismemberment.'

'Here goes!' said Sandhu, grabbing her notebook.

Thompson eyed Craft. 'As long as it's not from personal experience and not too technical.'

'What I'm about to offer is the psychology of dismemberment, the most common motivation for which is obviously ease of concealment or disposal. It can also be an act of pure rage against a victim, the killer almost certainly severely lacking in empathy for said victim.'

'You're saying he's a nutter.'

'If this was a one-off act, I might say that, somewhat rephrased, but given that we have a homicide series here, the overwhelming indication is that he is supremely organized and enjoys what he does. He is psychopathic, *not* psychotic.'

Thompson eye-rolled. 'I've heard a lot about psychopaths but I can tell you now, in all my years of policing, I've never met one.'

'Much more likely, you did not recognize what you were dealing with. Or, possibly those you did see had been identified as "antisocial".'

'And I suppose you've had direct experience of cases of dismemberment.'

'Yes, two.'

'Bloody hell—'

'A couple of Christmas turkeys.' She looked away from him. 'That was a joke.'

'Badly placed. I can't envisage anybody who's sane killing then dismembering another person *and* at the same time leading a life that passes for normal.'

'Given the likelihood of his being psychopathic, it is highly unlikely he would have experienced revulsion or any other negative emotional responses we might anticipate from such a deviant act. Zero anxiety, zero disgust would have been his response. This type of perpetrator is devoid of genuine emotion as part of his daily life experience. Think of it this way: no matter what he is doing – reading, playing football, destroying women – his blood pressure is likely to remain stable. I am not being judgemental when I say that almost all killers who indulge in this kind of activity are male.' She stood, went to the window to gaze out. 'Dismemberment is a *very* rare act in the commission of a homicide and there is limited research available.'

'I'm still waiting for some good news.'

She turned to him. 'I would not class it as "good news" but I have more theoretical information. There has been some analysis of the motivations of those who participate in such behaviour into five distinct types—'

'I can't recall a time I felt gladder,' Thompson muttered.

'The first is self-preservation. The killer's motive is to avoid discovery by concealment of his victims. Emma Matheson is a similar example. She was not dismembered, yet whoever killed her had a pre-prepared space in which to conceal her body. He secured her remains in order to fit that space. Which is one of the reasons I always believed the murder of Emma Matheson and the Forrest Park victims to be linked. The benefit to the killer in this latest scenario is that he required a relatively small space in which to conceal each part. No heavy-duty digging required. As already said, it is very likely he initially stored the body parts in a domestic freezer. Quite stylish thinking for a killer who is a planner and eminently sane.'

Thompson frowned. 'Not exactly my sentiments. Why didn't he conceal Alicia Franks in the same way?'

'Possibly he was interrupted. Other than that, I do not know.'

'What's the next type?'

'Aggression towards the victim in death suggests that the killer had negative emotions towards either the victim or to what she represented for him.'

She watched Sandhu's quick note-taking.

'The third motive is "offense-mutilation" where mutilation is itself the primary goal. Russo has not referred to any such behaviour, beyond that necessary to separate the body parts. In any event, offense-mutilation is indicative of a killer who is either psychotic and therefore not responsible for his actions, *or* is a member of an organized criminal fraternity who use dismemberment as a threat or discourager to others. In my view we can dispense with both types.'

Absorbing Craft's calm, non-emotional delivery and emulating it, Sandhu asked, 'This cutting up – what about people who kill animals for a living, like those with links to abattoir work? I mean, they wouldn't be bothered by doing it, would they?'

Craft shook her head. 'I understand you're thinking about the possibility of desensitization, but in the small number of studies available, there appears to be no occupational link.' Craft tensed at a distant yet penetrating sound. 'What was *that*? Did anybody else hear it?'

Sandhu nodded, looked to Thompson. 'Sir, it sounds to me like something's kicking off in reception.'

Dropping his pen on the table, Thompson headed for the door. Opening it, they heard a woman's voice in a high-pitched, unremitting scream. He was gone, speeding along the corridor, Craft and

Sandhu following. The scene in reception was mayhem. Members of the public who had come to Headquarters for any number of reasons were clustered together at its entrance, their eyes fixed on a female civilian worker lying on the floor next to the desk, a second civilian worker wide-eyed, hysterical, her voice now climbing to a high-pitched wail.

Pushing her way through the crowded entrance, Russo came inside. On a quick appraisal of the situation, she went to where Thompson was kneeling beside the woman on the floor and conducted a swift examination. 'I haven't got a clue what's happening here, but she's not physically injured.' She left him, heading to the screaming woman, took the woman's face firmly in both her hands. 'Yvonne? *Yvonne!* It's me, Dr Russo. Look at me! Breathe slowly with me – *slowly*, slowly . . . That's good . . . good . . . What's happened here?'

Still spaced-out, the worker pointed to an item lying on the floor behind the desk. Russo went to it, pulling on surgical gloves. 'Steve! You need to see this.'

He went to where she was pointing, lowered his face to the contents of the package she was holding, then quickly pulled himself away. 'This is . . . *madness.*'

Russo looked down at the small, bluish item lying within the embossed paper, fingers curled, nails dark. 'A to-the-point summation,' she whispered.

Thompson was facing Holdsworth across his desk. 'Sir, you need to issue an urgent appeal to women in this city about the Forrest Park area.'

'Saying what, exactly?'

On the verge of saying that it was bloody obvious, he went with a more measured response. 'They should keep away from it. That it is risky. Dangerous.'

Holdsworth stared up at him. 'Are you out of your *mind*? It'll just fuel panic and the press will stoke it up – to your professional detriment. I might add.'

'Sir, I won't be responsible for what happens if you don't!'

Holdsworth was on his feet. 'It's *your* name on this investigation, Steve, so the buck stops with *you*, got it? Given what we already know – that another woman has been murdered in that same area – and given the lack of leads, *both* our careers are on the line, possibly dead in the water as I speak!'

They eyed each other, breathing hard. Holdsworth said, 'There's one way to sort this, and that's for *you* to grow a pair, ASAP and find this madman!'

Thompson was at the door, wrenching it open. 'He's *not* mad!'

'Says who?'

Thompson was out of the office. 'Says Craft!' He pulled the door hard against its frame.

Ten minutes later, still riled, he was inside the pathology suite with Craft, Russo giving them her professional view of what had occurred earlier in reception. 'A good move sending both civilian workers home for the rest of the week, Steve.'

'It wouldn't surprise me if we never see either of them again.'

Russo lifted two large plastic boxes from the refrigerator and brought them to the examination table. 'Before their taxi arrived, I managed to get some details from one of them. The post arrived at around nine. The usual correspondence, including several packages, most of which were opened and logged. Nothing untoward noted in any of it. There was a sudden influx of people with inquiries so the package in question was temporarily placed in your tray, Steve.'

He looked up. 'Addressed to *me*?'

Russo shook her head. 'No. To "Professor Teigan Craft".'

Craft looked from Russo to Thompson. 'Why would anybody do that? Excluding people who work here, no one knows I'm at Headquarters.'

'Think again,' said Thompson. 'The media knows and their cameras like your face.'

Craft considered the many people employed at Headquarters for any who might have alerted the media about her: Ashton? Sullivan? They were both dislikeable, particularly Sullivan, who often disguised his misogyny behind a jokey facade, but surely neither would do something as aggressive, as professionally *risky*, as this? Both were involved in the recovery of the body parts. Was either of them sufficiently perverse to do such a thing as a joke? She shook her head, re-tuning to what Russo was saying.

'A fingerprint check matched this one to the hand located at the Forrest Park site. I'll start with what I know from the packaging.' Pulling on gloves, she lifted embossed paper from one of the plastic containers, laid it on the pathology worktable and pointed to it, almost fully opened out. 'You'll recognize this from the remains found at Forrest Park: Anaglypta wallpaper, circa the Seventies.

Bass is conducting a thorough examination of it for identification purposes' – she shook her head – 'but I doubt it will help us. This kind of paper has fallen out of favour over the decades. There is something else.' They looked to where Russo was pointing at a thin, snaking length of something dark brown in colour. 'This was wound several times around the Anaglypta containing the hand, then wrapped in brown paper, secured with Sellotape and posted here – and before anyone asks, there were zero fingerprints or partials on either side of the Sellotape or anywhere else for that matter. Which means we have a very forensically savvy killer.'

Thompson pointed. 'That thing wound around it is the same stuff used to secure Matheson's arms and legs prior to being pushed into the cupboard at Forrest Road.'

Russo nodded. 'It's very similar: thin, smooth, dark brown leather.'

'It looks unusual. What's it generally used for?'

Russo said, 'According to my search, it's mostly a handicrafts item – you know the type of thing which usually has beads or similar threaded on to it.'

Thompson looked unimpressed. 'That makes no sense. It sounds a bit "hippy" yet they were into peace and love.'

'What is "hippy"?' asked Craft.

'A Sixties wheatgerm-and-sandals type of thing – people who danced about, out of their heads on drugs.'

She looked at him. 'Were you hippy?'

'No, I wasn't!' he snapped. 'That was *well* before my time!'

Craft turned to Russo. 'I can't visualize what's being said about this leather material.'

'According to my online search, it is relatively fine, so it is ideal for decorating with coloured beads into necklaces or similar by people with too much time to spare in my opinion.' She nodded to Flood as he came into the room and pointed to the second box. 'Let's look at what it secured.'

Flood's gloved hands popped the lid. 'Some weird dudes around, guys.'

Thompson sent him a look, watched Russo lift out the severed hand and place it carefully on a glass sheet. No one spoke. It lay, small, the fingers bluish, curled towards the palm. Thompson broke the silence. 'Got anything to tell us about it, Lucia?'

She nodded. 'As you can probably see, it's a female left hand.' She pointed to it. 'These scratches on the third finger . . . here and . . . here are possibly indications of forcible removal of one or more items of jewellery.'

'Indicative of robbery as a possible motive?' asked Thompson, sounding hopeful.

'I doubt it. Fingernails well-kept.' She lowered her face closer to the nails. 'What do you call this?'

Craft said, 'It's a French manicure. You have DNA?'

'Yes. That was my first action. This hand belonged to an eighteen-year-old female named Lucy Greening who was reported missing by her family from Stratford-upon-Avon on the sixteenth of February three years ago, following her failure to return home from a job interview she told her parents was in Birmingham town centre. According to the parents, it later transpired that there was no job interview. Local police established that Greening travelled into Stratford where she went to a café. A waitress who still works there identified her from a photograph. Hardly surprising, she could not recall what Greening ordered, following which sighting, Greening has not been seen or heard of since.'

She tapped a nearby screen which flooded with light. A head-shoulders photograph of a young woman appeared, her hair long and blonde, her face open and pleasant. 'The hand was packaged and sent here first class from the Stratford-upon-Avon area, which might suggest that her killer was aware that she lived in the town.' She paused. 'Given the timescale involved, this young woman's remains had to be stored in a freezer.'

Craft said, 'She lied about the job interview. She was intending to meet someone there.'

Thompson's eyes were fixed on the hand. In his twenty or so years' investigative experience he had never encountered anything remotely like this. '*Why* would anybody go to . . . such trouble?'

Russo murmured, 'That is a question for your professor of forensic psychology. From my viewpoint, the more body parts we have, the more forensic information is available to us.'

Looking up, Craft saw David Brown in the doorway.

Russo gestured to him. 'David, come on in.'

Brown shook his head and looked at Thompson. 'I thought you'd want to know – officers in reception are waiting for instructions from you that they can let the people still there go, and there's been a couple of phone calls from a prison up north.'

'Those calls were for me,' said Craft. 'I'm in the process of arranging an urgent visit.'

'To where? For what?' asked Thompson.

'Insights into what we're dealing with here.'

She left the pathology suite, Brown following, went into reception, picked up the phone and confirmed her name. 'Yes . . . *yes*, I completely understand. As I already said to the two people I spoke to when I arranged the visit, I have done so many times—' A nod, a shake of her head. 'That is fine. I understand. Thank you.' She ended the call as Thompson appeared. 'The level of bureaucracy involved in the making of one straightforward prison visit is mind-numbing.'

Thompson gave her a look. 'Like to give *me* a hint as to what you're up to?'

She reached for her phone again, her attention fixed on its screen. 'Wait . . . Now I have an email, asking still more questions . . .' She quickly responded and put down the phone. 'Thompson, I have arranged a prison visit for us both for tomorrow morning. You need to be there as SIO. It is time you met a full-on psychopath.'

Coming into reception, Russo raised her eyebrows to him. 'There's a treat not to be missed.'

'I've got enough going on here—'

Craft eyed him. 'Thompson, if you, *we*, want to understand this case and what happened to Lucy Greening, and the other female victims, you need to be there whilst I talk to an individual who knows from direct experience what it means to dismember and mail body parts.'

SIXTEEN

Thursday 24 October, 9.15 a.m.

Thompson was driving with the air-con on, the weather having turned muggy overnight. 'You know what's causing this weather? According to the forecast this morning, it's the sodding jet stream.'

'Why do people talk incessantly about weather?' snapped Craft, looking as if she was awaiting an answer.

He glanced across at her. 'I *don't* and I hope this idea of yours is worth a two-hour jaunt up the M1.' Getting no response, he fell silent for the next half-hour. Leaving the motorway, he said, 'We should be there in around ten, fifteen minutes. What's your plan?'

'I don't have one, beyond getting inside, then out with something that helps us understand the psychopath we're searching for. I don't know what we might get. Possibly very little and a long journey for nothing.'

They drove on, a complex of buildings slowly coming into view: a large, dull, brick structure plus several smaller ones grouped around it, encircled by a high, pale wall topped with coiled razor wire. Thompson knew this was the largest Category A men's prison in the UK. He had never had a reason to come here. Today, even in hazy sunshine, it looked discouraging. Discouraged. It looked what it was. A warehouse.

As if intuiting his thinking, Craft murmured, 'Welcome to HM's Repository of Misery for the Antisocial, the Psychopathic and the Psychotic.'

He drove on, following signs to the admissions building and on to a blue-and-white striped barrier where he stopped, spoke their names, professional details, and reason for visit into a grille. A lengthy pause, broken by a disembodied voice directing them beyond the barrier to the car park, a specific parking space, and what to do on arrival there. With an upward glance as the barrier rose, seeing CCTV cameras ready to track his vehicle, Thompson drove directly to the designated space.

Getting out of the vehicle, Craft pointed to a low-rise building painted an odd shade of yellow-green some way off. 'We report to that place there.'

They walked towards it, Thompson feeling tension knotting his neck muscles. He glanced at Craft. She looked pale. 'You OK?'

She did not look at him. 'An impending migraine is all.'

The double doors of the squat building slowly opened as they reached them. They went inside, directed by two heavy-looking, uniformed guards, the peaks of their caps low on their foreheads. Entering a huge reception area, they saw two more guards standing behind a long table. One of them pointed to a white line painted on the floor. They went to it and stood, receiving intense scrutiny.

'Welcome, Detective Chief Inspector Thompson! Step forward, please.' Seeing Craft also move forward, he gave her a sharp look from beneath the peak, then held up his hand in a staying motion, '*Wait!*' Craft waited. He checked a small screen. 'We're expecting DCI Thompson and a Professor Titan Craft who is the initiator of this visit. Where has he got to?'

'*Teigan* Craft,' she snapped, again stepping forward. Four broad hands rose as both guards consulted details on a clipboard. Getting a signal to approach, she did so, one officer scrutinizing her Headquarters' ID, plus that of her university, both bearing photographs, then up at Craft herself. 'You are fully aware that this is a very high-security establishment?'

On a rush of irritation, she snapped, 'Of course.'

Thompson frowned at her, thinking that several minutes of their allotted time here had already elapsed and Craft copping an attitude was unlikely to speed up the process.

The second guard barked at them, '*No* phones. *No* cash. *No* credit cards. *No* keys. *No* personal items of any description allowed past this point!' He swiftly placed two grey plastic trays on the table in front of him, squared them up and glared at Craft. She deposited her handbag and Thompson his wallet, keys, a pen and a half-roll of mints. The guard pointed to chairs set against a distant wall next to an array of lockers. 'All other belongings to be deposited there!'

Craft shook her head. 'No, no. This is a professional visit and I need a pen and something to write on.'

The guards stared back at her, implacable. '*No* pens. *No* notebooks.'

They were watched to the lockers, watched as they placed their coats inside, then took seats, Thompson saying, 'I've never felt so welcome in my life. I hope this place is worth the aggravation.'

Craft spoke softly. 'Are you familiar with a murderer named Jerome Quirebell?'

'Who isn't? After killing his victims, he mailed some body parts to their families, saying he ate the—'

'He did not consume anything. It was concealed under floorboards in the house where he was living.'

'Even he's got limits.'

'I would advise you not to count on that with someone like him. Each of those families accepted delivery of a body part.'

Thompson shook his head. 'We're all waiting for something we've ordered online.'

They fell silent, distant shouts filtering to them from the antisocial, the occasional screams of the psychotic. After twenty minutes of squirming on chairs not intended for comfort, Thompson stood. 'I've had enough of this. That's a third of our time gone.'

The guards watched him approach, one of them saying, 'What can I do for you, sir?'

'We're still waiting for Jerome Quirebell to be produced—'

A nearby phone shrilled. Not taking his eyes off Thompson, the officer reached for the handset and spoke into it. 'Yeah, what's keeping you lot up there? Quirebell's visitors are getting restless . . . The *sick* bastard! I'll tell 'em.' Replacing the phone, he said, 'A bit of a hiccup. When staff went to fetch Quirebell from his cell, they found him in the middle of a conjugal visit – with himself – which necessitated a change of clothing. They're on their way down with him now.'

Craft was now aware of a sudden, intense pain inside her head. She slowly stood, approached the guards. 'I have medication inside my bag which I need—'

'*Stay*.'

She winced at the loudness of the word, watched him reach for a large bound volume and open it. 'Name of drug!'

Closing her eyes, she supplied the name, watched him flick numerous pages in the alphabetized book, saw him stop, run one blunt finger down the page, then thump the book closed, looking gratified. '*Prohibited,* due to lack of available information!'

Unwell as she felt, Craft was about to challenge him when there was a sudden, sharp *click* and a nearby door swung slowly open, an officer leaning into the waiting area.

'Quirebell's here.'

She and Thompson moved to the door which closed as they approached.

'There's a time delay,' said one of the guards, looking pleased with the arrangement. They waited. Another *click.* The door opened and they were waved into a corridor painted a dull mustard under the watchful gaze of a different officer whom they followed, Craft shallow-breathing a mix of bleach, sweat and a base note of urine. They entered a room containing four tables and four chairs, all bolted to the floor. The officer pointed to one of the tables. 'Have side-by-side seats at table number one! *No* physical contact permitted. *No* offers of help with his various appeals—'

'Unlikely,' snapped Thompson.

The guarded lifted his head, gazed at him from beneath his peak. 'Following the script, sir. Do not accept *anything* the prisoner might attempt to give you. *Clear?*'

They nodded, sat, and watched him leave the room. He returned in a couple of minutes, accompanied by an average-height male in fresh-looking, prison-issue, blue-striped shirt and beige chinos. The door closed and the guard stood to one side of it, thick, tattooed forearms bunched below his short-sleeved uniform shirt. Craft gazed at Quirebell, at the neat hair, the bland, smiling face.

'Hello,' he said quietly. 'It's a nice change to have visitors who are not my legal representatives. Thank you for coming—'

'*Shut* it, Quirebell!' snapped the guard. 'This is no garden party! You know the drill: you walk directly to table number *one*. You sit on the chair on the *left*.'

Craft glanced down at numbers stencilled in black on scarred grey vinyl.

'Any game-playing and you are straight back to the wing, *got* it?'

Quirebell nodded. 'Of course, officer.' He switched his attention to Craft and smiled.

She did not respond, watched him move slowly towards the table. After the authoritarian process they had experienced thus far, she had half-expected some means of restraint being applied to this inmate but there was none. Thompson introduced Craft, then himself. Quirebell did not look at him. 'How might I assist you?' he asked Craft quietly.

'I'm a forensic psychologist, Mr Quirebell. I am familiar with the offences that brought you here under three life sentences.'

He nodded, smiled again. 'I have knowledge of *you*, Professor Craft. Your name is on various tests administered by visiting psychologists who come here, with their black attaché cases full of little red and white cubes to fit together, their "guess the story" pictures, the "lie" statements in all other tests, including the interminable questions intended to evaluate psychopathy.'

'They don't impress you,' she stated.

He sighed, crossed his legs, both hands moving imperceptibly towards her on the table. 'They are all very limited people whose insight would be laughable if it were not so . . . annoying.'

'Prior to being sent here, that last test you just referred to yielded from you one of the highest psychopathy scores I have ever seen.' She looked around the room, then back to him. 'And here you are, a Category A inmate for life, Mr Quirebell.'

Thompson's stress level shot up, wondering why she was being so direct, so challenging, tensing his muscles at what sounded to him like the start of a face-off between her and this maniac.

Quirebell was staring at her, his face expressionless. He gave a light laugh and shook his head, looking directly into her eyes. 'Those tests provide a mere distraction when one has nothing more pressing to do.'

'They yielded a clear, objective representation of your personality, which fits with the offences you committed.'

His eyes drifted over her face. 'What exactly do you want from me, Professor Teigan Craft?' He leant forward, whispered, 'How might I be of assistance to you?'

She started at the officer's loud shout: 'Sit *back*, Quirebell! Keep your voice *up*!'

'We have an ongoing homicide investigation involving dismemberment.'

Quirebell tutted. 'How . . . distasteful,' he whispered.

The guard repeated, 'Voice *up,* or back to the wing!'

Craft breathed deeply. 'The killer recently mailed one of the body parts to . . . an investigative officer.' She watched his focus move for the first time to Thompson, a gleam in his eyes.

'I wonder, to what end?' he said. 'Who was the recipient, exactly?'

Determined not to indicate it was herself and thus feed his likely masturbatory behaviour, Craft shook her head. 'That is classified information, which I am not at liberty to divulge, but we would appreciate your insights on the mailing of dismembered parts. The evidence at your trial was that you demonstrated similar behaviour—'

'No, no,' he said, his tone now condescending. 'You are badly informed. I have no first-hand experience of such behaviour and I am currently engaged in the appeals process to have my homicide convictions overturned.' He paused. 'However, I would most certainly wish to assist you by giving your . . . dilemma . . . some serious consideration.' He gave her a penetrating look. 'Perhaps you are unaware that I have a degree in psychology from the University of Oxford?'

Craft picked up the guard's muttered, 'My *arse*.' She had already checked. Quirebell had completed two years of a psychology degree at a minor university prior to dropping out. She waited.

He brought his hands together, steepling his pale fingers, the nails immaculate. 'I appreciate that you have a problem and I certainly would want to help you. Of course, what I am offering you are my *theories* only.' The game-playing had now started in earnest. Craft knew the theory relating to dismemberment but this man knew the reality. She felt a sudden need for a pen. His tone switched to portentous. 'Reasons Killers May Forward Victim Body Parts to Others . . . Oh dear. I see that they have not allowed note-taking equipment. I hope your memory is good, Professor Craft.'

'It is excellent.'

His eyes drifted over her face. '*One!*'

Thompson started, more than ready to punch out Quirebell's lights.

'Such a killer has a fascination with the inner workings of the human body and' – he leant forward – 'he wishes to share it—'

'*Back*, Quirebell. Sit *back*!'

'*Two:* it is purposeful, in the sense that his motivation is sexual. He is a lust killer. *Three:* he is proud of his dismemberment skills and wishes to . . . exhibit them. *Four:* the key motivation is aggression towards recipients, particularly females, as is the dismemberment itself. *Five.*' There was a brief silence. 'He is a sadist and he wants to show the world that he is *God*.' He calmly eyed Craft. 'I hope that my explanation meets your requirements, Professor.'

She looked into his eyes, realizing that he would not go further. 'It does not. I want you to describe to me the attention-seeking, the grandiosity, the narcissism which supports what *you* did' – Quirebell's eyelids fluttered – 'and the fantasies *you* created around each of the female recipients receiving those remains. I believe that, despite all of your efforts, even they failed to move you to feel anything at all. Zero horror. Zero guilt . . . Zero pleasure.'

'Mmm . . . "believe" or is it a mere guess? You might be surprised.'

'I would not. You do not experience emotional responses, no matter what you do. Which is why you would continue to create more victims if you were free.' She saw something shift behind his eyes. 'You are an emotionless vacuum, Mr Quirebell, and always will be, no matter what you fantasize or do.'

Shallow-breathing, Thompson glanced at her, recognizing the extreme verbal prodding she was giving this monster.

'Which for *you* is a kind of hell, isn't it?' She saw the slick of sweat now on Quirebell's upper lip, the sole indicator that her words were having an impact.

'Time's up!' The guard pointed to Quirebell. 'You know the drill. You stand. You walk at a normal pace to me.'

Quirebell's eyes moved to Craft, drifting down to her left hand as they both stood. With the guard's attention momentarily on opening the door, he slid his hand across the table towards her, saying softly, 'Whoever you are seeking, he knows *you* and he has *you* in his sights. Take care, Professor Craft.'

She watched him go to the door, then disappear from view.

They walked in silence and drizzle from the main prison building to Thompson's vehicle and got inside, Craft preoccupied by Quirebell's glance at her hand and the ring there, wishing she had not worn it, hearing again his final words. She had overlooked a key rule: do not flag personal information about oneself to someone like him. Given his situation, he was no threat. Which did not mean that he was powerless.

Thompson took his first deep breath in what felt like hours. Being inside that place had left him drained of air, strength . . . life. He glanced at her. 'I heard what he said to you. Ignore it. He's a game-player, messing with your head, or anybody else's that he meets. Was it any help?'

She stared straight ahead. 'It confirmed my theoretical understanding of dismemberment. Having met him, I found it encouraging to know that he is an emotionless vacuum and always will be. The downside to that is the horrific lengths to which he must go in his attempts to feel anything. It is possible we are looking for a similar individual' – she glanced at Thompson – 'a soulmate, even.'

Thompson stared out of the windscreen at bleakness. 'I hope you're wrong about that – and him.' They sat in a lengthy silence, then Thompson asked: 'What do you think of what he said?'

'About the reasons for our killer mailing body parts? Each of the points he made had varying degrees of merit, but what he said about the killer we're looking for being a sadist with a God complex is correct.'

Out of energy, Thompson drove from the prison complex on to the main road to the motorway. 'I've learned something about you today, Craft.'

She looked at him. 'You have?'

'Yep. *You* are a rule-breaker.'

She said nothing. He waited.

'What did Quirebell give you?' He waited. 'Come on, Craft! I saw the slimy git slide his hand towards yours—'

'I do not perceive it to be rule-breaking but a legitimate part of my professional role to accept whatever information is offered to me in whichever way it is delivered.' She opened her hand. He looked down at the intricately woven band with the dimensions of a bracelet, executed in attractive, soft shades of peach and green. She brought it closer, her eyes moving slowly over other, darker threads within it. She gently pulled at one brown thread. It sprang out, short, coarse, curly—

'*Stop!*'

Thompson stood on his brakes as she pushed open the door, gasping in the damp air, almost falling from the vehicle. Thompson got out and came around. 'What's up?'

She pointed to the seat where the bracelet was sitting. He went to it, reached into the glovebox for a flashlight, gave the small item a close examination, took a plastic bag from his pocket, dropped it inside and looked up at her.

'What can I say? Rules are rules.' He passed her a plastic bottle of water.

She poured some over each hand, drank from it and threw up.

After some minutes, Thompson asked, 'Are you all right?'

She nodded.

He looked in the direction from which they had come. 'Tell me what we got from that, apart from me wanting to punch him?'

'I now know for certain that we're looking for a psychopath.'

'How does that help us?' They got inside the vehicle, Craft's face still without any colour.

'Psychopaths delight in playing games with authority figures. One of them, an American, is well-known for persisting in his game-playing almost to the point when he was taken to the electric chair.

We now have confirmation that we are looking for a psychopathic game-player.' Fastening her seatbelt, she looked across at him. 'And what people like that seek is other, like-minded individuals. I think the games are about to start.'

Inside the prison, Quirebell's neat head was bent over a very important task. He was writing a letter.

> My dear friend, or rather, soulmate?
>
> I hope this finds you as well and in good spirits as it leaves me. I understand what a troublesome time you are having and that a certain 'specialist' is making your life unnecessarily difficult. In my view, she is extremely arrogant and something must be done. I shall give this my fullest consideration. In the meantime, look after yourself, listen to all that is said for when your time comes. My admiration and best wishes go with you.
>
> Jerome.

SEVENTEEN

Friday 25 October, 8.40 a.m.

Thompson was already in his office when Craft came inside. 'Are you OK?'

'Of course.'

'That business yesterday at the prison—'

'Meeting Jerome Quirebell has me thinking . . .'

'The sick bastard—'

'About aggression demonstrated in this investigation. Alicia Franks, Penny Bristow and Lucy Greening were subjected to extreme aggression, yet Phillip Marsh and Emma Matheson were not. As I have said, we are dealing with a psychopath, so why the difference in those homicides?'

Thompson gazed at her for several seconds. 'You don't class being strangled to death or chucked under a train as acts of aggression?'

'I am referring to the *type* of aggression this killer showed towards

Franks and Greening. Bristow would have endured more of the same if he had been able to finish what he started.'

'To me, aggression is aggression.'

'It is not. We don't have the evidence, but I'm considering the likelihood that all three victims were subjected to some level of sexual aggression.'

Thompson felt his head tighten. 'You've read the pathology reports. There's zero evidence of it. What we know is that he hit both Franks and Bristow into the middle of next week, and probably the same for Greening.' He gazed at her. 'What's this about, Craft? Are you trying to reframe these deaths to prove some theory you haven't yet told me about? Or is it something about yourself?'

Her fingers rapidly tapping, she said, 'This is not about *me*. It is about a re-evaluation of these homicides—'

'That's where you're dead wrong. What we do in this building is we follow the physical *evidence.* It's about finding it, looking at what it is telling us. Right now, in the absence of evidence of sexual assault for Franks and the total lack of any confirmation by Bristow herself of sexual behaviour towards *her*, and much as *you* might want us to *assume* that there was a sexual motivation, it's not going to happen, because we don't build cases on assumptions.' He pointed at her. 'If you've got any ideas about seeing Bristow with the intention of getting her to "think again", *don't* do it, Craft. It could compromise any chance we have of building a robust case. We do our best with what the evidence is showing us. We don't interfere with witness recall and we *don't* provide the defence with the get-out that this whole investigation was compromised by witness interference! Is that clear?'

Craft snapped, 'I've already said that I have no intention of involving myself. But we must evaluate what we know, be prepared to . . .' she paused, '. . . think outside the box. Both Alicia Franks and Penny Bristow were struck on the head. Franks' body was tossed into a ditch that I suspect was full of water. Bristow was never formally interviewed by your predecessor.' She watched him reach for his coffee mug and walk away, calling after him, 'It's about progression of events, Thompson! It's about intuiting what was in a killer's mind at the time he attacks.'

He turned to her. 'My job's not about reading minds, looking for something I *want* to find. It's about actions which produce *evidence*.'

'What if there *was* a sexual aspect which Penny Bristow has blocked out? It happens.'

'Listen to yourself! This is *police* work.'

'Have you considered that at the time Penny Bristow was attacked she fully comprehended what was happening to her, until she was struck? We cannot assume that she remembers nothing.'

He stared at her. 'Are you saying that she's holding back information?'

'No. I'm raising the possibility that she is in no position, emotionally, physically or psychologically, to express the full reality of what happened, but we can't just leave it there.'

'Forget it. You approach Penny Bristow with that mindset and I'll have you off this investigation.'

'I'm not suggesting I—'

A voice made them turn. 'Is this a bad time?' David Brown was standing at the open door.

Thompson dumped his coffee mug in the sink and went to the table. 'The professor here is second-guessing motive on Franks and Bristow. How many homicides do you know about which never went to trial because of professionals riding roughshod over them and compromising cases?'

'I've never been asked for that kind of data, so I can't—'

'I'm *going*.' Craft reached for her coat and bag. 'I *won't* be restricted in what I do here by fears of what *might* happen months down the line! I'm going to pursue the Bristow aspect, with or without your approval!'

Thompson watched her leave, shouting after her, 'And I can't work with somebody who thinks it's OK to do as she bloody likes!'

Brown looked in the direction Craft had gone, then back to Thompson, his face shocked. 'Tell me I didn't kickstart that.'

'What? No, no. This is between Craft and me.'

12.30 p.m.

Craft came into the small building and headed for the receptionist who gave her a smile of recognition. 'Professor Craft! I saw your surname in the diary and guessed it had to be you. How are you?'

'I'm fine,' said Craft, unclear as to why she was being asked.

'I'll buzz you through. Lydia said to wait in her office. You know the way.'

'Thank you, Elsa.' Craft went through the security door, along the corridor to a comfortable room of soft décor and sat, getting her breathing under control, her words ordered.

Minutes later, the door opened and a woman came inside. 'Teigan!' Lydia Wadham gave her a swift hug. 'It's *so* good to see you. You look fantastic; a little pale perhaps, but aren't we all around this time of year.'

'I'm in a mess, Lydia.'

'Oh?'

'The police investigation I'm involved with, the SIO and I are in conflict and it's all a complete . . . mess.'

'I see.' She nodded. 'I do see, Tig: different professions with different objectives often collide. Not so long ago, I gave psychological training and advice to police officers on positive ways of engaging with sex offenders and I can tell you that some of it fell on *very* fallow ground.' She waited. 'Tell me about this "mess".'

'It's simple. The SIO and I are colliding over sex.'

Lydia grinned. 'Oh, dear. Poor Tom.'

'*What?* It's nothing to do with— That's a joke, right?'

'A tiny one. Go on.'

'The SIO and I have worked together OK so far, but now we have completely different agendas as to what should happen next. We can't even discuss it. He is accusing me of jeopardizing a positive outcome for the investigation because I want to do something that he says I cannot do.'

Lydia was silent for several seconds, then: 'Tell me if I'm wrong, but this sounds like police evidence and psychological theory on a collision course.'

'That's *exactly* what it is.' Craft sat back, her face now flushed. 'You have no idea how relieved I am to hear you say it. This is something you've experienced?'

'Yes.' She sat forward. 'I also know that your previous paper-evaluation cases did not involve collaboration with police officers and I suspect he hasn't worked closely with a psychologist so it's inevitable for there to be a degree of friction.'

Craft frowned. 'All I know is that he's impossible to talk to about any idea he perceives as representing even the slightest challenge to the investigation. Which, to me, is short-sighted and ridiculous.'

'He is what he is, which applies to you too.' She chose her words. 'He probably does have a point.'

Still irritated, Craft ran her fingers through her hair, saying nothing.

Lydia broke the silence. 'At a guess he's in direct conflict with you about your wanting me to work with the young female victim in his investigation. If so, I have to say I understand his viewpoint, Tig.'

'It *has* to be done, Lydia, and for two reasons: one, to try to help Penny Bristow lead a normal life; and two, to hopefully gain information from her which might help us stop this individual.'

'I understand. You don't need to convince me, so long as you accept that there is a risk issue here for when the case is taken to court. Your DCI is very much aware of that.'

'He is not *my* DCI.'

'He has responsibility for the whole investigation and everyone who is part of it.'

'It can't be right that he is able to veto my plans.'

'I saw you on the television news a week or so ago, so I knew you were involved in something big.' Seeing Craft's appalled facial expression, she said, 'Don't worry, you were only just within shot.'

'I try to stay as invisible as possible.'

'Which is not easy for you.'

'What do you mean?'

'Just words, Tig. Carry on.'

'The current homicide investigation is very complex. Two of the victims, a man and a woman, worked together years ago in London. For those deaths there is zero indication of a sexual motive. They died in different places at different times, from seemingly different causes, yet I suspect both deaths were linked and instrumental for their killer. Three other women have since been attacked not far from where that first female lived, a couple of months apart and within five months of the first woman's murder. One of those women is Penny Bristow who I spoke to you about. She survived the attack on her. I know it's a lot to take in, Lydia.'

'I'm no stranger to complex cases.' She stopped writing. 'Got it.'

'I want you involved in this for your psychological perspective on Penny Bristow, but also your expertise working with vulnerable women. There is every possibility that Penny Bristow's attack was sexually motivated but she was never formally interviewed by the police at the time, never examined for evidence of sexual assault and she is unable to confirm it currently.' She paused. 'We need your assistance on this.'

Lydia tapped her pen against her pad. 'When you mention "assistance", right there is where your SIO sees a problem.'

'He has a talent for seeing them,' snapped Craft.

'It is understandable. As SIO, the responsibility is his to take an investigation to court to obtain justice for a victim and also justify the investigative expense.'

'I thought justice was the sole reason!'

Lydia studied her. 'What is it, Teigan? Is there something else troubling you?'

'No.'

'OK.'

'Yes, there is. I have seen how much Penny Bristow struggles in her daily life. Somebody must help her.'

Lydia slow-nodded. 'I understand. You empathize with this young woman's difficulties?'

'I'm trying to do so. Help us, Lydia, *please.* Her current situation is that she has recovered physically but says she remembers nothing at all of what happened.'

Craft paused while Wadham looked at her notes then up at Craft. 'How bad is the current SIO's attitude to my becoming involved?'

'He's apoplectic.'

'As I said, I understand his viewpoint. He wants to protect any case he might present to the Crown Prosecution Service.'

Craft sighed.

'There are conditions: the SIO must be made fully aware of any proposal for my involvement and be satisfied with the conditions within which information is gained from her.' She stood. 'Come with me.'

Craft followed her out of the room, along a corridor and into another room. She looked around at soft shades on the walls, the comfortable chairs, some of them child-sized, absorbed its calm quietness. 'This is lovely, Lydia,' she said quietly, 'so soothing and . . . safe.'

Wadham nodded. 'I see children and adults here, in cases where memory for events has been compromised by physical injury and psychological trauma.' She gave Craft a direct look. 'Do you think Penny Bristow might respond positively to the quietness and peace in here?'

'I do. Her everyday experience appears to be one of extreme tension which I think is a current block to her recall.'

'If I agree to assist, Tig, she has to be aware of the key feature of this room, that her every gesture, every word she utters is being recorded.'

Craft's eyes sought out and found the tiny cameras in each corner of the room.

'Every single person who comes here to talk about an experience, regardless of age, is told of this feature because of the possibility that what is said in here could lead to criminal proceedings. Do you believe that this is a situation which might be acceptable to this young woman you've told me about?'

'She works for the Probation Service so I'm assuming that she is aware that verbal evidence needs to be preserved and protected.'

They returned to Wadham's office.

'I can tell you a little about her.'

Wadham shook her head. 'No. Put the information in a referral letter so there is a record of the presenting situation, what is required and that all meetings between this young woman and myself would be recorded in the interests of transparency.' She looked directly at Craft. 'It would be preferable if the letter was signed by your SIO.'

'What I know about her might help you understand her, Lydia.'

'Then it must also be put in writing to me.' She smiled at Craft's frustrated look. 'As I said, transparency is key and I want to safeguard your current investigation.'

EIGHTEEN

2.30 p.m.

Craft was waiting for Thompson to come into the office. She gazed down at the letter she had carefully constructed to Dr Wadham. Once she had Thompson's agreement to the arrangement and it was signed, she would send it. She sighed. Hearing the office door open, she placed a file over it.

'Afternoon, Craft. What are you up to?'

She stared up at him. 'Nothing. I don't know what you mean.'

He sighed. 'Just another way of saying "How's it going?" or, "You OK?"'

'Yes, thank you.'

He looked at her, his eyes narrowing. 'Good.' He went to a nearby filing cabinet. Hefting the investigative files out of the drawer, he brought them to the table and sat, arranging them in some kind of order.

Craft watched. Victim order. Taking his pen from an inside pocket, he opened a file and gazed down at its contents, intermittently turning pages. Eleven minutes elapsed, the silence in the room heavy. Suddenly he sat back. 'Right. I give in. What's up?'

'I don't know what—'

'Come on, Craft! There's something on your mind. Spit it out so I can get on with what I'm doing.' She frowned across at him. 'When I do tell you, you won't like it.'

'Put like that, I already don't!'

'Why are you shouting? Don't shout!'

He covered his face with his hands. 'Craft, it's *you* that's doing the shouting.' His hands dropped. 'Just . . . tell me what's got you in a tizz.'

'I don't tizz. I'm worried.'

'About?'

'Penny Bristow.'

He sat back, looking at her. 'Not that again!'

'Yes. Again. She needs to be able to talk about what happened to her if she has any hope of getting justice.'

'And you know as well as I do that if we get that far and she is considered or known to have been helped to recall her experience, we would have the defence down on it and us like a ton of bricks! It *can't* be done.'

'Yes, it can. It takes a lot of care and for whoever sees her to know the rules of evidence and how they are breached.'

'From my perspective, *anybody* talking to Bristow about the attack on her is going to be viewed in a bad light.'

She shook her head. 'What if whoever does so makes no reference at all to her experience and simply allows Penny herself to speak about it?'

He sighed. 'You heard her when we were at the house. She told us she does not want to talk about it.'

'I think she would, if the situation felt right to her.' She reached for her phone, tapped it, held it up. 'See this?'

He took it from her, looked at a photograph. 'What's this place?'

'It's where my colleague Dr Lydia Wadham works. She is experienced at putting witnesses at ease.' She took back the phone, showed him more pictures. 'This is the environment she provides, see? It's very relaxing. Very quiet.'

'What bothers me is what *she* might say to Bristow.'

'My understanding is it would be minimal. Her role is that of enabler. She would provide the calm environment, put Penny at ease and then allow the situation to develop.'

'What about the defence alleging she was led—'

'That can't happen.' She tapped the phone, pointing to another photograph. 'See the corners of the room, close to the ceiling? Those small black squares are devices which would record everything said inside that room.'

He sighed, took it from her, studied it. 'This kind of set-up is used by officers working with children who are witnesses to offences against them.'

'It works equally well for adults.'

He looked at her. 'You're certain that this colleague of yours won't say or do anything to compromise our case?'

'She is very experienced with this type of work so, yes, I am. I also believe she is our best chance for obtaining information from Penny.'

He handed the phone back. 'I'll think it over. Let you know.'

'No. It must be decided now.'

'From what you've said, if it's going to work, what does a day or so matter?'

'We need whatever Penny is able to recall.'

'And I'm the SIO here, unless you've forgotten. Like I said, I'll think about it.'

At home that evening, Craft was video calling Tom, telling him about the difficulties she was experiencing with Thompson. 'His sole priority is evidence protection, rather than how a victim-witness might be feeling or wishing to do.'

'He is the officer in charge.'

'I know that!' She sighed. 'I'm very conflicted about men at the moment.'

Tom laughed. 'Really? So, where exactly do I stand?'

She frowned. 'What are you talking about? You're not *a* man. You're my Tom.'

'Thanks for what sounds like a very dubious vote of confidence. Just out of interest, does the same judgement apply to your hero who does the wildlife programmes on the television?'

She stared at his face on the small screen. 'He's not a man in that sense, either, but he's also nice. Like you.'

'Nice, and neuter.'

She grinned, lay back against cushions. 'Not at all. It's been a very tiring day. I'm hoping that Penny is able to give us something we can use to catch this man. She is the best chance we have of getting evidence against him, possibly our only chance. I want Penny to meet Lydia and if anything comes of it, I'll show Thompson the recording and go *na-na!* but in a serious way, because he's being a total pain and I won't like him until I like him again.'

He shook his head, smiling. 'You do know that you are the quirkiest woman I've ever known.'

'How many?

'Mmm?'

'How many quirky women have you known?'

'Just you.'

She relaxed against the sofa cushions. 'You're such a great person, Tom, yet you're the only one I know whose ankles Percy nips. If it continues, I shall have to take him to an obedience class.'

She listened to his soft laugh.

'Tom, the other thing I haven't told you is . . .' She held up her left hand, wriggling the fingers. 'I'm wearing it.'

He looked at her, his face a study in blankness. 'You always wear red nail polish.' She laughed. '*Tom!*'

'Oh, you mean, the *ring*.'

They both fell silent. 'I love you, Tig.'

'I know.'

'Don't you *dare* end this call, like you often do when I say that.'

She grinned into the phone. 'I love you to HD189773B and K2-186 and back, Tom.' She added, 'They are both stars,' and ended the call.

NINETEEN

Monday 28 October, 10 a.m.

Thompson came into Headquarters, looking preoccupied.

'Morning, sir!'

He stopped, turned to the officer on reception duty who grinned at him.

'Professor Craft's been here since . . .' she ran her finger down a list, '. . . five ten a.m.'

'Good for her.' He headed for his office, seeing a light on inside. Opening the door, he saw her sitting at the table in a pool of light, surrounded by papers, blonde head bowed over textbooks. She looked up.

He said, 'Good morning,' took documents from his tray and brought them to the table. 'You OK? You look a bit tired.'

She did not respond.

He continued, 'I've considered this idea of yours for sending Penny Bristow for therapy and the answer's no.'

She stared at him. 'Are you *insane*? I've told you. It is *not* therapy and we need whatever information is inside Penny Bristow's head about the man who attacked her. We need it *now*.'

'You think your opinion that it's a safe thing to do and a recording of what she says is going to stop a defence barrister raising questions and objections? If you do, you must be greener than I thought.'

She frowned. 'How does colour enter the equation?' Impatient, she slid printed sheets towards him.

He shrugged off his coat, dropped it on to the back of his chair and sat, rubbing his face with both hands, blinking at the printed sheets. 'Just tell me.'

'Dr Lydia Wadham has already seen Penny once, on Saturday, and she has reported that Penny felt sufficiently safe and relaxed to talk about her ordeal.'

'You knew my attitude to a witness being spoken to and yet you *still*—! How . . .'

'Read it! It indicates how scrupulous Dr Wadham is in her work, that she understands the police evidential stance. She has a video recording of that meeting which demonstrates that Dr Wadham's involvement was directed solely at ensuring that Penny Bristow was relaxed, her role otherwise unobtrusive.' She leant forward. 'It has taken just one session for Penny Bristow to confirm that the attack on her was sexual in nature although it did not involve intercourse.'

'Jesus *H* Christ! Why didn't she say so at the time?'

'You know why! She had suffered two blows to her head, plus the police officer in charge of her case never asked her, and she probably preferred not to face it! Do you think it is easy to just *say* stuff like that? Her own memory spared her, until such time as she felt sufficiently safe to allow herself to know what happened to her!'

Thompson was on his feet. 'If this gets as far as a courtroom, I hope you're prepared for accusations of witness influence.'

'It won't happen, but *if* it does, we can counter it. Read Dr Wadham's letter. You'll see how careful she was in her approach.'

'Yeah, and I know the lengths barristers go to, to raise doubts about witnesses.' He was silent for a few seconds. 'Just . . . *tell* me what she got from Bristow.'

'Penny recalled being taken to the hospital and treated for her physical injuries and later discharged home. We know that no one asked her to give an account of what happened to her at that time or subsequently, including the police. More relevantly, Penny did not want to hear those words from her own mouth. She put that whole experience to one side. She now remembers arriving home by taxi from the hospital. Her boyfriend was there and he looked after her. As far as he knew, she had been attacked physically but nothing further. She went to bed, exhausted. Her boyfriend slept in the sitting room. Penny Bristow awoke very early and she touched the injuries to her upper face and head.'

'And?'

'She described her hair to Dr Wadham as "feeling crisp, stiff to the touch". Penny knew what that meant and she did the one thing she felt able to do at that time. She took a shower to get his semen out of her hair.'

Thompson let his head drop back. 'We could have had DNA.'

'Penny Bristow had never been hit in her life until then. It changed her whole world view. I suspect that that's when she put the whole experience away from herself.'

Craft watched him shake his head.

She leant towards him. 'Thompson, she was in survival mode. The only way she had for dealing with an experience she never wished to revisit because of the trauma of it. The safe, calm situation Lydia Wadham provided helped her face the memory of that whole experience. You should be applauding Penny.' She reached for a sheet of paper. 'Here, verbatim, is what she said to Dr Wadham after she fully realized what had happened to her.'

He took the sheet and read it:

> It was in my hair and my head hurt terribly. But I had no other damage or pain anywhere else. I put it all away from me. Did not think about it. Left it. Got a haircut. Lost my boyfriend. Gradually, what happened, what really happened was gone. It felt like it had been left on the salon floor. I never wanted to think about it ever again. I didn't dare.

Craft asked, 'Do you recall the case of the London taxi driver who picked up female fares, plied them with alcohol and who-knows-what else? It took some of those women *months* to make sense of what had happened to them and to report it, which is very similar to Penny's experience. She had a serious head injury and was in no fit state to process what was done to her and then, after a while, it was so much easier not to think of it at all.'

'What about Emma Matheson's homicide? Does this change your view of what happened to her?'

Craft shook her head. 'No. Her murder was not sexual. I told you. It was *expedient*.' She reached under the table, brought out two sealed brown bags. 'These contain Penny Bristow's clothes from the day she was attacked. Because there was no indication of it being a sexual attack, they were put into a plastic bag and given to her mother at the hospital. Fortunately for us, at a time of such family upheaval, her mother simply put them away, forgot about them, just as Penny "forgot" what had happened to her. Thompson, we *might* have DNA here.'

He pointed to pages of her neat writing. 'What's all this?'

'I'm developing a psychological profile of this killer. Two, in fact. One which profiles him as a rapist, and the other as a killer.'

Thompson reached for a thick, soft-covered publication lying on the table beside it, read the title, *Criminal Investigative Analysis*

– *Sexual Homicide.* He pointed. 'It says here that this is from the FBI.'

'It is.'

'How did you get hold of it?'

'The FBI sent it to me.'

He muttered, 'Why did I bother asking? These two profiles will give us his name, will they?'

'You are now being sarcastic. What they will give us is clarity around the type of person he is in terms of his personality and as a sexual offender, that he might have previous convictions for rape.'

The desk phone rang. Thompson reached for it. It was Holdsworth. 'Yes, sir. I'll come now.' He listened, his eyes on Craft. 'We're still working on it. Nothing specific yet.' He ended the call, reached for his notebook, his eyes on Craft who was halfway out of the door, brown bags in hand. 'Holdsworth's demanding results. I'll tell him we've got a potential DNA result coming.'

5.30 p.m.

Craft had brought case information home. It was now spread out on the dining table. Her eyes moved over it, then on to the notes she had made so far which had produced an outline of the individual they were searching for. There was no need for two profiles. Penny Bristow had been fortunate: this was an individual with a rape-kill mentality. She read what she had written:

> This is a male whose self-esteem is low, who routinely experiences emotional disconnection from others, whose aggression towards females is off the scale. A man who has learned to conceal his emotional deficits behind a façade of geniality, plus an array of social skills; a sham which enables him to coexist within society, until such times of his choosing when his massive, inner rage is unleashed, perhaps towards a partner, more likely to a stranger.

She shook her head, inserting the word 'female' before 'stranger'.

> People in his life believe they know him. What they know is the façade he has developed over the years. That is, until he creates a particular situation in which to show his true self.

She stopped reading. 'And God help whoever is with him when he does.' She dropped her pen on to the table and brought both hands to her face, at the edge of exhaustion. She took a deep breath, looked down at all that she had done to generate a sexual homicide profile: an evaluation of the crime scene details; what was known about the victims; how they were found; the weapon used and the forensic detail if available. Despite the sketchiness, the unavailability of some detail she continued with the assessment of the attacks on Franks and Bristow as purposeful homicide, including the likely scene dynamics where possible. Now, for the third time, she read the most specific profile she had ever put together, based on what had happened to the known victims in the investigation:

> This investigation involves repeat homicide, specifically the deaths of Emma Matheson and Phillip Marsh, neither of which is judged by this evaluator to be sadistic in nature, but rather a means to an end. The death of Alicia Franks indicates a sadistic offender. The dismembered remains of Lucy Greening, also in Forrest Park, reinforce this.

Craft frowned at her own words. Was she able to be this confident? She pressed on:

> Those two homicides and the attack on Penny Bristow are linked by modus operandi as indicated by the perpetrator's behaviour during the attacks.

Craft sat back. It felt right. As right as she was able to make it. Craft was now fully aware of police officers' dislike of anomalies and their incessant demands for proof. From Thompson's viewpoint, she still had nothing. She looked down at the profile. This was a mere tool, a means to clarify thinking, as much for her own benefit as anyone else's. She resumed writing:

> This offender is a rapist-killer, fully in control of what he does, the exception being Penny Bristow. She is a potential source of information for this investigation.

Craft paused, aware of the implication of her written words.

> The possibility of continuing risk to Penny Bristow must be addressed and some means of protection put in place. Finally, given my opinion that Emma Matheson is dead for reason/s which are known to her killer, exploration of her connection to Phillip Marsh, his subsequent death, and the fact that he and Emma Matheson were in a relationship suggests that the motive for his homicide was also expedient. Given the current investigative timeframe, I advise that focus remains on the most recent deaths and attack as potential sources of information. This offender is highly aware of the forensic implications of what he does and adjusts his behaviour accordingly.

She looked up at the lights in other apartment windows and shook her head. Who does not know about forensics? It is a mainstay of every television crime show. She sat back, her eyes on what she had written. Where might this killer be? She had no advice to give on his geographical location. What she did have was an awareness of his knowledge, his skills and the kinds of people who were most likely to have them, her thoughts going to several possibilities: biologist, archaeologist, anthropologist, a chemist, a medical researcher . . . a police officer?

Craft's phone vibrated on the table. She snatched it up, hearing Thompson's voice. She closed her eyes. 'What do you want?'

'A hint of civility wouldn't go amiss. Anything to report?'

'Only what we both already know – that every time either of us makes a definitive statement about these attacks it leads to friction between us. You need to provide Penny Bristow with some level of protection.' She waited for a response, not getting one. 'Despite knowing your antipathy to profiles, I have continued with mine for the clarity it gives *me,* in terms of what I believe his intentions were.'

'Is that scientific?'

'I don't bloody care at this stage! I'm constructing a summation of all he *is* and all we *know* he has done and if you'll get off the phone, I can continue with it.' She ended the call.

An hour later, the profile was complete. She whispered, 'I don't give a damn for anomalies. Right now, this is as good as it gets.' In the darkness of her apartment, sitting in the pool of light from her desk lamp, she read:

> The organization within these attacks is evident. This perpetrator plans each homicide of his targeted victims, which, of itself, is indicative of stalking. He seizes control of victim via initial verbal manipulation which quickly progresses to physical force and significant brutality.

'And so far, the only exception to that smooth progression is Penny Bristow.'

Craft switched off the desk lamp, plunging the room into darkness. She stared out of the window at the neatly kept grounds of the apartment complex, a few windows still lit. She whispered, 'I'm starting to *see* you. To have been directly involved with Emma Matheson and Phillip Marsh so many years ago suggests that you are somewhat older than I thought. Perhaps well into your forties now? The timing of your attacks suggests that you are in employment. You have a good level of intellect as evidenced by your planning abilities. Initially you present as physically acceptable to your victims.' She paused. 'So . . . what do I have? An educated, employed, perhaps late forties male, a details person with a visceral hatred of women . . . self-controlled in his daily life . . . sufficiently charming to con the unwary until that persona drops away and he shows his true nature in darkness and seclusion. And not forgetting that you have a bathtub, a freezer and privacy.' Another glance out of the window at the darkened grounds. 'You live alone, don't you?'

She reached for her phone and rang Thompson's number. 'I'm about to email my thoughts to you. Do *not* raise objections around lack of evidence or any other perceived deficiencies.'

'I'll have a look at it and let you know what I—'

'He's "Mr Normal" and no one knows otherwise until it's too *damned* late. I'm going to bed.'

'It's only half ten.'

'I don't care what time it is! What have *you* been doing all *bloody* evening?'

'What's with the language, Craft?'

'It must be the company I'm keeping!'

'How about early tomorrow morning we take a ride in my car?'

'Given the circumstances of this case, that sounds somewhat inappropriate . . . Where?'

'To a nice, historic town not far from Birmingham?'

'I'll be at Headquarters at seven a.m.'

Ending the call, she showered, pulled on pyjamas, switched off lights and lay down; her last conscious thoughts were of Lucy Greening.

TWENTY

Tuesday 29 October, 9.30 a.m.

Craft was inside Thompson's vehicle travelling along the motorway, a gantry sign indicating the Stratford-upon-Avon exit coming up soon. She looked across at him. 'We're on our way to see the Greening family?'

'No. I've already talked to them. It's a long time since their daughter disappeared and the local police ran out of ideas in a matter of weeks.' He reached under his seat, brought out a file. 'Have a look through this. It's information the Stratford SIO emailed me.'

She took it from him, opened the worryingly slim file, the first item an eight-by-ten photograph of a young woman with fair hair, regular features and excellent dentition smiling up at her. 'What do we know?'

'Lucy Greening. One month short of her nineteenth birthday when she disappeared. She worked as a beautician and lived with her parents and younger brother close to Stratford town centre. Lucy broke off her engagement to her boyfriend ten weeks prior to her disappearance.'

'Wait. Russo found marks on her ring finger which suggested the possibility of something being forcibly removed. What do we know about this boyfriend?'

'He was a year older than Lucy, employed as a trainee chef in a Stratford restaurant. The break-up was amicable, according to both families, and he managed to persuade Lucy to continue wearing the ring in hopes of her changing her mind.' He glanced at Craft. 'She didn't.'

'Her killer took her ring as a trophy.'

He shrugged. 'My guess is he flogged it.'

'Where are we actually going?'

'First to a dating agency Lucy Greening was registered with. They're expecting us.'

She waited. 'You are *not* serious! Why would an attractive, almost nineteen-year-old female have anything to do with such—'

'Ever been involved with one, Craft?'

'Certainly not,' she snapped.

He grinned at her. 'You know what they say: "Don't knock it till you've tried it." We've also got a witness who saw Lucy the same day she registered with the agency, so we'll have a chat with her, after which the local police have agreed to talk to us.' He drove to the police station. 'I've arranged to leave my car here. Parking's a mare in this town.'

They left the police station car park and walked in the direction of the town itself. Within minutes they had navigated crowded pavements and were inside a small, walled courtyard containing just two business premises: one a women's expensive-looking clothes shop, the other a discreet frontage with neatly scripted letters on its door: The Agency.

Craft pointed to it. 'Very subtle.'

His facial expression disapproving, Thompson pressed a button to one side of the letters and they heard it ring inside. The door clicked open. They went in and were met by a cheerful-looking woman. Thompson showed his ID and she led them inside a pleasantly warm room of pinks and pale yellows and sat at a desk. 'Please – have seats. I'm Caroline Wells, the proprietor of this agency. I have all the information available on Lucy Greening.' She looked up at them. 'I was truly horrified when I learned she had disappeared and now *this* dreadful news.' She shook her head. 'Here we are. This is the contract between Lucy and the agency and our recording of her.'

Thompson said, 'You were never asked for the recording once she'd disappeared?'

'Apparently, Lucy kept her involvement with the agency a secret from family and friends. No one knew she had registered with us. As soon as we realized that she was reported missing, I contacted the local police myself. I took the recording with me and they made a copy of it. It is for our internal use only. Our method for assisting people to present well. You might be surprised how many people can't do that. We show them their recording and help them see how they can improve their personal presentation. We find showing rather than telling works best.'

'And these are never released to other customers?'

'*Members*. No. We pride ourselves on the confidentiality we provide.'

'We need to view the recording of Lucy.'

'Of course.' A minute or so later, Craft and Thompson were looking at the on-screen face of a young woman. 'This is Lucy. She sounded very pleasant on the phone, which is exactly how she proved to be when I met her in person. She told me that having broken off her engagement, she realized that her work as a beautician was not providing her with many opportunities to meet young men.'

Thompson and Craft watched as the on-screen Lucy Greening came to life, her smile wide as she reached up and pushed back her hair.

'Oh, golly . . . I'm . . .' She shook her head, laughed. 'I don't know what to *say*. This is harder than I thought.' They watched her take a breath. 'OK, my name is Lucy. I'm a fully qualified beautician and, er, I love my job, but it limits the number of people I meet during worktime.' She smiled. 'I'm talking about men. When I'm not working, I like to get out into the countryside for long walks with Stuey, my Labrador, who is two years old and . . . that's probably irrelevant . . . I enjoy music, romantic films and eating out. My most memorable experience last year was being at the Royal Albert Hall for the closing night of the Proms, which was a present from my parents . . . I read a lot when I have the time. My favourite authors are Jane Austen, Charlotte Brontë and Georgette Heyer . . .'

Wells aimed a remote at the screen, freezing Greening's image. 'You can see from her presentation that Lucy was a well-educated, very engaging young woman, attractive, full of life, somewhat romantic in her attitudes.' She paused. 'When we found out she had disappeared, it was unbelievable. I mean, she was so vivacious, so likeable. So . . . alive.' She looked away. 'It's too dreadful to think about.'

'You set up some introductions for her?' said Craft.

'No. We were still in the process of doing so when I saw a news item on the television about her having disappeared . . . Just . . . terrible.'

'We need to take this recording with us,' said Thompson.

Craft and Thompson walked down the narrow pathway and out on to the busy street. Craft broke the silence. 'That is one of the saddest things I have ever seen. She was so lovely in life, so . . . alive, and we know what was done to her.'

'Buck up, Craft. There's somebody else who saw Greening that day.' He pointed ahead. 'She works in that coffee shop up there. I phoned to check; she's in work today. Come on. Looking like a wet weekend's not helping anybody.'

Pulling a face, Craft followed him up the busy street and into the coffee shop where three baristas were serving a queue of customers. Thompson by-passed it, headed to the head of the queue and held up ID.

One of the baristas nodded, pointed to herself, then at a distant table. 'Give me five.' Going to the table, they sat in silence. The young woman arrived within a couple of minutes and sat opposite them. Thompson introduced himself and Craft. She said, 'Sorry, this is our busy time. You want to know about that woman I saw, the young one that disappeared.'

'Tell us all the details you remember.'

'It was a Friday and we had a rush on here. One of the servers had not turned up for her shift so it was mega busy. In the afternoon it calmed down, which is when she came in. She ordered a cappuccino and a toasted sandwich, paid, took the coffee' – she pointed – 'to that table over there. I toasted the sandwich and took it to her. We exchanged a few words, and I said, you know, being friendly, something like, "You look happy" and she said she was. That she had done something she had never done before – she had registered with a dating agency. That surprised me. She looked so young and attractive, but' – she shrugged – 'each to her own, yeah?'

Thompson was sitting, pen poised. 'That it?'

'No. She asked if I knew the agency and I said I knew of it as it's just down the road, and she was like, "Oh, don't tell me it's an awful place!" and I laughed, told her that I thought it was probably sound. She seemed happy to me, like, excited, you know? She told me a bit about what it was like at the agency and I said that it sounded nice, no riff-raff around there, and we both had a laugh. She was very "up", looking forward to introductions from it. That's when I saw that a queue was building up so . . . that was it. I went back to serving.'

Craft and Thompson left the coffee shop.

'I agree with what she said about that agency being respectable. It's probably irrelevant to our investigation,' Craft said.

'It might well be, but I want confirmation from local cops. See what they know.'

They returned to the police station, this time going up the shallow steps and inside the modern brick building. Thompson gave their names to the officer on duty. Within a couple of minutes a female officer appeared, they shook hands and she gestured for them to follow her. Inside a corner office overlooking one of the main traffic islands, she said, 'I'm DCI Claire Jackson. I was SIO on the Lucy Greening investigation. I have all the information which was at our disposal at the time Lucy Greening was reported missing. What would you like to know?'

Thompson asked, 'Did any names emerge as part of your inquiries?'

'Just one that merited any real attention. Timothy Aldous Robson.'

'I know that name,' said Thompson.

She took a photograph from a plastic wallet and passed it to him. 'I'm sure you do. He is a Birmingham resident but at that time he was working regularly here, which is how he came to our attention. He had set himself up as an electrician, picking up inquiries via his phone. After two complaints about him, we got him in here for interview.'

Thompson and Craft exchanged looks.

'The first complaint we received about him was from a female householder who alleged that whilst he was at her house, ostensibly as an electrician, he called her into the kitchen and pointed at the internal workings of her gas boiler. Whilst he was doing that, he sexually assaulted her. She described his actions as smooth – so smooth, in fact, that it took her a few seconds to fully realize what was happening. The second woman he assaulted the following day described him as "very free with his hands" and that prior to that he had photographed her without her consent when her back was turned to him.'

'What tipped her off as to what he was doing?'

'Apart from sounds from his phone as he took them, she saw his reflection in the glass door of her oven.'

'Was there any violence?'

'No. Both women asked him to leave and he did without any problem. We arrested and charged him, went to court and he was given a two-year sentence.'

'Oh? That's more than I would have expected.'

'He was already on the Sex Offender Register for two previous cases of similar assaults.' She looked at her watch. 'I'm due in a meeting in five minutes but I'll get the information we've got brought here and you can read through it. There's not much. If there's anything you want to take with you, I'll arrange for it to be photocopied.'

Over an hour later they left the building, Thompson looking irritated. Craft gave him a sideways glance. 'I'd have thought you'd be pleased to know—'

'Yeah, I'm overjoyed that Robson was "unavailable" for both Franks and Bristow, having been banged up for two separate sentences of several months.'

'It's obvious you're *not* overjoyed.'

He turned to her. '*Is* it, *really*? And why do you suppose *that* is?'

'You know I don't do sarcasm, and I don't understand why you're so irate about being given information which has saved us wasting time on Robson.'

She watched him walk away, talking over his shoulder.

'Everything is equal, to your way of thinking, Craft. Most of us on difficult cases appreciate the occasional buzz we get from situations panning out, because they are very few and far between.'

'No. I don't get it.'

'Jesus *wept*.'

2.45 p.m.

Ashton, Sullivan and Sandhu were in the office and David Brown was making himself coffee. He glanced up as Ashton tapped his phone and held it out to Sullivan, saying, 'Seen this one?'

Sullivan took the phone from him. 'Bloody *hell*! Look at the booty on that! Ooh-la-la! That's French for "I don't mind if I *do*".'

Sandhu, her hands over her ears, was reading information in a file in front of her.

Brown came towards them. 'What you two are doing is unacceptable, given there's a female present.'

There was a combined, 'Ooooh-er!' from the two male officers, who squared up to Brown. 'What's it to *you*, Dave?' asked Sullivan.

'You've got an office upstairs. If you come in here you go with the flow, right?'

Coming into the office, Craft stopped on seeing Brown, his face angry. 'No! It isn't! This is a shared work environment and what you are doing is unacceptable.'

Sullivan turned slowly to Ashton. 'Hear that, Ash? What do you think?'

Ashton's grin disappeared as Sullivan moved closer to Brown. 'I'll tell you what *I* think: our civilian computer tapper is bang out of order.' And to Brown, 'When *you* do *our* job, that's when *your* opinion matters. Until then, shut the fuck up!'

Sandhu leapt to her feet. '*You* shut up! I'm sick of hearing your voice, Sullivan!'

Brown moved to her side as Sullivan approached. 'You are way out of order, Sullivan.'

The door opened and Thompson came into the office, seeing Sullivan matching Brown for height but using his imposing musculature to steer the data analyst in the direction of the door. '*Hey!*' Thompson shouted as Sullivan moved smoothly past Brown and on to the kettle.

'Like a coffee, sir?'

Craft looked at Brown's flushed face.

Thompson pointed to Ashton and Sullivan. 'Have you pair finished checking all retail outlets within two miles of Forrest Road, like I told you?'

'Nearly, sir.'

'"Nearly" means no, you haven't. Get on with it!' He watched as the two officers headed for the door, Sullivan with a swagger, the door slowly closing on them. 'What was that about. David?'

'Just some joking around that went too far.'

Thompson studied him, saw Craft looking confused, her eyes going from Brown to Sandhu and back. Getting her attention, he pointed to the door.

Craft followed him into the corridor. He turned to her. 'Tell me what that was about.'

'I . . . it happened so suddenly. I didn't fully understand what was happening until I realized that Sullivan was attempting to intimidate David.'

'Did Brown initiate it?'

'He objected to the way Sullivan spoke in front of Officer Sandhu.'

They returned to the office. Thompson sat looking across at the young officer. 'Sandhu, I want a written account from you of what just happened here involving DC Sullivan.'

'Yes, sir.'

He turned to Craft. 'And I'd like your ideas on our next investigative steps.'

'I'm waiting on some forensic information from Penny Bristow's clothes—'

He reached for the desk phone on its first ring, mouthing, 'Bass,' to Craft. 'Yeah . . . yeah, she's here . . . so, what's the result? . . . OK. It is what it is. I'll let her know.' He put down the phone, his eyes and hand still on it. 'Penny Bristow's clothes. The DNA on it looks to be hers and hers alone.'

Craft stared at him. 'No! Other DNA must be there! Tell Bass to check again!' She was on her feet. 'I'm going up there to talk to him.'

Thompson let her go. If she chose to be wilful, she could deal with the fall-out. He had enough to do without protecting her from herself.

Fifteen minutes later, Craft returned to the office to find it empty. The atmosphere she had left in the forensics lab was not positive. She had demanded Bass retest Penny Bristow's clothing. He had refused. She had persisted and the situation had ended with his telling her to leave the lab. Going to the table, she reached for her bag and took out several files. She spread them out and selected one, soon losing herself in the detail, her usual method of choice for coping with frustration. When she next looked up, she saw that almost two hours had elapsed, during which she had achieved nothing apart from committing the details she had read to memory. The office was now in shadow, except for the small pool of light where she was working.

She flinched as the door suddenly swung open and David Brown appeared. Seeing her, he said, 'Hey, I hope the row you had earlier in Forensics had nothing to do with me.'

'No. That was all me, single-handedly alienating Bass. Want coffee?'

'Please.'

'Real coffee?'

'Even more, please.'

She headed for the cafetiere. A few minutes of silence and she was pouring coffee into two mugs and bringing them to the table.

Brown raised the mug to his mouth and sipped. 'Mmm . . . that's good.'

Craft asked, 'Have you had time to think about our case?'

'I'm really busy analysing the last twelve months' arrest rates, looking for an explanation of a general increase in housebreaking, which so far appears to be due to a lack of follow-up after the event and a low level of officers on the streets, but I have been giving it some thought.'

'Is there anything you can tell me?'

'How about I pull my ideas together and email them to you?'

'I'd really appreciate that.' She paused. 'Do you enjoy your work, David?'

He shrugged. 'I don't think "enjoy" comes into it that much. It can be interesting at times.'

'Why did you choose data analysis as a job?'

'It wasn't a choice. I initially opted for a computer science degree and applied to Imperial College London and Durham. Both were oversubscribed but Durham offered me a combined criminology-data analysis course, which I accepted.' He raised his hand. 'And here I am.'

Craft eyed him. 'Are you married?'

He grinned, dark brows climbing. 'That's direct.'

'I know. I get criticized for asking personal questions.'

'Oh? By whom?'

'My mother.'

'No. I'm not married. I almost was.'

There was a brief silence. She waited, at a loss how to move the conversation on when he spoke.

'July, 2019. That's when I was due to get married.'

'What happened? Sorry, I'm doing it again.'

He shook his head. 'No problem. Her name was Suzie and the previous winter she decided to take a temporary job as a ski instructor in Italy because it paid well.'

'I tried skiing. I loved it but my boyfriend thought it was hideous.'

Brown shook his head. 'I never got the hang of it, either.'

'So what happened? Did you and Suzie break up?'

'She died.'

Craft stared at him. 'David, I-I'm sorry. I don't know what to say.'

'There's nothing to say. She had dinner with some other instructors then left the restaurant alone to walk along a path that ran high above the road. They returned to their apartment complex, realized Suzie wasn't there and reported her missing. She was found at the side of the road. She had slipped. Fallen? No one knows. The medics said she might have survived if she had been found quickly but . . .' He stood, reached for his mug.

Craft looked up at him. 'I'm so sorry, David, and sorry I asked you.'

'Don't be. It was ages ago and you weren't to know.'

She watched him rinse mugs, revising her impressions of him. Quiet. Business-like. Separate. Self-contained. She should have known there was something in his background. He was coming back to the table.

'Do you live alone?' she asked.

He shook his head. 'I have a housemate. He helps with the rent, works at the university, keeps normal hours, doesn't drink as far as I can tell, and he's no trouble.' He hesitated. 'After Suzi died, I didn't handle it very well. It wasn't what I expected of grief. I was on constant high alert, expecting something bad to happen, phoning my parents every day to check on them. It was a crazy time.'

'Hypervigilance. It's a fairly common reaction to sudden trauma.'

'That's what the doctor eventually came up with.' He shrugged. 'It's a pity I didn't know you then, Teigan. You would have sorted me out.' He looked at his watch, reached for his coat and bag 'I'm off home. See you tomorrow.'

'David, I *am* sorry.'

He turned to her. 'No need. Like I said, it was ages ago. There's enough sadness in the world without dwelling on things, right?'

'I'm sure there's somebody for you, David.'

He paused in the doorway. 'I'm sort of looking.' A brief smile and he was gone.

After another hour, feeling dispirited, she packed away the files, stowed textbooks in her bag and fetched her coat. The moment she arrived home, she would ring Tom. It was not something she normally did but this evening was different. She felt unsettled. She needed to hear his voice.

TWENTY-ONE

Wednesday 30 October, 10.30 a.m.

Craft came into the small clinic, drive by the possibility that the destroyer of the young female victims in the investigation knew them to some degree. Going to the receptionist, she said, 'I need to speak to Dr Lydia Wadham now about a young woman she is seeing named Bristow. It is *very* urgent.'

The receptionist told here to take a seat. 'It might take a couple of minutes to contact her and see if she's able to speak to you.'

Craft paced, listening to the receptionist's voice, trying to intuit from her words and tone if Lydia was available. It did not sound hopeful. The phone went down.

'Dr Wadham says she can see you in fifteen minutes if you're willing to wait.'

Checking the current time on her watch, Craft nodded and left the clinic for the main hospital. Inside the café, not buying anything, she sat gazing out of the window. If Lydia was able to confirm that Penny Bristow had indicated to her a readiness to talk to the police about the attack on her, Craft would set it up at Headquarters, with Sandhu conducting the interview with Penny.

'Tig?' Craft looked up to see Lydia looking concerned. 'I understand you need to see me urgently about Ms Bristow. Has something happened?'

'What? No. I must know more about the progress you have made with her.'

Lydia's facial expression changed. She turned with a curt: 'Follow me.'

Craft did so, back to the building and Lydia's office.

Once inside, Lydia turned to her. 'What on earth is the matter with you, Teigan? I was busy with a client referral and I left her because your urgency suggested something had happened.' She sighed. 'So far, I have seen Penny for an introductory meeting. During it, I encouraged her into a relaxed frame of mind. She was very receptive. She voluntarily spoke a little about what happened to her, which I put in a letter to Headquarters for you and your SIO, and which bodes well for when she comes to talk to me again.'

'Has she specifically said that she has more to say? Has she mentioned any male names? If not, is there any way you can speed up the process?'

'You know better than that! This kind of work takes as long as it takes. What *is* going on, Teigan? Why the impatience?'

Craft paced, running her fingers through her hair. 'The situation at Headquarters is very demanding. We need investigative progress and it occurred to me that Penny might have mentioned a name or something which would be relevant to me, yet perhaps not to you.'

'I do not release information piecemeal. That first meeting was to familiarize her with the setting here, and she did voluntarily and very briefly talk about what happened to her but that is all I'm willing to say at this stage.'

Craft turned and left the office.

'*Tig!*'

Driving at speed into Headquarters' car park, she looked for David's car but could not find it. She was expecting an email from him giving his thoughts on the investigation. It had occurred to her that he might have something which she had overlooked. Going straight to the office, not finding an email from him, she returned to reception. 'Has David Brown arrived?'

'No. He's on sick leave.'

'Since when?'

'This morning, as far as I know.'

Craft quickly nodded. 'Give me the sign-in for his computer. I need to look at the data he has gathered in the last few—'

'Sorry, no can do.'

'What? Why not?'

'It's confidential.'

'I work with him!'

'Yes, and all info relating to you in relation to your work here is confidential.' The officer watched Craft leave and head in the direction of Thompson's office.

Her colleague arriving for desk duty asked, 'What's up?'

'The professor is demanding access to David Brown's computer and she's well ticked-off because I refused. Thompson is a nightmare to talk to, so I'm glad he's gone out, and Holdsworth is shouting on the phone, wanting the media moved from the front entrance – and all I've got is you for company.'

'How about a cuppa and a biscuit?'

'Mmmm . . . go on then. Make it two biscuits.'

Craft came into the office and began searching among the many files on the table, moving some and turning pages of notes. She was stopped by a list of names. Looking down the list of names under the sub-heading TEMPORARY PERSONNEL she soon came to that of David Brown, her own name a few lines below it. She quickly copied the contact details, returned the files and documents to their original positions and quit the office.

Ten minutes later, she was parked on one side of the road, her gaze fixed on nearby houses. Seeing the house number she wanted, she got out of her car, went directly to it and rang the bell. The door was opened by David Brown, looking pale and tired. 'Teigan?'

'David – you look dreadful!'

'You're welcome to come in, just keep your distance.' He went ahead of her and she followed him into the warm sitting room. 'It's just a heavy cold. Take that chair over there.'

'David, I can see you are unwell. You don't need me—'

He pointed. 'Sit. My housemate is upstairs and he's OK, but I'd rather not cause you headache and a throat full of thistles. Anyway, enough of that. Let's switch topics or I'll get well into moan mode. It's nice to see somebody who doesn't look like she's at death's door. Although, I'm guessing this is not a social visit.'

'I was expecting an email from you with further thoughts and ideas on our investigation?'

He shook his head, winced. 'Sorry about that. After I saw you yesterday, I started feeling rough, but I did give it some thought.'

The short pause was broken by Craft. 'Did you come up with anything?

'I started thinking about the type of person this killer might be. I don't profile so this is my clumsy version of it: male, obviously, an individual who is both very interested in women but who also denigrates them. Someone who is able to engage with women on a superficial level but, and I know this sounds contradictory, he is also very coarse in his views of them – possibly even directly to them. If he is married or in a relationship, I would anticipate some level of domestic violence, maybe verbal, possibly physical.'

She waited, then: 'Did anything more specific come to mind?'

He grinned at her. 'If there were, you would already know because my terminal would have released a confetti storm and a chorus of *Hallelujah.*' Seeing her face, he added, 'That's a small, not very funny joke.'

'I understand.'

'What's on your mind, Tig?'

Conscious of his use of Tom's name for her, she said, 'I'm considering that it is someone I know.'

He stared at her for several seconds, turned away then back. 'Who?'

'I won't give a name, but it's someone I believe is physically and possibly sexually challenging to females.' She shook her head. 'Forget what I just said. Do you have any more thoughts?'

He gazed at her for some seconds. 'This is all entirely speculative, you understand. In my opinion, this killer is a mature male in his late forties.'

Craft gave this some thought. No male in his forties came to mind. 'Might he be younger than that?'

Brown gave this brief consideration. 'I doubt it. If that were the case, your theory that he also murdered Emma Matheson and some guy in London she worked with years ago doesn't work, does it? He would be *way* too young.'

She could see the point he was making. 'What's your theory, David?'

'Easily forty-plus. Other than that, he has no more than secondary education, although he might have acquired work skills. Marital status uncertain, but given what we know about his offences, he has the freedom to come and go as he wishes. Which might also apply to him as an employee.'

'What type of work do you see him involved in?' she asked.

Brown shrugged. 'Given what I've said, and this is only a possibility, he might be some kind of service provider who visits people's homes, which would provide him with an opportunity to select a victim.'

Craft's thoughts went back to the individual identified in Stratford-upon-Avon, a sex offender she had not told him about because that individual was ruled out. 'You're suggesting that this killer knows his victims?'

He shrugged. 'I'm evidence-driven. That's my job. I suggest a search of offenders with similar offence histories who may have been apprehended prior to any homicide. My advice would be to particularly follow up those known to have stalked their victims.'

She absorbed his words.

He said, 'You look unconvinced.'

'I see him very differently as a male who seizes sexual opportunities. Not someone who takes his time choosing a victim.'

'You're looking stressed, Tig.'

She sighed. 'The only aspect of this killer I feel confident about is his personality. I've analysed brain scans of males who have exhibited similar behaviours. When they talk about their offences in detail, they show only minimal brain response.'

'You're not serious? I thought people like him got a kick out of, you know, "reliving" offences.'

'Yes, but what I'm saying is that they do not feel any guilt associated with what they do. Because they are psychopathic.'

Brown was looking thoughtful. 'How different someone like that is from you, me, most other people.'

'I shall know him if I meet him – make that *when*.'

He grinned at her. 'I really like your positivity, Tig. I hope you do.'

She stood. 'I need to get back to Headquarters. When are you next in?'

'As soon as I no longer feel and look like roadkill. It can't be soon enough for me. I'm adjusting a little too easily to doing nothing.'

Midnight

A heavily built, dark-haired woman walked quickly along the road skirting Forrest Park. She had just finished a hectic A & E shift at the hospital and this was a direct route to her house. Replacing recollections of patients with thoughts of home, her bed and the electric blanket already switched on by her husband who was waiting for her, she glanced into the park, undecided whether to go some way into it and reduce the time it would take to reach home. She hesitated, eyes skimming the dense trees. She had seen it recently on the television news, about a woman being attacked there. Maybe not. She walked on, her flat shoes continuing their rhythmic movement.

'Evening.'

Her eyes darted to her right and a man in a padded ski jacket, a scarf over his lower face, in one hand a lead, at the end of which was a red setter. She recognized its breed because she and her husband owned one. She opened her mouth then closed it again. *Don't engage. Walk on.* Words she had said many times to her two daughters.

He watched her as she continued away from him, his voice low. 'Those shoes would not have saved her, would they, Buddy? They never learn, and I'll tell you why. They think they're the strong ones. The ones in charge. You can never truly know a woman until you have her and she's . . . gone. That's the single, best, the *only* time you really have them.' He gazed up at the rising, tree-covered land on the other side of the road. 'And I celebrate their failure to learn.' He gave a gentle pull on the lead and man and dog turned and went back the way they had come.

TWENTY-TWO

Thursday 31 October, 9.15 a.m.

Thompson walked through reception hearing his name being called. He turned to Holdsworth. 'Sir?'

He got an abrupt: 'My office.'

Thompson followed. As soon as they were inside, Holdsworth said, 'I don't need to tell you that media interest in this investigation is growing daily but I'm not seeing much if any progress.'

'We're doing all we can, sir. It's a very complex investigation but we're well into it.'

'What about this Greening woman who went missing in February three years ago?'

'Professor Craft and I have talked with the SIO in Stratford-upon-Avon where Lucy lived. The one individual the SIO mentioned who would have been of interest was already in prison when all the attacks took place, plus we've checked out a dating agency Greening signed up with and I'm confident it's on the level. In fact, she didn't get as far as an introduction from them.'

'I'm getting pressure from above and I don't like it. Make this Stratford angle your focus, as of now. Given the nature of what was done to this Greening woman, I want results. Get a shift on!'

'Sir.'

Thompson went to his office to find Craft already there. She looked up at him, pointing to three slim, manila files. 'These arrived by courier from Stratford police half an hour or so ago with an accompanying memo. I've been reading through them.'

'The old speed-reading coming into play?'

She frowned. 'I absorb information extremely quickly.'

'Course you do. Tell me what you know.'

She pointed to the file open in front of her. 'This one is of particular interest because it covers what is known of Lucy's life until the time she disappeared.'

'Give me the gist. Any ideas gratefully received and all that.'

She gazed at him. 'Reserve your bad mood for Holdsworth, whom I suspect deserves it, not me.'

A silence formed between them. She turned pages and he saw the narrow, bright red band around her right wrist. He had noticed it before, had asked her about it once. She had told him it was a method for controlling stress and anxiety. He had considered getting himself one. Maybe he still should?

She was speaking. 'This file immediately got my attention because it's flagged; see here?'

He looked to the manila cover, saw where she was pointing to a red sticker at the top right-hand corner. 'What's in it?'

'I was about to find out when you walked in. I'll do so now.' She read close-printed lines, picking up the clatter of cups and spoons, the low rumble of the kettle heating up. Within a further ten minutes, coffee in front of her, Craft passed some pages to him. 'Read what I've highlighted.'

He took them, looked down at Lucy Greening's face, seeing how open it was, surrounded by curling, blonde hair. He found himself searching for a word to describe it. He held it up, thinking of his own daughters. 'See this?' he asked. 'Greening was an attractive young woman but with none of that pouty, false-eyelash-batting business that's always on the television.' He tapped the statement, highlighted by Craft. 'At the time she went missing a friend described her as "very straightforward, a bit guileless". The same friend told

Stratford police that Lucy had met somebody she liked not long before she disappeared.'

He reached for the desk phone, tapped a number and waited, fingers drumming the table. 'This is Detective Chief Inspector Steve Thompson from police headquarters, Birmingham. Am I speaking to Sarah Reeves who lives at . . .' He read out the Solihull address.

Craft could hear the woman on the other end of the line. 'This is Sarah Reeves. Is this about what happened to Lucy? Lucy Greening?'

'We need to have a talk with you, Miss Reeves.'

Craft picked up a single word from the phone. '*Finally.*'

'Is it possible for a colleague and me to visit you this morning?'

Thompson listened, then nodded. 'Thank you, Miss Reeves. We appreciate it.'

He ended the call. 'That's a bit of luck – she works from home and she sounds like she wants to talk to us.'

Forty minutes later, Thomson and Craft was parking outside the small, neat-looking townhouse, Thompson saying, 'I'll do the intros, get the ball rolling, then feel free to come in whenever you like.'

At the front door, Thompson took out his ID and rang the bell. The door was opened by a young woman who confirmed her name, giving them an apprehensive look as she invited them inside. Thompson took out his notebook. 'Like I said on the phone, Miss Reeves, I'm DCI Steve Thompson and' – he gestured in Craft's direction – 'this is my colleague, Professor Teigan Craft, who's a forensic psychology expert.'

Craft nodded, seeing the young woman's apprehension climb further.

Thompson sat, his full attention on the young woman. 'We understand Lucy Greening was a friend of yours. What can you tell us about her?'

There was a brief silence before she responded. 'Lucy . . . was a great person. Clever, hardworking. I knew she was a bit unsettled because she had finished with her boyfriend and wanted to meet someone else. I told her that that was a good decision.'

'Why did you say that?' asked Craft.

Reeves shook her head. 'I didn't think he was right for her. He was the same age as Lucy, but immature.'

'Does he live locally?'

'He did until he joined the army about six months ago. Lucy didn't seem all that upset about the break-up. She told me she was thinking of going to a dating agency in Stratford. I told her she didn't need to do something like that, that she was lovely, funny and clever and kind . . . she just laughed.' She looked up at Thompson. 'It was on the news that she had been found.'

'Yes. In an area of south-west Birmingham called Forrest Park.'

Reeves looked startled.

'As far as you're aware, did Lucy have any connection to that area?'

'No, none at all, as far as I know.' They watched tears form.

'We've taken over the case from Stratford-upon-Avon police, Miss Reeves. Tell us whatever else you know about this dating agency Lucy was thinking of joining.'

She gave him a distracted look. 'I don't know anything about it. I thought I'd talked her out of it. I told her that men who joined those kinds of set-ups were probably weirdos or on the make, but she laughed, said I was being old fashioned.' She stopped, more tears coming.

Craft asked, 'Do you know the Forrest Park area at all?'

Reeves looked up again.

'I'm asking because when my colleague first mentioned it, your response suggested it might hold some significance for you.'

'I . . . no, not really. It's just something Lucy told me . . . about someone she had met.'

They waited. Craft prompted, 'What did Lucy tell you?'

Reeves took a breath. 'She said he lived in a nice part of Birmingham . . . lots of trees.'

Craft swiftly reminded herself that Birmingham generally was home to multiple trees. 'Was she any more specific about it?'

'No.'

'How did she meet him?'

'I don't know but . . . Lucy was a bit of a romantic and I could tell that whoever he was, she liked him a lot. She never mentioned a name . . . she said he told her that Birmingham wasn't at all what people said about it. That it had lots of open space and woods and that he wanted to show them to her . . . and he said that there are a million trees in the city, which I thought was ridiculous until I looked it up online and . . . it's true.' She looked up at Thompson.

'He said he wanted to show her the true Birmingham, to share his deep love of the outdoors and his adoration for trees.'

Craft tensed. 'He used the word "adoration"?'

'Yes. It sounded weird to me. Who "adores" trees? Even if you like them, you don't go around telling people you "adore" them, do you?' She shrugged. 'Lucy just laughed. She didn't take any notice of what I was saying. She said he was in tune with nature and very sensitive. To me, he sounded odd, you know . . . strange. I've never met a guy who talked like that and I told her so. She wouldn't listen. She said that she had agreed to meet him, that he was going to share his wonder and love of trees with her. *Weirdo!* That's why I reacted like I did when you said where she was found.'

They drove back to Birmingham. Thompson said, 'Your thoughts, Craft.'

She did not respond. After another fifteen minutes, she said, 'How about a drink? You might need one when you hear what I have to say.'

He redirected the vehicle away from Headquarters to the High Street. Within fifteen minutes they were inside the small, almost deserted pub, Thompson bringing drinks and bags of crisps to the table, seeing Craft's eyes fixed on a solitary drinker staring into his glass.

'Not the kind of place I anticipated,' she said, 'but at least it is quiet.'

'I've been in here once and I'd say that's usually a signal for a fight about to start.' He nodded at the drinker. 'Think we can handle him?' He saw her face change. 'Joke.'

She reached for one of the bags of crisps and opened it. 'Have you any thoughts on what Sarah Reeves just told us about this man Lucy Greening had met?'

'The tree hugger? Yeah. So, what?'

Craft sat back, sipping gin and tonic, suddenly exhausted.

Thompson studied her. 'What's up? You look like you've lost a tenner and found a fiver.'

Putting down her glass, she chose her words. 'Thompson, I'll start with a few pertinent words and see how you respond. Here goes. Forest. A love of trees, a wish to express that love, that *adoration* . . . Why are you grinning like an idiot!' she snapped.

He looked at her, still grinning. 'If that's your take on setting up a joke, you don't have one clue how to do it.'

'I don't do jokes and I *wasn't*!' she hissed, provoking a start from the morose drinker.

Thompson frowned. 'Don't go mardy on me. Just tell me what you're on about.'

'*Dendrophilia*.'

'What's the age of trees got to do with anything?'

She let her head drop forward, looked up at him. 'OK. How about this? There are many ways of experiencing and expressing sexual attraction, Thompson. For some people, it's about a particular type of person. For others, it might be an inanimate object – close your *mouth*. For some, admittedly a very small percentage, the tree is a phallic symbol. I met one such person, a dendrophile, when I did my clinical training' – Thompson was still staring at her in disbelief – 'and he freely admitted to me that trees were a significant source of sexual gratification for him.' She took another sip of her drink. 'In fact, I wrote a paper on it which was very well received—'

'What is it with you psychologists and sex!' He glanced around. The worse-for-wear drinker stirred, opening one eye.

She gave Thompson an impatient look. 'It is a recognized *paraphilia*. Paraphilias involve recurrent, intense, sexually arousing fantasies, urges and behaviours towards non-human objects.'

He was staring at her, bewildered.

'Think of it as a fetish—'

'I don't want to think of it, full stop!'

'Dendrophilia is literally a love of trees which involves sexual attraction and arousal . . . Why are you getting so heated about this?'

'*Why?*' He downed his drink. 'This is probably everyday stuff to you—'

'Actually, it isn't.'

'—but not for *me*! In all my time on the force, I've never come across it.'

'You have now, and the likely reason you haven't is that it isn't illegal—'

'Whoever does stuff like that should be locked up!'

'*Shhhh*,' she said, pointing to the now-restless drunk. 'Although, thinking about it, if you ever found someone engaged in it, you could probably arrest them for indecent exposure.'

Thompson ran his hand across his eyes. 'Thanks for the image. Where does that get us, if anywhere?'

'It gets us to a name I know.' She took out her phone.

TWENTY-THREE

Friday 1 November, 5.30 a.m.

Craft gasped herself awake, images of dissected body parts floating through a dark forest filling her head. She sat up, perspiration on her chest, her heart pounding. She had spent the latter part of the previous evening thinking about geo-profiling, dendrophilia and what it meant for this killer in terms of his comfort zones and understanding of place. Heart rate settling, she recalled Thompson's resistance to the dendrophilia angle. More thoughts followed. With Lucy, this killer had changed his MO. Why? He had left Alicia Franks' body intact in a ditch, while his attack on Penny Bristow had been incomplete, leaving her alive. Was he worried that that incompleteness might bring the police to his door?

She shook her head. If he followed the news, it was unlikely. So, what meaning might dismemberment have for him? Could it be an *homage* to the sexual satisfaction he derived in that area? Or was that simply expediency due to the ease with which he was able to conceal the body parts there? Was it about his visiting that park, gazing at the places he knew held buried remains? A kind of offering to the trees he adored? Was he living a short car journey or a brisk walk away from it? Wherever he was, knowing what he had done to Lucy Greening, did he feel that he still had ownership of her? The suddenness of the revelation was such that she gasped again. Once Lucy Greening's death was a buried secret, he could revel in the knowledge of what he had done and where he had left her. He had made Forrest Park into his own private fiefdom.

She left the churned duvet and headed for the shower.

7.35 a.m.

Craft was following the path from the main hospital to the low-rise building just visible now to talk to a man who was a friend of Tom's. A man she trusted as much as she trusted Tom. Arriving at the entrance, she rang the bell and was soon admitted by a man in nursing uniform.

'Hello, Professor Craft. Nice to see you again. You know where to find him. He's expecting you.'

She walked the long shiny corridor to another on the right and followed it, looking out at a garden of rock formations, small plants nestling among them, the small metal water feature which spun and sprayed in the summer months now still. Craft liked to come upon things she had not seen in a while. It gave her a sense of continuity. That there were reliable patterns to life.

Reaching the open door with its nameplate Professor Richard Grierson, she knocked and leant into the room.

'Tig!' A genial-looking man stood, motioning her inside. 'You look lovely as always. Come in! Have a seat.'

'I've reached the stage in the investigation I mentioned on the phone, which is giving me nightmares.'

He looked surprised. 'That's not my experience of level-headed you.'

'It was mine at around five o'clock this morning.'

'I was intrigued by your phone call yesterday.' He held out a shallow box towards her. 'Real Turkish Delight. A little early in the day, but try one of them. You'll only need one . . . Oh, and don't pop it in whole whatever you do, or you'll be incapable of speech for the next half-hour.'

She grinned, took a square, bit into it. 'Mmm! Got nuts.'

They sat in companionable silence for a couple of minutes, then Craft said, 'Tell me what you know about dendrophilia, Richard.'

He swallowed, then paused. 'Excluding individuals who are self-confessed tree-lovers and merely like and enjoy being around trees, it will come as no news to you that we're talking sexual fetish.'

She nodded. 'I need to understand what it is that prompts individuals to express their love for trees in a physical way, a sexual way. It sounds very risky – and potentially painful.'

'You're right about risk and pain,' he said, 'but not all such individuals express their attraction directly. There is so little formal research available, but the accepted understanding is that most with such an attraction choose to express it via engaging in sexual behaviour with a partner out of doors.'

She considered this. 'When would it be regarded as a paraphilia?'

'I would say when those who have a sexual interest in trees take it to a physical level and act out that interest towards an actual tree. It could be said that if others are unaware of it as a fetish, they may not realize what they are witnessing.' He paused. 'If we think about it, the reason that dendrophilia is poorly understood and under-researched is that whilst most people might regard it as very strange behaviour, it arguably has no "victim" and thus no explicit harm is caused.'

Craft turned the last few comments over in her head. 'But what if we can't say that? What if there is a situation in which a dendrophile chooses to demonstrate that arousal to, say, a female and harms her?'

'I hear what you're saying, Tig, and such a situation does create a very dark picture, but you know me, dry as dust researcher, I'm back to the significant lack of research in the area, and I am unaware of any instance of sexual violence directed to another individual in such a situation. We just don't know what implications there might be to others, if any.'

She gave him a direct look. 'What I'm doing right now, Richard, is trying to frame some serious questions about it.'

'I understand, Tig, but you're going beyond my knowledge.' He hesitated. 'Have another Turkish Delight,' and offered the box to her.

She shook her head, thinking over what he had said. 'You're saying that it's possible that such a person, a dendrophile, would initiate sex with another person out of doors where there are abundant trees, as a kind of proxy behaviour?'

'I'm saying that it is likely. Your guesses, your theories are as legitimate as anyone else's. It's not considered unlawful behaviour, yet anyone reported to the police for being *in flagrante* with their tree of choice, *might* risk arrest for lewd behaviour.' He smiled. 'I think I know what this is about. Tom told me that you're involved in a police investigation and I've seen reports on the news recently.'

She nodded. 'Right now, I'm doing the best I can, considering all possibilities, whilst operating on the premise that all information is good because it could move us forward. I have considered suggesting a litter collection at the crime scene for indications of sexual behaviour, you know, condoms and the like, but it would be very expensive and time-consuming and possibly tell us nothing, given the lapse of time.'

'I'm sorry I can't offer you any research which might assist. My comment earlier about a dendrophile's behaviour being concealed within an agreed al fresco union – a "proxy" as you suggested – is possibly the way in which most dendrophiles legitimately meet their sexual needs. Have you checked police records for arrests involving outdoor sex?'

'That's my next action.' She stood. 'Thank you, Richard. You have told me more than I knew when I arrived.' She looked at her watch. 'I need to leave.'

He walked her to the door. 'Bye, Tig. Don't go down to the woods alone, don't work too hard – oh, and say "Hi" to Tom for me when you see him.'

10.25 a.m.

Craft arrived at Headquarters distracted and in low spirits which the last half hour had done little to lift. A records search had yielded no arrests for outdoor sexual behaviour in areas similar to, and including, Forrest Park. Having shared her knowledge of dendrophilia with Thompson and his key investigative officers, the response had been largely disbelief, with several nudges from Sullivan to Ashton. Sullivan's eyes had been fixed on her each time she glanced in his direction. Still preoccupied by her waking thoughts, her attention turned to her investigative notes. Richard Grierson had suggested the possibility of sex out of doors as a way a dendrophile might express his paraphilia. Was it possible that Alicia Franks and Penny Bristow had come across such a scene in Forrest Park which had shocked, frightened them and placed them in danger?

Thump! Thump! Thump!

Flinching at each *thump* she glared at Thompson, balancing on the rear legs of his chair, throwing an old tennis ball from one of the filing cabinets against the nearest wall then catching it. '*Must* you?' *Thump.* She was on her feet. 'I cannot focus in here.'

Thompson lowered his chair, the tennis ball rolling unheeded across the floor.

She said, 'We have this *wrong*. We have been viewing these Forrest Park cases as essentially stranger-homicides and getting nowhere. Emma Matheson and Phillip Marsh knew each other and their killer knew *them*. I think the Forrest Park cases are no different. Those victims were not chosen at random. I think their killer had some kind of prior contact with them.'

Thompson studied her, got to his feet, pointing to his officers. 'I want you doing second visits to family members, friends and work associates of Emma, Alicia and Penny. Sort out between you who goes where, but your brief is to collect full biographical information about the interests these victims had, the schools they attended, higher education establishments if any, friends, the places they've lived, the clubs and other organizations they belonged to, the churches they attended if relevant, their Drs, dentists, other health contacts they had, including mental health – in short, every human contact they had. And yes, I know you've already done some of it, but a further visit might confirm prior contact between these women and their attacker. In which case, it could open up this investigation. Be careful how you raise some of these issues but I want it done, ASAP.' Getting a chorused, '*Sir*,' he added, 'This is not routine information collection like previously. I want you asking the questions and *listening* to what you are being told. Analyse all that you get and if anything, *anything* claims your attention, query it until you are entirely satisfied you've got all the available detail. There's a logic to these women's deaths – a killer's logic – and you'll find it by listening with *this*'– he tapped his right temple – 'staying alert for the smallest possibility, the most insignificant nuance.'

His eyes still fixed on them, he said, 'A single link is all we need to give us an investigative angle, a direction. Query any incidents in the lives of these women which caused them concern. Don't look to me for ideas as to what they might be. Your job is to find out. I want to know about these women's lives from birth to death because *somewhere* in that information must be the answer to who killed them.'

He waited as they made quick notes.

'I didn't choose any of you to be on my team but I'm trusting you to be sensitive and thorough. Do not sit on information which seems relevant.' He pointed in Sandhu's direction. 'Give it to Officer Sandhu for processing.' He moved quickly across the room. 'If she's unavailable for any reason, give it to David Brown.'

Brown raised his hand to them.

'He'll hold on to it, and David? If you can spare the time, look through it and see if it raises any queries for you.'

Getting a quick nod from Brown, Thompson turned to two extra officers. 'Get over to Stratford-upon-Avon. Collect detailed information on the same issues I've just outlined from Lucy Greening's wider family, plus all others who knew her. Her homicide is the most recently discovered, so tread carefully with the immediate family.' He looked at all the officers. 'Get going!' He watched them leave the office then turned to Brown. 'I know you've already got a remit for being here, but if you could find the time to look through what they get—'

'I am pretty busy but I'll make a start by switching to case management software and adding a crime scene scanner—'

'And you'll be looking for links?'

Brown shook his head. 'That's the computer's job. If they're there they'll show up and we're on our way.' He stood. 'I'll fetch what's needed from my office.'

'Good man. Get it set up, soon as you can.'

As Brown left, Craft said, 'What about the geo-profiling I suggested a while ago?'

'You mean mapping the attacks to see what it yielded in terms of roads, housing, shops et cetera? It's already been done. It gave us nothing.'

She shook her head. 'As I said to you previously, geo-profiling is a different concept.'

Thompson sighed. 'Tell me again how that works.'

'It's a particular way, a personal way for us to analyse the areas in which we know he is operating, but from *his* viewpoint. Think about it, Thompson. Consider the area in which you live. You have a mental map of its features but it is not comprised merely of roads and houses. They each have a personal relevance for you: the neighbours you get on with and those you don't, the routes you prefer when you take walks and why. It came to me early this morning that we must establish the personal relevance of this killer's geographical space, specifically the Forrest Park area.'

'How do we do that when we don't have a clue who or where he is?'

'We look at his behaviour and what it is telling us about him.' She went to the wall screen, activated a large map, and pointed to several similar items. 'These black flags show the deposition site for Alicia Franks' body and also Penny Bristow's attack' – she moved her finger – 'and these red flags represent the places in which Lucy Greening's remains were concealed.' She looked at Thompson. 'To have a hope of solving this case, we need an understanding of what this whole area represents, what it *means* for this killer. It's *his* killing field. As a process-focused killer, he spends time with his victims prior to and after killing them. We know he spent significant time with Lucy Greening's remains. We know what he did to her. By dismembering her, he kept her *close.* He could walk around that space whenever he needed to, relive that whole experience. My question: could he be local?'

'Pretty risky behaviour if he is.'

'Where is the risk? I've visited that park and seen few people there. It is not a "park" in the general sense. It's fairly challenging terrain. Whoever killed Alicia Franks and Lucy Greening believed that by concealing their remains he could hold on to them and the memory of what he did.' She paused. 'He must be aware that he has lost "ownership" of Lucy. You need to stake out that area for any regular visitors.'

'Do you really think it's possible that he could live very close to the park?'

'I don't know. He may live some distance away, but what I am suggesting is that wherever he lives, he creates opportunities to visit or simply gaze in the general direction of Forrest Park to relive what he knows he has done there.'

'The more I hear about him, the more convinced I am he's a nutter.'

'I doubt it, but don't run with the idea he's some kind of genius either. Average intellect is probably closer to the mark.'

Thompson grunted. 'The problem with "average" is that it's a big net that catches a lot of people.'

Craft had left the office and was inside her car, feeling frustrated. She had reviewed details of police visits to residents in the general area of Forrest Park but they had yielded nothing. There was no way they could take her theory forward that this killer was local by calling at every single house and apartment within, say, a two-mile radius of Forrest Park. It was too time-consuming and a potential failure if he lived outside it. And the kinds of questions which really needed to be asked would create fear and panic. Yet there was another possibility with a more focused objective. One which might provide this killer with another equally legitimate reason to be in that general area. His workplace.

Phone in hand, she tapped the number of the estate agent which had provided information on Emma Matheson. A pleasant female voice gave the estate agency name. 'How may I help you?'

'This is Professor Craft from police headquarters.'

'Hello, Professor Craft! You and the police are still working in the area.'

'Yes, and I have a query. How many male individuals does your agency employ?'

'That's an easy one. None.'

'Oh. Why is that?'

'In our experience, men aren't attracted to suburban work locations like ours, whereas it suits our female employees because they live locally and we are close to shops and childcare facilities.'

Craft thought about this. 'In the last three or so years, has your agency employed any short-term or temporary male staff?'

'No, none. It's company policy that we don't employ short-term or temporary staff because of the nature of our business. We store a lot of confidential information, plus we have keys to properties on the premises which need to be easily available to everyone who works here. I'm sure you'll understand what I'm saying.'

Craft did. She was also disappointed. 'Can I assume that what you've just said is pretty much the policy followed by other estate agents in this area?'

There was a pause. 'There's only one in this general area but you need to talk with him directly about that.'

Craft wrote down the contact details, thanked the woman and ended the call.

Within minutes she was on her way to the address she had been given, a small parade of shops to her left claiming her attention. She pulled into the narrow service road and drove slowly along until she came to an estate agent's premises. Getting out of her car she went quickly to it, noting the lack of interior lighting and the CLOSED sign on the door. Returning to her car, about to drive away, she looked up to see a man at the now open door of the premises. She quickly left her car and headed towards him.

'Sir? Excuse me! If I could have a moment of your time?'

He turned, eyeing her up and down. 'If you're selling anything, I'm on my way out.'

'I'm part of a police investigation. If you are the owner of this business, I would much appreciate talking with you.'

He glanced at the ID she was holding towards him. 'I can spare you two minutes.'

'Thank you, Mr . . .?'

'Wyatt.' He held the door open for her and she went inside.

'I'm Professor Teigan Craft. I'm part of an ongoing police investigation in this area.'

'If this is about one of our For Sale properties being vandalized, it's about bloody time.'

'No. My query is not property-related, it is employee-related.'

He pointed to a chair and sat opposite her. 'We have occasional turnover of staff like any other company. What do you want to know?'

'Have you employed any short-term or temporary staff during the last say five years?'

She saw his face change. 'It's a case of having to! Nobody wants to do a week's work for reasonable money these days. They all want five figures and bonuses.' He eyed her. 'Are you asking about male or female temporary staff?'

'Male.'

'Time was, you could run a family business like this, in an area like this without having to second-guess everybody who comes through the door.' He shook his head. 'I do the best I can here but we're always short-staffed, and you know why?'

Craft waited.

'Because there's another estate agent pretty close to this one and they pay top whack to whoever they employ. It sets a precedent! One I can't compete with. What exactly are you after?'

'The names of any temporary employees you've taken on in the last, say, five-plus years.'

'That's easy. Two of 'em. A youngish chap, student. This would be maybe ten or so years back now but I remember him like it was yesterday. Guess what he did.' Wyatt did not wait for a response. 'He disappeared, having helped himself to five hundred quid! After that, I took on a single woman, figuring she would be more reliable. She spent most of her time here on her phone, so I had to get rid of her.'

'What was this young male student's name?'

'I can't remember.'

'Did he have references?'

'People looking for temporary work rarely have 'em. I use my own judgement and, in his case, I made a big mistake.'

'What can you tell me about him?'

Wyatt shrugged. 'Like I said, he was a student. I'm no good at ages but I doubt he was more than twenty. On the tall side, well-spoken, pleasant. That about covers it.'

'Do you have any other details on him, Mr Wyatt?'

He was looking put-upon. 'No offence, but I need to get on with my day.'

There was a brief silence.

'What can I tell you . . . like I said, well-spoken, educated, made me wonder at the time why he wanted casual work around here. He gave me some tale about being at medical school.'

'What exactly did he say about that?'

Wyatt gave her an impatient look. 'This is a one-man band I'm running here. I don't have time for gabbing.' He sighed. 'Hang on, I might be able to find some paperwork for him. Give me a minute or two.'

As Wyatt left, Craft's focus switched to the clock on her phone. She watched its slow progress.

One minute.

Wyatt did not reappear. Irritated, she watched a further one-point-five minutes elapse.

He was back, waving a single sheet. 'Got it! I knew I had his paperwork somewhere.'

Craft took the 'paperwork' from him. A single, multi-creased sheet of paper torn from what looked to be an exercise book. She read the words on it as Wyatt continued.

'He seemed to relate to clients OK. As I said, pleasant, although he wasn't one for chatting, which suited me.'

She looked at him. 'Mr Wyatt, it says here that he gave his name as "Harry Shipman".'

'Yeah. So?'

'The name wasn't familiar to you?'

'Why would it be?'

'He told you his father was in the forestry business. What exactly did he tell you?'

'According to him, his dad had been offered a million quid by some government department to buy part of the land he owned and develop it into a recreational area which would offer accommodation for nature lovers from the inner city. He seemed to think that was funny. I did wonder if he meant one of them nudist type places.' He shook his head. 'Too bloody cold in this country for that malarky. According to the news, we're all stuffed unless we cover the whole sodding country in trees and wind farms.' He sighed. 'Anyway, when he hopped it with the money, I checked on what he had told me about his dad. I couldn't find anything that matched what he said.'

'When he told you about the trees, how did he seem?'

Wyatt looked flummoxed. 'Meaning?'

'For example, did he appear proud of his father?'

She watched him consider it. 'I never noticed anything like that. Like I said, he laughed. I noticed it because generally he didn't strike me as your light-hearted sort, you know.' He paused. 'But it did make me wonder why his dad wasn't shelling out a few quid to him. My guess is that it was all lies. I'm just hoping I never bump into him when he's a qualified Dr.'

Craft gazed at him. 'Is it possible that that was also a lie?'

'Now you mention it, probably.' He sighed. 'What I just said about him, by the time he was here a week, there had been hardly a word out of him; he just got on with the job and at the same time was robbing me blind! If I ever see him again, I'll nail his bits to the nearest *tree*!'

She gave him a direct look. 'I would advise you against any such course of action.'

He frowned at her. 'Don't you know a joke when you hear one?'

'Mr Wyatt, is there anything else at all that you recall about this man which was odd or stuck in your mind?'

'Nothing beyond what I already said. A lot of the time I wasn't here. You can't let temporary staff loose in For Sale properties.'

Craft reached into her coat pocket and handed him a card. 'If you do recall anything else, please ring me on that number.'

She pulled over to the side of the road and took out her phone. Thompson picked up her call.

'I've just finished talking to a man called Wyatt, an estate agent in the general area of Forrest Park, who has confirmed my suspicion that most people are useless when it comes to the small indicators and anomalies of another person's character.'

'A bit harsh, Craft. Have you ever thought that your attitude to people could do with a brush-up?'

'He employed a young male of about twenty some years ago, supposedly a medical student who said his name was *Harry Shipman.*'

'You're having me on!'

'He stole five hundred pounds, then disappeared. Who in their right mind would accept without a single thought or reference an unknown male applying for a temporary job who claims to be a medical student whose father owns a forestry business and whose name is Harry Shipman, for God's *sake*!'

'All right, calm— Forestry business?'

'I *am* calm. You were not inside my car as I drove away, *screaming* at the sheer lunacy of it. I'll do an internet search later in relation to this forestry angle, but I can tell you right now that, whoever that young man was, he played that estate agent for a fool.'

'Sounds like he was a real game-player.'

'Exactly!'

'And trees are cropping up again.'

Back at the apartment, hours later, Craft scrolled the on-screen information a third and final time then sat back. Sure enough, according to her search, there was no forestry business run by anyone called 'Shipman'. What she and her colleagues had was a killer with an extremely warped sense of humour.

TWENTY-FOUR

Monday 4 November, 10 a.m.

Coming into Headquarters, Craft was aware of a subtle buzz in the air. Going directly to Thompson's office, she found him staring out of the window. 'What's happening?'

'Nothing, as of yet. Read this.'

She took the printed sheet from him and quickly absorbed the detail of a visit made by Ashton to the family of Alicia Franks. The family had described a problematic incident involving Alicia seven months prior to her death which related to an experience she had had with a man named Justin Wetherby that quickly morphed into a stalking situation after she refused to see him again. It lasted one week before Alicia's father witnessed Wetherby loitering outside the house and warned him off with the threat of police.

Craft looked up. 'Get him in.'

'He's already here.'

'I *must* be part of that interview.'

'Who's arguing? *You* could start a row in an empty room.' He turned from the window and headed to the door. 'Come on.'

Craft followed him upstairs and inside an interview room where he gave her an evaluative glance. Much of the time, she was right on top of everything, yet there were times she seemed to struggle. Right now, he needed the sharp version. He turned to Ashton who was coming into the room. 'I want you observing the interview.'

Ashton glanced at Craft, then back to Thompson. 'You're the boss.'

She watched him go. 'He doesn't want an observational role, either.'

Thompson reached for the desk phone, spoke into it. 'Tell the duty sergeant that DCI Thompson and Professor Craft are waiting in Interview Room One for Justin Wetherby . . . On second thoughts, don't mention Professor Craft.' He ended the call. 'We don't want to look like we're spoiling for a fight.'

Craft asked, 'What else do you know about Wetherby?'

He pushed the sheet across to her. She absorbed the biographical details and those relating to Wetherby's caution: his age – thirty-eight; status – single; employment – estate agent, among several others . . .

Picking up footsteps approaching the door, Craft watched it open and a man of robust built with an arrogant facial expression was ushered inside.

Thompson said, 'Have a seat, Mr Wetherby.'

The accompanying officer said, 'Sir, we're still waiting for Mr Wetherby's legal rep to arrive.'

Wetherby glanced at Thompson. 'She's on her way.'

His eyes settled on Craft, a steady click of high heels sounding from beyond the door.

A woman entered. Craft absorbed the smooth, long blonde hair, the expensive-looking suit. The woman placed her briefcase on the floor and took the chair next to Wetherby, her words clipped. 'My name is Felicity Gordon. I am Mr Wetherby's legal representative. If this interview has begun without my being present, I shall make an official complaint on his behalf.'

Having heard a lot of lawyer bluster over the years, Thompson merely said, 'Thanks for coming. *Now* we can make a start.'

She ignored him, her attention on Craft. 'Who is this? Why is she here?'

'This is Professor Teigan Craft, forensic psychologist, who is working with us on our current major investigation.'

'What has that to do with my client?'

'Professor Craft is assisting me because she is generous with her forensic psychology skills,' snapped Thompson.

Craft's eyes were on the solicitor. If Gordon was as hot at her job as her presentation suggested, she would already be aware of the police investigation into Alicia Franks' death. Gordon made no response. Not so hot.

Thompson continued, 'We have a statement made by Gerard Franks, father of Alicia Franks, and we need to discuss it with Mr Wetherby to obtain his account of a situation which occurred between him and Alicia Franks.' This got him a dismissive glance from the solicitor. There was zero indication that she was aware of the significance of the name. Thompson opened the file in front of him and took out some handwritten details. 'This is your client's statement concerning his relationship with Alicia Franks, who is now deceased.'

Craft's eyes went to Gordon's face. Connection now made.

'DCI Thompson, if you are entertaining *any* thoughts of connecting my client to an historic homicide investigation which has featured recently in the news, this interview is at an end, pending my receiving full disclosure.'

'That depends on how forthcoming your client, Mr Wetherby, is about his relationship with Alicia Franks.' It was an 'Open Sesame!' moment.

'Hang on!' Wetherby looked from Thompson to Craft and back. 'You must have all the info on my caution, which was a stitch-up by Alicia's old man' – Craft's eyes were fixed on his face – 'and I don't see why I've been asked to come here, which, by the way, I've done *voluntarily*—'

'With your solicitor,' observed Craft.

The solicitor snapped, 'Which my client is perfectly entitled to do! In my opinion, this whole situation is *extremely* heavy-handed. We all regret Ms Franks' demise, *but* my client's very brief involvement with her was a long time prior to it. If you have any evidence, anything which specifically connects him to her homicide' – Wetherby gave her a look, his face tense – 'I demand to see it, after which this interview will end—'

'Hang on!' said Wetherby. 'I want this sorted here, *now*.'

'Mr Wetherby!'

He shook off her hand. 'I don't want any messing about. I know how the police work: "give a dog a bad name", and he's in the frame for anything.' He transferred his attention to Thompson. '*You* tell *me* why I've had to come here and what you think you've got on me!'

Thompson said, 'Tell us about your relationship with Alicia Franks.'

His solicitor snapped, 'Do *not* respond to that.'

Wetherby eye-rolled at Thompson. 'We had *one* date! You'll have a job making anything out of that!'

'That depends on what you tell us about it, Mr Wetherby.'

Wetherby glared at him, his face reddening. '*One* single date. We went for a drink at a city centre bar. I offered her a lift home. She said yes. I took her home!'

'You took her directly home, following this "date"?'

Wetherby's eyes strayed. 'The area where she lived was close to a park. It isn't your ordinary kind of park, laid out with grass and flowers. I've seen athletic types there, running.'

'You know it well,' observed Thompson.

Wetherby shook his head. 'No. I'm just describing what I saw of it as I drove past it to work. It seems to attract extreme running types.'

Thompson studied him. 'Tell us about your contact there with Ms Franks.'

Wetherby pointed at him. 'I don't know what you mean by "contact"!'

'OK, give us your version of the . . . *rendezvous* you had with Ms Franks.'

Wetherby's face suffused. He said nothing.

'Mr Wetherby, we don't seem to be progressing, given your reluctance to respond to what I'm saying. Are you prepared to give us a clear account of what occurred between you and Ms Franks that evening?'

Wetherby stared at him, then: 'If it gets me out of this bloody place, yes.' A brief silence ensued. 'Like I said, we went to a bar for a drink, just the one. I offered her a lift home. She said "yes". I drove her to where she told me she was living. That park was on the route to it.' He sat forward, eyes fixed on Thompson. 'It looked to me like a good place for us to park up and get . . . better acquainted—'

'Mr *Wetherby*.' His solicitor was looking vexed. 'I must caution you against giving information that has not been specifically requested!'

Thompson eyed her. 'Your client has a caution. We're getting to that.' And to Wetherby: 'Come on. Tell us what happened at that park.'

Wetherby ran his hands over his hair. '*Nothing*. We had a bit of a cuddle, you know. It was a nice night and that park is private, if you get what I'm saying. Everything was OK as far as I was concerned, but she got a bit . . . She said she could see something, somebody moving around among the trees. I tried to calm her down, like, but she kept pointing over my shoulder. I looked round and all I could see was trees. Not a soul there. It was a tree that got my attention, like all white on its trunk, and it looked like a good place to me—'

'For what?' snapped Thompson.

Wetherby looked at him with dislike. 'What's the big deal? She agreed to me giving her a lift. She got in my car under her own steam. I keep a travel rug in the boot; I spread it out on the ground' – he caught sight of his solicitor's face – 'but within five minutes she's out of the place and running off along the road saying somebody was watching us.'

'What did *you* do?'

'I followed her in my car. She got in.' He looked up at Thompson. 'Would she have done that if I'd done something she didn't like?'

'I ask the questions, Mr Wetherby. Tell us about the caution you received in respect of Alicia Franks.'

Craft watched his face suffuse again, saw anger flare in his eyes.

'What a bloody fiasco! I dropped her off at her house that night. The next day or so, I go back to see how she is because I'm concerned about her.'

Thompson said, 'According to our information, Ms Franks' father had to come to the door and insist that you leave.'

'Yes, because *she* had obviously said something to him about me that wasn't true!'

'Such as?'

'How should I know, but he was a big bloke so I left.'

'According to our information, you went back to that house, *twice,* demanding to see Alicia and were also observed to be hanging around—'

'You've got this all wrong! I just wanted to talk to her. Sort out why she was refusing to talk to me. I'm not the sort of bloke who goes around attacking women!'

Wetherby and his solicitor had left and Thompson and Craft were back in the office. Craft broke the silence. 'What do you think he did to Alicia Franks?'

Thompson shrugged. 'Who knows? We've got no evidence and she can't tell us.'

'It sounds like he sexually assaulted her when they reached that park.'

'But we don't *know* that and his version is that Franks got spooked by somebody who was there.'

'What if it was him? What if *he* was there, this man who eventually killed her? If you had put some real pressure on him—'

'Familiar with rules of evidence, are you, Craft? We ask questions. We get answers. We write them down. That's what we do.'

'Wetherby referred to a specific tree. He does not appear to me to be the type of male who is into gardening or flora and fauna, yet you did not take the opportunity to question him further.'

He stared at her. 'What are you on about?'

'Do not ask me what I'm "on about"! It's obvious. I've already told you that this killer is into trees—'

She watched him stand, roll his eyes.

'Not that again—'

'Yes! It is!'

He pointed at her. 'You tell me which one of us is SIO here! *This* is *my* investigation. The buck stops with me. Once you go back to your university and do whatever you do there, my job is to conduct investigations, including this one, as *I* see fit.'

'Yes, but you are aware of the possibility that this killer *is* a dendrophile—'

'Stop right there!' He stared at her. 'I don't *know* that and neither do you.' He watched her, on her feet gathering papers together, pushing it all into her bag, fetching her coat and pulling it on.

'I cannot do this! I cannot work with somebody who ignores my advice.'

'Same here.' They stared at each other. Thompson said, 'Craft, you're clever and you know stuff that I don't, but *I* say what's relevant to this investigation and what isn't.' He watched her grab her bag and head towards the door, speaking over her shoulder.

'This was a mistake from the start. I cannot work with *you*.'

The door opened and David Brown came inside. He looked from Craft to Thompson. 'Sorry, am I interrupting?'

Thompson pointed to him. 'I've got a question for you, Dave. Do you know what a dendrophile is?'

Brown looked at him, then at Craft. 'At a guess I'd say it's something to do with trees – the ages of trees?' In the ensuing tense silence, he said, 'I need to collect a file I left here, if that's OK.' He walked quickly to his desk, picked up a file and went to the door. 'See you tomorrow?'

They stood, silent, as he left.

Thompson looked to her. 'Hear that? I just asked somebody who's got a criminology degree, who's smart, who does police-related work and *he* couldn't answer the question.' He looked away from her. 'These murders are bad enough without coming up with outlandish theories that nobody but you ever heard of. We don't look at information in the same way, you and me, but rather than get Holdsworth in a tizz, I suggest we work separately from now on. I'll investigate as I see fit and you follow up whatever seems relevant to you.' He watched her to the door. 'Craft?'

'I heard. I agree.'

She arrived home to an empty apartment, switched on the heating and made herself a snack she did not want. No Percy. No Mother. And now, if she chose to, she could free herself of the investigation. Tell Holdsworth . . . what? That her efforts were being blocked by Thompson? Her face set, she could hear her mother's voice in her head, telling her she should see it through. Annoyed, disconcerted, confused as she was by Thompson's attitude towards her, she would not let go of her role in this investigation. She owed it to Emma, Alicia, Lucy and Penny to stay with it. She also owed it to herself in this, her first experience of collaborative police work. Despite the difficulties she had encountered she now knew that she had the necessary knowledge and skills. And she wanted to do more of it in the future. She would not let this investigation go.

TWENTY-FIVE

Tuesday 5 November, 7.30 a.m.

Craft came into Headquarters, not looking directly at anyone, feeling like an interloper. She still had a role here but she also knew that, for Thompson, she did not belong. Coming into the office, she saw Dave Brown making coffee.

He looked up. 'Hey, you're early. Want coffee?'

She shook her head. 'I've got a lot to do. I have a question for you, David.'

'Ask away.'

'How many actual serial homicide investigations have you assisted?'

He looked surprised. 'I'll have to think.'

She removed her coat, hung it up and came to the table. 'I don't need an exact answer, just a rough idea.'

'I'm just going through them. I was data analyst on a few in the London area – the West End Ripper. The Croydon Strangler. The Kentish Town Arsonist.'

Craft stared at him. 'Those were all really high-profile investigations.'

'I was responsible for the computer data analysis only. Nothing directly investigative.' He shrugged. 'You probably know that the Croydon Strangler is still out there. Serial homicides are the most difficult of crimes to bring to a positive conclusion. The main difficulty is trying to track down an offender without any known connection to his victims.'

'Is that your general experience of serial killers, that they kill randomly?'

'Yes. Why?'

'My view of the current investigation is that somehow the victims are linked to their killer.'

He looked doubtful. 'That doesn't fit with my direct experience. I know what you're saying – that a single item of data can make all the difference in terms of informing an investigation. A prior meeting between victim and killer, some kind of situational link, even something totally indirect such as a note or a phone call from a killer in the absence of face-to-face contact can start the ball rolling but, in my experience, such subtle links are mostly not there.' He shrugged. 'Every investigation I was data analyst on, there was zero evidence of killer and victim having any connection, either direct or indirect, prior to the homicide.'

'Surely there has to be *some* form of contact in order to select a victim?'

He nodded. 'I hear what you're saying but these killers are highly motivated and they have a modus operandi to fit their needs in any situation. Example: a US serial killer who enticed, kidnapped and murdered his victims without anyone being aware of what he was doing because he abducted his victims from crowded shopping malls. As soon as he saw a potential victim, that was it and she was none the wiser – until he struck.'

'You're suggesting that the killer we are pursuing selects and kills in the total absence of any prior contact?'

'I think it needs consideration. Think about it. In the very short time available between observation and his striking, he attracts no attention to himself, follows at a distance. If he has a particular preference, such as the park area where those women were found, he ensures that he is invisible. The less "contact" between him and a victim, the less the likelihood of his being observed until – *bam*!'

Craft started.

'She's gone and no potential witnesses are any the wiser. One must admire, or rather *acknowledge*, the psychological awareness, the skill, of such an individual.'

Craft frowned. 'Must I? My question to you is how was the killer you've just mentioned able to choose the right words, the right gambit, if what you are saying is accurate: that he approaches a complete stranger and persuades her to go with him? That makes no sense to me.' She pointed to the whiteboard. 'Look at those names, David. I see young women robbed of their futures, family members' anguish as they try to deal with their loss. I see nothing admirable about it.'

His face serious now, he said, 'I mis-spoke and I apologize if I sounded flippant . . . but if you run with the hounds as we do, and for long enough, in my case, looking at everything on a computer, it's difficult sometimes to always keep the terrible human suffering behind the stats and the families whose lives have changed for ever at the forefront of your mind. Any death is a catastrophe.' He looked away from her and she recalled what had happened to his girlfriend.

'I'm sorry, David. You know what it is like to lose someone.'

'No apology needed. I was also going to make the point that, given the work we do, we risk becoming habituated to violence and death. Suzie was a victim of bad weather and bad luck.'

'I still think that there had to be some connection here between this killer and his victims, or else how to explain the deaths of Phillip Marsh and Emma Matheson?'

'Have you considered that your theory for them might be wrong, Tig? I struggle to see a connection between those two victims and the later, younger ones, due to the age disparity.' He picked up several files. 'Sorry, I need to go and see Holdsworth. He's waiting for the burglary-related information from me.'

She watched him go through the door, then spent the rest of the day going through her textbooks before gathering them up, sudden activity starting up inside her head following what David had said. She shook her head. *Enough! I'm too tired.* When she was thirteen years old, her mother had taken her to see a specialist who had proclaimed, among other things, that she had left-brain dominance as an explanation for her ease with mathematics. She had always had an affinity for logic, for facts. Which is why art materials bought for her were rarely used. She shook her head. Whatever had caused that rush of activity inside her head just now was gone.

On her way to the door, Sullivan suddenly appeared, filling the door space, his eyes fixed on her. She became very still. *See, Ma? I can 'do' imagination. I can intuit – and right now I don't want to be here—'*

'Going somewhere?' he asked.

'I've finished for the day.'

'So have I, for the next three months. What do you know about me being suspended?'

'Nothing.'

'Don't tell me that wanker, Thompson, has never mentioned it!'

She headed to where he was still blocking the door. 'Please move aside. I want to leave.'

He looked down at her, his eyes moving over her face. 'In my book, he's out of his depth with this investigation. What do you say?'

'Let me through, please.'

He glanced at the wall clock, looked back at her. 'Holdsworth's another wanker but he's in charge and he'll be watching to see that I leave. I want to know what has been said about me. How about we meet up for a drink to discuss it? It feels like we've got off on the wrong foot, you and me.'

'I do not think so.'

'Oh, we have. If you knew me better instead of jumping to conclusions or listening to Headquarters' gossip, you'd—'

'Let me *pass*.'

He pushed the door wide, still blocking her way.

'Come on! I'm not stopping you.'

She went closer, squeezed past him, feeling his heat, her heart banging her chest.

Reaching her car, she got inside and looked back at the building, seeing him appear at the entrance. She engaged central locking, continued to watch him to his vehicle, staring as he opened the door where he turned, pointing his index finger at her for several seconds before getting inside and driving off, engine revving. Watching his taillights fade, she breathed for the first time in what felt like hours.

Coming into the apartment, she closed the door and stopped, picking up tiny *tik-tik-tik* sounds, feeling a sudden rush of joy as Percy ran to her. She had forgotten her mother's call earlier that she would drop him off at the apartment. She knelt, whispered, '*Hello,* Per-*cy.* It's lovely to see you!' She picked him up and carried him into the kitchen. 'Are you hungry?' Hearing her own voice break, she busied herself with the puppy's needs and watched him eat, closing her mind to the whole, awful day. Leaping as her phone rang, she reached for it.

'Tom!'

'Hi, Tig! I'm on my way home. I'll be with you in an hour. Tig? Is everything OK?'

'Yes. Fine . . . I've missed you.'

TWENTY-SIX

Wednesday 6 November, 8.30 a.m.

Thompson looked up as his office door swung open and Craft came inside. Not looking at him, she put down her bag, shrugged off her coat and hung it up. He tried to evaluate her current mood following yesterday. She seemed much as usual, except for the tiredness. 'Holdsworth has received some intel about a male sex offender who was released on licence two weeks ago, following a four-year sentence.'

She did not look at him. 'Oh?'

'Holdsworth wants him talked to.'

'Because?'

'Because he sexually attacked women in places very similar to Forrest Park and not long prior to the attack on Alicia Franks.' He waited, getting nothing.

She glanced at him. 'So? What do you want?'

'I want you and me on the interview with him.'

'I understood that we are going our separate ways on this investigation.'

'We are, but he's due in in half an hour and I want you there . . . I want your insight.'

'If he's just completed a four-year prison sentence, he can't be the individual we are searching for.'

'I know. I want to talk to him because if there's one thing sex offenders do, besides offending, is they *talk*. To each other. Why wouldn't they? They have interests in common which most non-offending people don't have. What better than to while away the days in prison, reliving what they've done and exchanging ideas with other cons on the best ways of operating? I want to get into all of that with him.'

She nodded. 'OK.'

'He's due here in fifteen minutes. Grab yourself a strong coffee while we're waiting and read through what we've got on him.' He pushed a file towards her.

She asked, 'Do you want to plan our approach?'

'We'll wing it. See if a bit of spontaneity loosens his mouth.'

Twenty minutes later, they were facing Colin James Tempest inside Interview Room 3, Craft peripherally eyeing him as Thompson made introductions. 'This is Professor Craft, who is assisting us with our current investigation.'

Tempest's hand shot out. 'Pleased to meet you both.'

They shook hands with him. Craft suddenly aware of his perspiration on her hand.

Thompson was speaking. 'I'm Detective Chief Inspector Steve Thompson. This is not an interview, Mr Tempest, more an exploration of your offending experience.'

Tempest grinned, pointing at him. 'I get it. You're looking for that geezer who's killed those women in a park somewhere, right?'

'I thought we'd start with you telling us about your offences, so we understand where you're coming from.'

'Glad to. You won't get no avoidance or denials from me. I did the full sex offender programme during my sentence.'

'Let's start with your offences, shall we?' prompted Thompson.

Tempest nodded. 'I've taken full responsibility for what I've done. That's a big part of the programme. I did four years inside and got released on licence two weeks ago.'

'Tell us about your first victim.'

Tempest looked pained. 'I don't like the word "victim". She was a grown woman, about, I don't know, thirty-five, same age as me. Just for the record, I never hurt nobody, right? My usual mode of offending was to go into parks and see what turned up.' He frowned at Craft making notes and pointed. 'Make that *who*. It sounds better.'

Craft amended her notes as Thompson continued, 'So, you cruised around open park areas—'

'I never "cruised". I don't like that word either. What I did was get to a park entrance, do a bit of watching and waiting and if I saw somebody, an attractive woman, I went for it, so to speak.'

'What did that entail, Mr Tempest?' asked Craft.

He shrugged. 'A bit of a once-over to start with. Example: if I saw you, I would think, "Yes, very nice, but probably a bit too tall. Too risky".'

'Let's keep things impersonal, Mr Tempest.'

He shot Thompson an aggrieved look. '*She* asked me, remember?'

Thompson massaged both temples, a sure sign for Craft that he was irritated. 'Let's talk about the mates you've got who are sex offenders.'

'Not any more. That's a rule of the programme: zero fraternization. It's obvious, in'it? Hang out with people like that and before you know it . . .' He stopped. 'I don't get what you want from me.'

Thompson sent Craft a quick glance.

She said, 'When you were sent to prison, it is very likely that early on in your association with people of similar interests to yourself – which might not have been considered "fraternization" back then, because you had not yet completed the treatment programme you mentioned—'

'I know what you're getting at and you're right: you can only change when you know what to change *to*. Yeah, before I done the programme I had a couple of mates inside, well, not mates exactly. We'd chat, you know, talk about women.'

'Who were they, these mates?' asked Thompson.

Tempest raised both hands. 'Hey, no names, no nothing.'

'We don't want names. What we want is a sense of how you and these mates got to the stage of advising and supporting each other.'

Tempest nodded. 'I get it. Here's a f'r instance, like I just said, don't choose women taller or bigger than you. Don't move in on them without having an escape route planned.'

'Again, no names,' said Craft, 'tell us about some of the other sex offenders you knew prior to your prison sentence.'

He frowned at her. 'I don't like being classed with "other" sex offenders. I've done time, learned the ropes of offending and how it can sneak up on you and before you know it – I'm not going down that road again.' He shrugged. 'One or two of the lads told me about this bloke they'd seen around parkland and running trails.'

'Can you describe him?'

'I never saw the bloke so how can I do that?'

'What made him stand out, sufficient to claim your associates' attention?'

Tempest grinned. 'This bloke was the business, apparently. Well-dressed and well-spoken. A bit on the posh side.'

'He wasn't a college lecturer by any chance?' asked Thompson.

Tempest frowned. 'Dunno, but now you mention it, he looked the part, but get *this*. Somebody told me he was in the force.' He nodded. 'Yeah! How about *that*.' He caught Thompson's eye. 'I know now from the programme that sex offending is what they call "global". It involves all types of people of all ages and all types of work. Course it does. Offenders are people, regardless of background, education, IQ – that's another variation—'

'What else do you recall about this man?'

Tempest shrugged. 'That about covers it. He was a cop. A big bloke. Any chance of a cup of tea?'

Ten minutes later, Thompson was sitting with his hands over his face. 'I'm hoping you'll take what I'm about to say as my unvarnished view of what we've just listened to.' He blinked. 'We're not just dealing with the "dirty-mac" brigade—'

'If we ever were.'

'It's across all strata of society.'

'Well said,' murmured Craft.

Thompson eyed her. 'Well patronized.'

'What do *you* think of what this friend of his said about a sex offender on the force?'

'It happens. You know about Sullivan's temporary suspension?'

She nodded.

Thompson said, 'But in his case, it's about his attitude to females rather than any explicit sexual actions.'

Craft's brows rose. 'That is a fine distinction you're making. Has there ever been any complaint about Sullivan which confirmed aspects of his behaviour as intentionally sexual, rather than sexist?'

'I'm temporary here, so I don't know, but I doubt it.'

Craft was recalling Sullivan's recent behaviour towards herself. 'How long has he been stationed here?'

'A couple of years as far as I know. Why? You're not thinking there might be some connection between him and these homicides?'

'Come on, Thompson. You know I can't say that, based on hearsay from a dubious source.'

He folded his arms, looked down at the table. 'I agree. All we actually got from Tempest was a possible well-spoken bloke who's part of the force and hangs around parks in the Birmingham area. It's not enough.' He glanced at her. 'Tempest tells a good tale about what he learned in prison, about offending and how to avoid it. What's your bet as to where he might be in two years' time?'

'Like you, a high probability he'll be reoffending, possibly arrested again.' She reached for her phone, tapped a number, and waited. 'Hi, Penny. Teigan Craft. I'm sorry to have to call you but I want to ask you a question. You've been to Headquarters where I work. I'm assuming that if you had seen anyone who looked remotely like the man who attacked you, you would have said so?' She listened to Bristow's words, which she had on loudspeaker so Thompson could hear, thinking how much stronger her voice was compared to the first time they had met her.

'Of course I would! I saw several men moving around the building, but none of them looked remotely like him. What keeps me going is that if I ever saw him, I might recognize him.'

Call ended, Craft was now considering an idea she had had previously when Penny Bristow's memory of her attack was still compromised. She now had confirmation from Lydia that Penny was confident in her recall of her attacker's face. She looked up at Thompson. 'Is there a possibility, anything to be gained, by inviting Penny Bristow here to do an e-fit?'

'Yes, if you think she's up to it.'

'I do. I'll phone Penny tomorrow and see how she feels about it. It's only very recently that she has recovered her memory for the attack on her and in my view she's still rather vulnerable to the possibility of seeing her attacker's face begin to materialize.'

He watched her as she got ready to leave. He didn't ask her where she was going. Two days ago, he had drawn a line between them which she accepted. She would do her thing and he would do his. It was better this way. It reduced the risk of personality and other clashes.

TWENTY-SEVEN

Thursday 7 November, 9.15 a.m.

Tom watched Craft place her phone on the bed, eyes fixed on it as she quickly slipped a sweater over her head and tucked it into her trousers. 'Oh, hi, Penny. I thought I would update you on a possible way forward. One of the officers in the forensics department at Headquarters is an expert at producing likenesses from witness descriptions.' She smiled. 'Yes, you are right, it can produce some very odd-looking faces at times, but I'm confident that Headquarters' trained personnel can do a good job.'

Penny Bristow's voice came into the room. 'I'm really keen to do this, Teigan. When shall I come in?'

Craft thought of the terrified, emotionally scarred woman Peny Bristow had been only a short time before. 'I think we need to be cautious on that, Penny. If it is an effective e-fit for our purposes, we need to be sure that you are sufficiently resilient to cope with what is produced.' She listened to silence. 'Do you understand what I am saying?'

'Yes. You're concerned that if it's really lifelike I'll freak out, but I want to do it. I want him caught.'

'Leave it with me, Penny.' She ended the call and sat beside Tom.

He said, 'You're looking pensive.'

There was a short silence. 'I am. I am feeling . . . highly emotional.'

He kissed her. 'Tell me.'

'You know Mr Bartholomew from the apartment next door?'

'I know of him. Mid-fifties or thereabouts?'

'No, that's his son who comes to visit him. Mr Bartholomew is *really* old. About, I don't know, eighty-something, and he's got a friend.'

Tom fist-punched the air. '*Go*, Mr Bartholomew! Every eighty-plus man needs a female—'

'A *male* friend, Mr Chowdhury, who is around the same age and lives in the apartment above this one. I saw them yesterday, walking together in the grounds . . . one using a stick, the other a long umbrella for support.' She looked up, suddenly tearful. 'They looked so . . . contented, Tom.' She fingered away tears.

'Tig? What is it?'

She shrugged, shook her head. 'It's just nice to see older people with good friends, who have their lives, their worries, challenges, all . . . sorted out.' She got up from the bed. 'Now, I must sort mine. I'll see you later.'

Twenty minutes later she was inside Headquarters, the officer on reception waving to her. 'Professor Craft? Got something for you!' She was holding up a small, clear evidence bag, a single key on a small fob nestling in one corner. 'It was found close to Forrest Park so I thought that either you or DCI Thompson should have it.'

Craft carefully took the bag from her. 'Where, exactly? Who found it?'

The officer pointed. Craft turned to a middle-aged man sitting nearby, getting to his feet. She went to him. 'Good morning, Mr . . .?'

'Brooksby. I was on my way to work when I saw it, just lying there.'

'Where, exactly?'

'It was lying in grass about halfway along the park. It's a wonder I saw it at all, but I did, thanks to the sun.'

She waited. 'The sun?'

'Yeah. It's bright this morning for a change and I saw the glint of it on metal. Everybody round there knows what's been happening inside that park, so I thought I should bring it in.'

'That's very public-spirited of you, Mr Brooksby.'

'No trouble at all. Any chance of a reward?'

'No, but we need your fingerprints before you leave.'

Craft came into the office, finding it deserted. She placed the plastic bag on the table and lowered her face to what was inside: clearly a Yale door key attached by a metal ring to a small, rectangular fob. She stared at colours: green, white, red.

The door opened and a forensic officer she knew by sight looked inside. 'Bass says you want an e-fit done.'

'Yes. We have a witness who is keen to do it but still somewhat vulnerable so I'm considering leaving it a few days.'

'I'd advise you to do it soon as, while recall is still strong.'

'I'm not too worried about that because she's actually in the process of regaining her recall.'

'OK. Let me know when.' He glanced around the office. 'No David Brown?' He grinned. 'When you see him, tell him he's won twenty-eight pounds thirty from the forensic department's lottery ticket.'

The door closing on him, Craft reached for the internal phone and spoke to the officer on desk duty. 'Is David Brown due in this morning, do you know?'

'Doubt it. He phoned an hour ago to report that his house has been broken into.'

Replacing the phone, she reached for her bag and headed for the door.

Fifteen minutes later she was ringing Brown's front doorbell. He opened it, looking better than he had, but harried. 'Tig! Come on in, but mind where you step, there's glass in places.' She came into the hall and followed him inside the sitting room. The place was a mess.

'David, I'm so sorry.'

He shrugged. 'It happens.' He held out his hand to her as she stepped carefully over a scattering of books.

'When? How?'

'My housemate and I were both out overnight. I stayed at a mate's house because I'd had too much to drink to drive home. I came back early this morning and realized I'd lost my front door key. Anyway, long saga short, my housemate arrived within minutes.' He pointed to the ceiling. 'He's up there, checking his room to see what's gone.' He pushed his hand through his hair, looking around the chaotic room. 'I can't sort this out, I've got too much on at Headquarters after taking time off on sick leave.'

'Have the police been?'

He shook his head. 'Would you believe they don't routinely attend for break-ins.'

'Did you tell them who you are?'

He raised his brows, grinned. 'As in, "Look here! I am David Brown the eminent data analyst and I demand service!"'

Getting what he was saying, she smiled, then: 'Is this yours?'

He looked down at the key on her palm, then looked up at her. 'Where did you find it?'

'I didn't. A man found it in grass on the edge of Forrest Park on his way to work this morning and brought it into Headquarters. I had an idea it might be yours because of the fob colours – green, white and red, and . . . it occurred to me that it has personal relevance for you because of your girlfriend's death. It's been forensically tested. Nothing.'

He took it with a whispered, 'Thank you. Whoever broke in here probably threw it away.' He shook his head. 'And, not content with stealing your stuff, they give you extra jobs, like sorting out the mess they left and replacing glass. I'll need to change the locks as soon as I can, in case they made a copy of the key.'

'Can I help at all?'

'You're being here is a help – and I appreciate you finding it. The fob means a lot—' He stopped, gazed around. 'It looks to me like it was a hurried search, books and stuff flung around. I'll sort it.'

'I'll help you. What's the rest of the house like?'

'It's mainly this room that was targeted.'

They picked up books and other items from the floor, placing them on shelves. Turning, she saw him looking at the key and fob. 'Does your housemate know anything about what you're working on at Headquarters?'

'Mmm? No. I don't discuss my work with him or anyone else.' He looked up at her. 'You're not suggesting that he has anything to do with this?'

'No. I'm merely following trains of thought as they arrive.' She headed for the door. 'Are any of the rooms upstairs in disorder?'

'No, and you've spent enough time on my problem. How about I finish sorting this room and I'll see you at Headquarters?'

Craft nodded. 'Oh, guess what? Today is your lucky day. You've won twenty-eight pounds something on the forensic department's lottery.'

He laughed. 'I think I'll carry on with the day job for now.'

She walked to the front door then stopped on a sudden thought. 'What is your housemate's full name?' He gave it. 'Thanks. See you later.'

Back at Headquarters, Craft had typed Brown's housemate's name into various databases and got nothing. *You're too suspicious of everyone and you might have offended David by asking about him.*

There was still no sign of Thompson. Not that she was anticipating or looking for him. It was evident that they could no longer work as a team.

She took the soft-cover textbook from her bag and opened it at Post-it marked pages, wanting to read again the FBI material, particularly that which focused on what American theorists call 'Lust Murder'. She re-read the general characteristics, the attitudes, the beliefs of such killers: *Devaluation of the victim. Devaluation of society in general. A world viewed as unfair and unjust. A general view of life as unjust and inconsistent. An obsession with dominance via aggression.*

She stared out of a nearby window, translating it to suit the current investigation, speaking words out loud to hear and evaluate them. 'We are looking for a male malcontent, a resentful individual who feels he has been unfairly treated in and by life and who, in consequence, relies on violence to dominate those he most blames.' She sighed. 'Which are *women*, apparently. Or, are they the easiest to blame? To hurt?' She sat back. 'And we don't have a single individual in the frame who matches that profile. Maybe the profile is wrong? Have *I* got it wrong?' She turned pages, coming to a printed sheet about aspects of organization within serial homicides, her eyes moving over her own word-processed words.

All the evidence we have points to this killer being intelligent, socially competent to engage his victims, at least initially. He is also sexually competent because he left his semen on Penny Bristow's hair, yet he leaves no other forensic traces. Nor did he conceal the remains of all his victims. He left Alicia Franks in a ditch, yet still visible if one really looked . . .

She thought again of Ozymandias, King of Kings: 'Look on my works, ye Mighty, and despair!' She had told Thompson, 'That is what this killer is saying to us. Yet so far, *we* have demonstrated zero mightiness in our investigation of this case.'

He had not liked it, had merely looked at her, then left the office. She shook her head. She was certain now that the killing of Emma Matheson had a different motivation to that of the attacks at the park and that it linked to that of Phillip Marsh. She felt her heart rate accelerate. 'Unless – I have this completely wrong?' She stared straight ahead. '*Please*, no. Not at this stage of the investigation.'

She looked down at what she had read. 'Four people have died, another almost did, and I'm making a complete mess of this.' Her heartbeat thudded inside her head. 'I was cautious. Careful in my theorizing.' She shook her head. 'I have not got this wrong. Yes, he is predominantly an organized killer, yet the fact that he left one of his park victims, Alicia Franks in a ditch at the scene suggests *some* disorganization.' She frowned. Or was he *displaying* her as his 'work'? Hard on this came another thought. What if these were not spontaneous attacks? That he had made it his business to follow them in preparation for doing so? He could have learned enough of their movements to engage them in basic conversation, disarm them. Her head pulsed. 'Did you watch them? Did they see *you*?' She thought of Alicia Franks and Lucy Greening, both ruined. Lost for ever. Alicia. Lucy. Which of those young women was most likely to behave in the way Craft was now contemplating? It was obvious: Lucy Greening. Because she was so young and was seeking a partner.

She reached for her phone.

TWENTY-EIGHT

Checking the house close to where she was parked with the details on her phone, Craft got out of her car, locked it, approached the house and rang the bell. She waited, seeing a shadow on glass. The door was opened by a woman in her mid-forties. 'Come in, Professor Craft.'

Craft went inside, seeing a subtle familial likeness in this woman's face to one of the photographs at Headquarters. 'Mrs Greening, I'm very grateful to you for allowing me to visit.'

'Not at all. Please, go straight ahead.'

Craft did, coming into a large, sunny kitchen.

Mrs Greening followed. 'I was pleased when you phoned. Really pleased.' She looked suddenly uncertain. 'I'm hoping that you have some news? About what happened to our daughter?'

Craft said, 'We are exploring all possibilities in this investigation, Mrs Greening. It's why I'm here. To look at Lucy's belongings, her room, if I may, to get a sense of her. How do you feel about that?'

Greening nodded. 'Of course. Her bedroom is just as she left it. People often say that, don't they, but it's true. Nothing in there has been changed.'

Craft watched her regain control.

'Can I get you anything, before you make a start?'

'No, thank you. I would just like to see the room.'

'Of course. Follow me.' They went upstairs to a large front-facing bedroom. It was neat, orderly, the bedlinen immaculate. She watched Greening's mother walk slowly around it, touching a curtain, pulling gently at the smooth pink bedcover. 'I come in here most days. My husband thinks it's a bad idea, but . . . it works for me. Mostly.'

'Is this as Lucy left it?'

'More or less. Her bed was unmade and there were one or two items of her clothing on the floor from the morning she went. You know what young women are like. Always in a rush, not bothered about tidiness . . . We thought she might have met someone who . . . took her away, so my husband took the clothes to the local police station, in case there was a chance that they might find something on them, but they didn't.' She brought her voice under control. 'If I can help at all, Lucy was very open with us, with me in particular.'

'In the period leading up to what happened, did Lucy mention any changes in her life?'

Greening shook her head. 'Sorry, I don't know what you mean.'

'I mean anything small, like acquiring a new friend or—'

'We didn't know she'd gone to that dating agency. We liked her boyfriend, the one she had before. I thought he was ideal for her, but she said no. If she had mentioned joining an agency, I would have told her not to have anything to do with a place like that. They put photos up or show them to men . . .' She stopped, breathless. 'I'm sorry. Please, look at anything you like. I'll be downstairs.' She turned away.

'Mrs Greening? Do you know if Lucy kept any sort of diary of her life?' She watched Greening's slow headshake.

'No. Nothing like that. If she did, it would have been on her phone . . . but we don't have that either. It was taken.'

Craft watched her walk to the door without a backward glance, saying, 'I'll make some tea,' and go downstairs.

Craft looked quickly around the room, went to the double wardrobe, opened it, searching pockets, the insides of shoes and boots, the drawers beneath full of neatly folded T-shirts, sweaters and underwear never to be worn again. She crossed the room to a chest of drawers. Same story. Tights in packs, others laundered, a soft envelope-shaped item made of white satin. Her pulse-rate climbing, Craft reached for and opened it, gently removed the contents: two sets of matching underwear, bras and pants, silky to the touch, a designer label on each, both unworn. Had they been bought for the enjoyment of someone Lucy regarded as special?

Craft replaced the underwear, then dropped to her knees to peer beneath the bed, lifted the mattress, looked under it, let it fall back into place. She turned slowly, eyes moving over the whole room, seeing for the first time a mid-height dado rail running along each wall. Returning to the wardrobe, she went to the wall it was standing against and, placing her head against its side, she peered within the narrow space between wardrobe and wall. Sliding her hand into the space, fingers moving, lower arm protesting at the narrowness, her fingertips brushed against something. Removing her hand from the space, she looked again, seeing nothing. Placing her hands either side of the wardrobe, pressing her lips together, she lifted it a couple of centimetres from the wall and heard the whisper of something slide almost soundlessly down the wall.

On her knees again, she pressed her forehead against the wardrobe and stared into the narrow void. Reaching into it, shoulder protesting, she gripped the small item and carefully brought it out. A slim book. A notebook. Her fingers quivering, she opened it, seeing dates, lines of neat handwriting, notes which appeared to relate to a period of weeks including the four days prior to the day on which Lucy Greening disappeared. She took it to the bed and sat, began reading, turning pages, reaching the fourth one. She started at Mrs Greening's voice coming from somewhere on the stairs.

'Do you take sugar?'

Her heart thudding, Craft quickly closed the book, slid it inside her bag. 'No, thank you! I'm coming down now.'

Reaching for her bag, closing it and looping it on to her shoulder, she went to the door, had a quick look back at the room, then continued down the stairs and on to the kitchen. Mrs Greening had laid out tea and cake on the table. 'Have a seat, Professor Craft.'

Craft did so, lifting her cup, quickly replacing it on its saucer, aware of the tremor in her hand.

'Which cake would you like? There's Victoria sponge or maybe a slice of Millionaire's cake? It's not that chocolatey and you're very slim anyway.'

Craft watched a slice arrive on the plate beside her. She picked up the cake fork and slowly began to eat, listening to Mrs Greening's voice. 'I like to bake. My niece is coming later and she loves chocolate cake. How about you? Are you enjoying it?'

Craft left the house ten minutes later, went to her car and sat, light-headed, inside it. What she had just done was shocking. Against every rule. After a few minutes' deep breathing, she started the car and drove away from the house. Ten minutes later she quickly pulled into the side of the road, getting an irate hoot from the car following. Coming to a halt, she opened both windows and pulled air into her chest. She had stolen evidence from Lucy Greening's family.

Arriving home forty-five minutes later, she parked her car and hurried into the apartment complex, very aware of her bag against her side. She knew she should deliver the notebook directly to Headquarters. She also knew that she would not. She wanted to look through it, read every single word, analyse it, weigh every possible connotation, and do it here. Now. Removing her coat, dropping it on to a chair, she fetched unused nitrile gloves from the kitchen, pulling them on and carefully removed the notebook from her bag. Her prints were already on file at Headquarters but she still needed to limit her handling of it. She opened the small book and read the words on the fourth page. Lucy Greening's words. She sat back, her eyes still fixed on them. Words written by a young woman just days prior to her disappearance and death. Lucy Greening was the youngest victim by several years and Craft had anticipated that, being the youngest, she was the most likely to commit her thoughts to writing. She gazed down at neat words.

> God, I'm so happy!!! Is it possible? Does this kind of thing ever really happen? Someone has comes into my life and he is my soul-mate. So understanding. So lovinG. My life, my world hAs changed for the betteR. He is my destinY. I am ecstatic because I know now that there is someone for me, someone loving, who loves me. Yes! My extra-special someone: my SXXXY

A tiny heart drawn beneath the final 'x' left Craft in no doubt that what she was reading was Lucy Greening's heady, breathless declaration of love. A young woman who had craved romance and now believed she had found the man who would give it to her. She read it again, pondering the odd capitals. She copied them on to a separate sheet, studied them, her heart hammering as she circled each one, seeing a name form. One that she knew.

Thompson needed to see this, but first she had to follow up what appeared to be another potential lead which had been on her mind. Reaching for her phone, she tapped on an international number. Her call was picked up. Craft introduced herself, speaking slowly to get the words right and to make herself understood.

'I need to speak with someone about a possible homicide in your jurisdiction involving a young woman.' She gave the names, listened, shook her head. 'No, I believe this case is from approximately three years ago.' She gave the general location details she had. Several minutes of silence followed, then a voice speaking excellent English said, 'Apologies, caller, but the details you have given are not linked to any homicide on our database. If you could provide additional details, I can search again, but as of now, I cannot help you.'

Murmuring her thanks, she gave her email address and ended the call. Grabbing her coat and keys, she left the apartment. Twenty minutes later she opened the office door, let it swing slowly, silently open, seeing a lone figure sitting within a small circle of light. It leapt up.

'Bloody *hell*!' Thompson stared at her. 'What are you trying to do? Give me a bloody heart attack!' He dropped back on to his chair. 'It's gone nine. Why are you here?'

She sat opposite him, gazed into his face, seeing for the first time the impact the investigation was having on him. 'I have some information.'

He shrugged. 'Follow it up and leave me to do the same.'

'I think you need to see this.'

He looked across at her, dropped his pen on the table. 'Being my own worst enemy, go on.' He watched as she slid an A4 sheet towards him.

'Read that.'

He briefly eyed it. 'So? It sounds like it's been written by some lovesick teenager.'

'That's exactly what it is, but much more.'

He waited. 'If there's a point to all of this, can I have it?'

She tapped the sheet. 'Those are Lucy Greening's words.'

He frowned at them. 'Who says?'

'I do.'

'Where were they?'

'Inside a notebook at her mother's home.' She reached into her bag and brought it out. 'Take a look.'

He made no move to do so. 'Greening's mother gave it to you?'

'No.'

'So how . . .?' He watched Craft's gaze shift away from him, whispered, 'What have you done, Craft? *Don't* tell me you took it!'

'I did.'

He stared at her. 'You can't *do* that! You can't go into a murder victim's family home and just *take* something! Are you *nuts*?'

'No. I want this investigation brought to its conclusion.' She opened the notebook, turned pages and pushed it towards him, tapping one of them. 'These are Lucy's actual words, her writing.' She watched his eyes move along the lines.

He looked up. 'If Lucy Greening did write this, my response is still, so what? I've got two teenage daughters and they're always on their phones or iPads, fingers in a frenzy and going barmy if I or their mother go anywhere near to them. It's what teenagers *do*.'

'Lucy was eighteen and she was desperate for romance.' She pointed to the book. '*This* is evidence that she found it.'

'Who says? It looks to me like a bit of fantasy.'

'What she has written here is confirmation that she believed she had found a man she wanted and who wanted her.'

'Like I said—'

'You need to *really* look at it!'

He gave her an irritable look. 'I *have*. I've read it three times—'

'Read it *again*.'

She watched him do so. 'What do you see?'

'Nothing beyond some odd capital letters.'

'They are a young woman's way of concealing personal information about someone she has met.'

He frowned at her, looked at the words again, then reached for his pen. She watched him slowly track the words, circling capitals. He sat back, looking at them, then up at her. 'I don't believe it.'

She pointed to them. 'G-A-R-Y, and then, at the end, S-X-X-X-Y. I think those are kisses disguising Sully. Lucy Greening *had* met someone named "Gary". Someone she called her "Sully—"'

'No, no, no. I know what you're thinking and it's off the wall!'

'Why? Because he's one of your officers? This is a deceased

young woman and *this* potentially implicates Sullivan who is already suspended for his attitude to females.'

'A temporary suspension, initiated by *me* because I'm fully aware of his attitude and I don't approve of it. Where's the proof she and Sullivan ever met?'

'It's *here.* In what she wrote!'

He closed his eyes. 'Like I said, this is a young woman who clearly fancies some bloke. Or it could easily be made up.'

'Oh, come *on*! Someone she has met, who has the same name as one of your officers? This is no coincidence, Thompson. Where was Sullivan working at the time Lucy Greening was murdered?'

'He had just transferred here from the Met. So what? This isn't proof of anything and Greening herself can't confirm it.' He shook his head. 'She was living in Stratford-upon-Avon. How the hell would she have come into direct contact with Sullivan?'

'I can't answer that, but she knew his *name*! How do you explain that? It's telling me that they *did* meet. Check all available reception diaries, all officers' notebooks for this period of time . . .'

'You don't think I've got enough to do! That kind of search would take *days.*' He fell silent, then: 'Craft, I know you're bright and keen, but this isn't the way forward and it's giving me a real headache.' He watched her delve into her bag and snapped, 'Not *that* kind of headache!' His eyes fixed on her. 'What you're telling me sounds like pure Agatha Christie. I'm in the *real* world here, wondering how the bloody *hell* I use this information without letting on exactly how *you* came to be in possession of it.' He fell back against his chair. 'Don't you *get* it? You *stole* it from Greening's mother's house.'

'She doesn't know it exists.'

'You don't know that and so *what*? She has to know that it's been found and right now I'm thinking how I square what you did to get hold of it and I'm coming up empty!'

'In which case, the rules of evidence are wrong. Stop shouting.'

He put his hands to his face, rubbed his eyes and blinked at her. 'You can't rewrite rules to suit yourself. I don't question your intellect, I don't question your determination to see this investigation through to an arrest, but you can't ride roughshod over rules!'

'You are rejecting out of hand that Gary Sullivan might be involved with Lucy Greening's death, despite *knowing* how he behaves around women and for which *you* suspended him?'

'That was Holdsworth's final decision and as I've said, it's temporary. As of now, he reports here once a day.' He stood, went to the window, looked out on darkness and rain. 'You won't want to hear this, but there are a lot of Sullivans in the world. In the force. Even if I accept what Greening wrote, there's no proof she's talking about the Sullivan who works here. Gary is a common enough name. I can name *four* without trying that I've worked with over the years.'

'What about "Sully"? That should convince you to at least explore it – and do not go on about "*evidence*" because I'll *scream.*'

He gazed at her. 'I know how hardworking and determined you are. I also know how impulsive, how certain you can be about things without fully weighing them up.' He studied her face. 'OK. I'll make some inquiries myself about Sullivan' – she brightened – 'but I'm not saying I think you're right.'

'I *am* right.'

'*Leave* it!'

TWENTY-NINE

Friday 8 November, 6.30 a.m.

Penny Bristow was out of bed at six thirty. In the last few days she had begun to feel so much better. Not having received any update from the police about her case and still waiting for a date to do the e-fit, she was going to Headquarters to demand whatever new information they might have. She searched her wardrobe for clothes which said, *I am a strong woman.* Selecting the grey suit and a white shirt, she got dressed. A critical glance in the full-length mirror confirmed the weight loss indicated by the suit trousers. She straightened, pulled herself to full height. 'No more sandwiches instead of proper meals. No more lying around in leggings and jumpers!'

A nod to her reflection and she left the bedroom. Within ten minutes she was inside her car taking more deep breaths. Police headquarters held few good memories for her but getting an update on the progress of her case and helping with the e-fit would mean that things were moving on. That she was moving on. She focused on her driving and was soon moving along the road to the police headquarters, the huge building coming into view. Entering the car park, monitoring her breathing, she got out of the car, locked it. Shoulders back, she headed for the entrance.

Coming inside, she saw the long queue of waiting people. Joining it, she gazed ahead, trying to estimate how long she might have to wait. The man in front of her turned round. 'This is what we pay our extortionate rates for.'

She gave a quick nod, not wanting to encourage him. The queue moved slowly forward. She now had a better view of the reception desk, the three females talking to those at the head of the queue— She froze. She was looking at the man who attacked her at Forrest Park. He was talking to another large male. A wave of heat spread over her. She stared at the man who had almost ruined her life. *They have arrested him! They want me to see him and confirm that it is him!* Her heart thumping, she looked around the large area for the officer in charge of her case, the tall, blonde psychologist helping him, then back to the men still in easy conversation. *Please, God, no. He works here. He's a police officer.* Hardly aware of what she was doing, she backed away, into a woman standing behind her, turned and headed for the exit, bumping into people, getting tuts of annoyance. She made it to the doors and outside, leant against the wall, thinking that this was a nightmare she would never be free from. All the people working in this massive building . . . and he was one of them. Another realization crashed into her head: he could get hold of her contact details. He could . . .

She reached home with no memory of how she got there, went inside the house, double-locked the front door, chained it, went into the sitting room and sat, emotionally, physically spent, trying to block the memories of the man and what he did to her. Later that afternoon, she knew what she had to do. She got out her phone, rang the direct number she had been given. Her call was picked up. 'Dr Wadham, this is Penny—'

'Dr Wadham is unavailable until Monday. Please leave a message including your contact number—'

Feeling abandoned, she cut the call, then thought of the tall, blonde psychologist who had been very supportive. She had her phone number. Reaching for her phone again, about to tap it, she stopped. This man was a police officer. She was aware from her work with the Probation Service of the force's attitude to complaints against serving officers, its determination to protect its own. The phone slipping from her hand, she closed her eyes. Helpless.

Thompson was in a meeting with Holdsworth about progress. Craft was alone in the office finding it difficult to settle to anything. Her head propped on one hand, she leafed through her notes, hearing the door open.

'Did you manage to convince Holdsworth that we're on track?'

Getting no response, she looked up. Sullivan was filling the doorway, his eyes fixed on her. Instantly on her feet, she said, 'What are you doing here? You're suspended—'

He came towards her, his eyes fixed on hers. 'If it's any of your business, I sign in daily and I've got a question for you. What have you been saying about me to the boss?'

She seized her coat, pulled it on, gathered her belongings and dropped them into her bag, aware that he was closing in on her, so close she could feel the heat coming off him. Not looking directly at him, she quickly went around him and on to the door. 'I have nothing to say to you.'

He also moved quickly, light on his feet for such a large man, and reached the door before she did, blocking her exit. Still not looking at him, she said, 'Move out of my way. I want to leave.'

'Who the *hell* do you think you are! You've said stuff about me and—'

'Let me *pass*.'

'Answer me!'

She was lightheaded. 'I've nothing to say to you—'

He seized her upper arm. 'I won't ask you again! What lies have you been spreading about me?' He shook her.

She hit him in the chest, saw anger flare in his eyes, felt his grip tighten.

'You're supposed to be smart. In my opinion, *you* are bloody odd, I don't like you and it's time somebody put you in your place!'

She swung her bag, caught him in the face. He released her. She staggered backwards. He grabbed her, pushing her to the floor, was now on top of her, glaring down at her, his breath hitting her face as he grasped her neck.

'You can't be that smart or you'd never cross *me*.'

Gasping for air, she fought him, feeling his grip loosen.

Pulling away from him, she staggered to her feet. 'Is that what you did to Lucy Greening?'

'You're out of your fucking mind!' He lunged for her.

Whirling from him, she slipped from his grasp, a wave of dizziness hitting her. She yelled, 'You've just proved to me exactly what I know you are!'

He pointed at her, finger quivering. 'I won't let you get away with this! I've got mates here who'll tell me what you've been saying!' He glared at her, breathing heavily, and aimed his foot at her lower leg.

She yelped, heard the door open then close. She looked down at the reddening area close to her ankle. Straightening, she put her weight on it. It felt sore. Picking up her bag and the items which had spilled from it, running a quick hand over her hair and face, she took deep breaths, slowly opened the door and checked the corridor. Deserted. Walking into reception, eyes down, she went quickly out to the car park. Getting inside her car, she locked herself in, waiting for her breathing to settle. The first thing she would do when she arrived here tomorrow would be to make an official complaint against Sullivan.

THIRTY

7.30 p.m.

Tom was home. Craft had not yet told him about what had happened to her. Hearing the shower running, she went to her phone and tapped Thompson's number. He picked up. 'Don't tell me you're still working.'

'No. I'm home. I . . .' She searched for words.

'Craft, if you've got something to say, just get to it because my dinner's going cold.'

'I need to report an assault.'

'Verbal? Physical? By whom and to whom? Keep it brief.'

'Verbal and physical, by Sullivan to me.'

'Say, again?'

She closed her eyes. 'Sullivan physically assaulted me late this afternoon.'

'*What?* When you say "assaulted"—'

Out of patience, she snapped, 'He kicked me. On the leg.'

'Where are you?'

'At home.'

'Stay there, I'll come—'

'*No.* Tom is here and I haven't yet told him—'

'Meet me at Headquarters in around thirty minutes.'

'I can't. I just wanted you to know—'

'*Be* there, Craft.'

She looked at her phone. He was gone.

Tom was coming into the room. 'How about we eat out?'

She reached for her coat, moving quickly in the direction of the front door. 'I need to collect something from Headquarters, I won't be long.'

Feeling his eyes on her, she was through the door, down the single flight of stairs and out into the car park. Twenty minutes later she was walking into Headquarters, feeling wary, a growing soreness in her ankle. The officer on reception looked up at her, did a double-take. 'You on the night shift now, Professor?'

'No.' She continued to the office and sat, getting her breathing under control. This was a first for her. She had never needed to report anyone, least of all an officer. Thompson had to know what had just happened. The door flew open and Thompson was standing there, looking at her. He came and sat opposite her. 'OK. Give me all the details.'

She did, watching his quick note-taking. 'Hang on, let me get this straight. You were in this room with Sullivan and he suddenly kicked you because . . .?'

'I hit him with my bag.'

He looked up at her. 'You, what?'

'I hit him. With my bag. He was saying things to me—'

'*You* hit *him*?'

She covered her face with her hands. '*Because* he grabbed me by my arm, then pushed me to the floor!' She looked at him, pointing to her neck. 'He put his hand *here*, would not let me go. He said he would check with officers here what I was saying about him. He got up, kicked me – and he left.'

'Was anything else said?'

'I said he had done something similar to Lucy Greening, holding her neck.'

Face set, Thompson continued writing, then put down his pen. 'You accused him of killing Greening?'

'Sort of. Why?'

'That's *my* question. You're saying you've got evidence that he killed Greening?'

'Yes! The note she wrote about him, plus I know Sullivan has the personality characteristics which make it feasible.' She watched Thompson quickly read what he had just written.

'So, he says things to you that you don't like, you hit *him* and he gets you down on the floor.' He looked up at her. 'Craft, I've checked. Two weeks prior to Lucy Greening going missing, Sullivan had a broken arm following some skirmish while he was arresting somebody.'

'No. That's not possible.'

'Like I said, I *checked*. He was taken to A and E.'

She stared at him. 'What kind of "skirmish"?'

'He saw a known suspect get out of a vehicle, gave chase, there was a struggle, he made the arrest and was knocked to the ground by the suspect's mate. He landed on his right arm. He's a big bloke. Heavy.'

'I know that firsthand!'

'He was put on desk duties for the next two weeks and was seen by Human Resources twice within that timeframe.'

She looked at him, frustrated. 'Wait! You are not based here, yet you know all these details. You've been checking up on him!'

'I have. I got the facts.' A silence grew between them, broken by Thompson. 'I'll deal with Sullivan and what he did to you, but I need you to make an official complaint about him in writing, then put the incident to one side so that you're open to any other leads which come our way in this investigation and which might pan out . . .'

'I am a professional. I *know* that.'

He stood. 'First thing tomorrow morning, I'll have Sullivan in here to give me his view of what happened between the two of you' – he saw Craft's mouth open – 'but there is no way he will convince me that his actions towards you are acceptable. He's already on temporary suspension and this is not going to help him get back here. One more thing. Take the whole of the weekend off.'

* * *

Thirty minutes later, Craft came into the apartment. 'Tom?'

'In here!' He was in the sitting room. 'What was so urgent at Headquarters?'

She shrugged. 'Something I had forgotten to brief Thompson about.' She glanced at him as he came to her.

'Is everything all right, Tig? Your look very stressed. You need to take time off.'

She shrugged. 'I'm . . . tired. I'm going to bed.'

Monday 11 November, midday

Craft was diverting her attention from the investigation, at the same time waiting for a call from Thompson confirming that she could go to Headquarters. Hearing her phone ring, she reached for it. It was Tom, to say that he would be late that evening. Ending the call, she wandered, aimless, around the apartment, sat at the piano, played a few notes, abandoned it, went to the window to look out on the cold day.

Her phone rang again. She picked it up. 'Craft?' It was Thompson. 'Get yourself to Headquarters!'

'Why?'

'Just . . . get here.'

Craft came into Headquarters, picking up the downbeat atmosphere. Seeing the faces of two officers on reception, she asked, 'What's happened?' They avoided looking at her directly.

One said, 'DCI Thompson will brief you.'

She went directly to Thompson's office, saw him coming out of it. 'What's going on? What's happened?'

'I'm on my way to see Holdsworth. You need to be there.'

She followed him along the corridor and upstairs, wondering if some key investigative information had suddenly become available. Thompson's mood and the general atmosphere inside the building suggested not. Following Thompson into Holdsworth's office, Holdsworth's face, the grimmest she had witnessed to date, was further confirmation.

They sat, Holdsworth looking intently at them. 'I've just diverted four officers here to deal with calls from the media. The brass is demanding action on this investigation. It wants results.' Craft frowned at 'brass', guessing that the superintendent was in trouble. No. Not Holdsworth. Her gaze moved to Thompson. *This is about us.*

Holdsworth said, 'There's no way to soften this: if there's no significant development leading directly to an arrest within the next *seven* days' – he looked at Thompson – 'you'll be removed from the investigation and' – his focus switched to Craft – 'the same goes for you, Professor.'

Thompson made no response.

Craft stared at Holdsworth. 'That is totally unfair! We, the whole investigative team, is working very hard, doing everything possible—'

'With zero progress.'

'It is a very complex investigation.'

'And I'm being leant on to get it sorted! Which is what I'm about to do right now. Take this for what it is, an ultimatum. I want *action*. I want a *result* leading directly to an arrest. If either of those don't happen in the next *seven* days, both of you are finished here, is that clear?' He paused. 'This city wants to know what this force is doing about these homicides of vulnerable females. If there is *still* nothing, if you can't make it happen within the next seven days, *maximum*, there will be a clean sweep of the whole team and another officer from outside this force will take over as senior investigative officer. That's it.' He stopped, breathing hard.

Craft eyed him. 'This is grossly unfair!' She saw Thompson get to his feet and head for the door. She stared after him, aware of Holdsworth's eyes on her. Still irate and now helpless, she stood and followed Thompson, her shoulders back, head held high, pulling the door after her which slammed against its frame.

Thompson said, 'You think that's going to help?' They went down the stairs.

'It helps *me*,' she snapped.

They came into the office, Craft still fuming. Thompson said, 'If you think this is about fairness, think again. Our energy would be better used thinking how we get this mess to a conclusion.'

Arms folded, she stared at the endless notes she had made, thinking about the hours she had spent. 'I cannot stand this place a minute longer. I am going home.'

He watched her go.

* * *

Craft was home, on the phone to Tom. 'And Holdsworth has put us on seven days' notice and he's already got someone waiting to take over the investigation.'

'Tig, I'm so sorry to hear it but I'm sure you and DCI Thompson have done all you can. You could not have worked harder.'

'If that were true, we would not face being dispensed with. We've missed something.'

A brief pause and Tom's voice came again. 'All I can say is that knowing you as I do, you've done everything possible. It could be one of those cases which are never solved and remain in people's consciousness for years.'

She shook her head, thinking of the victims who were as real, as known to her, as anyone else in her life, particularly Emma Matheson and Penny Bristow. She had let them and the other victims into her consciousness, her emotions. This was not merely a job. And what Tom was describing – she would not allow it to happen.

After another minute the call ended and she went to the dining table on which she had spread all the information she had. To *miss* something suggested that it had to be here, something she had not picked up on, not fully appreciating its relevance. 'I've been over it multiple times,' she whispered. 'Is it possible that I *have* missed something? That I made an error?' She poured more coffee, brought it back to the table, chided herself for her negative thinking. On many occasions in her life, Craft had had to acknowledge her difficulties. She also knew her strengths: a hyper-attention to detail, a laser-like ability to recognize patterns within information and, during this investigation, thinking outside the box. She rotated her shoulders, breathed deeply. No way would she walk meekly away from it.

THIRTY-ONE

Tuesday 12 November, 2.30 p.m.

Craft walked into Headquarters, picking up on tension. She went directly to Thompson's office, saying, 'I've decided: I'm going to see Holdsworth to demand that he gives us more time—'

'Take my advice and don't waste the time we've got.'

She frowned, eyeing his suit, white shirt and tie. 'You look very formal.'

'All part of my master plan to be nobody's victim. I've got a meeting with Holdsworth in two minutes who is about to confirm the actual date when I'm for the chop.'

'He can't do that! We haven't yet had the seven days he promised. I'm coming with you.'

'You haven't been invited.'

'I don't *care*.'

As they approached Holdsworth's office, the door opened and he emerged with another man. They watched as the two shook hands. Thompson whispered, 'Not wasting any time, is he?'

Craft studied the man's smart appearance, the way he held himself, his tone as he said, 'Sir, I can assure you right now that once I start here, there won't be any wasted time on my watch.'

She gave him a furious look. He turned away from Holdsworth with barely a glance at them and went down the stairs. She and Thompson went into the office. They were not invited to sit. 'That was DCI Rollaston from Worcester Constabulary, your successor on this investigation.'

'Not until seven days have elapsed,' snapped Craft, 'which is what you promised us.'

'That still stands. Rollaston has a week's holiday arranged, but following that I hand the whole investigation over to him.'

Thompson saw Craft's mouth open and sent her a quick headshake.

Holdsworth looked away from them. 'That's all.'

It was early evening. Thompson had left for the day but Craft was still there, on her phone to Tom.

'That sounds extremely autocratic.' he said. 'You've worked so hard.'

'Not hard enough, apparently. I'll be home soon.'

Call ended, she sighed. 'Why can't I get a hold of this case? Why can't I *see* . . .' She reached for a stack of notes, tapped their lower edges on the desk, like the women who deliver television news, then placed them squarely on the table in front of her, her notebook uppermost. She opened it and read a few paragraphs, shook her head, thinking of the waste, the loss, and one of the victims such a young age.

11.45 p.m.

Her phone rang. Without looking at it she knew who it was. 'Hi, Tom.'

'When are you coming home?' He sounded worried. Annoyed? Without seeing his face, she was unsure. Not waiting for her response, he said, 'Tig, you're still investing too much of yourself in this case in view of Holdsworth's attitude—'

'That is precisely why I'm doing it. I won't be dismissed from it, Tom.'

'I don't see that you have much choice now. You, your colleagues, have done all you can. It's possible this case is beyond a solution. You've done enough. Come home.'

She closed her eyes. 'What if I haven't done enough?'

'Knowing you, I doubt that, but if it were the case, it's too late, Tig. The decision has been made.'

The call between them ended. Tom had a valid point. There was a lesson for her here. A lesson in failure on a case she had never wanted yet had accepted as a challenge. She gathered her belongings and left the office.

A while later, she glanced at the bedside clock. Four a.m. She got quietly out of bed, sudden activity starting up inside her head, willing her to retrieve a word, a phrase she knew was there, yet still inaccessible, tapping its presence, just beyond reach. She shook her head. It would not come. Telling herself to stop, she lay down. After ten more minutes she was out of bed again. The words inside her head were prodding and pushing, refusing to leave her alone, her own memory functioning as gatekeeper, locking her out. Frustrated, she went to the kitchen, not sure why, once she was there. She recognized what was happening: tip-of-the-tongue phenomena, and that her efforts to force retrieval were pointless. If it came at all, it would happen in its own time.

Wednesday 13 November, 8.00 a.m.

Tired, listless, Craft was staring straight ahead as the door opened and Thompson came inside, his face matching her low mood. 'I'd drop the early mornings if I were you, Craft. No point now.'

'So why are you here?'

'As SIO I need to sort out all the information we've gathered, ready for handover in a few days to DCI Rollaston.'

She felt a sudden surge of anger. 'If *he* succeeds in this case where we haven't, I'll—'

He looked across at her, waiting. 'Yeah? What will you do?' He shook his head. 'Give it up, Craft. I'm ready to go back to my usual base in north Birmingham.'

'What about the car-ringing investigation you were promised?'

'It's now history: six arrests.'

'Oh.'

'Cheer up.'

She sent him a warning frown.

He said, 'You can get back to your university and whatever you do there.'

She thought about it, chin on fist. 'It feels like ages since I was there.'

'You'll be back there in a couple of days and you'll forget all of this.'

'I won't.' She sent him a quick glance. 'I thought I would not like being part of a team but it's been OK. Apart from our likely failure.'

He stood, gathered up files and headed for the door. 'My advice is don't class it as failure. It happens. You're young. You'll have other chances of investigative work, if you want it.' The door closed on him as the words she had been searching for and failing to retrieve clicked into place: *Ages. Young.*

She seized her notes, turning pages, her eyes drilling down at line after line until . . . she had them. They were both here. Two keys to open this investigation wide. She needed confirmation. Reaching for her phone she checked the time: 9.02 a.m., selected a number, waited as it rang out, was picked up. 'Harrison Marsh, how can I help—'

'This is Teigan Craft. I need to speak to Helen Drew urgently.' After a short wait she heard a different voice, one she recognized.

'Helen, this is Teigan Craft. Yes, I'm fine. I need to check some historical information you gave me about an intern who worked at Harrison Marsh in London. Do you recall his exact age?' The reply, when it came, was the one she hoping for.

'He was just short of his seventeenth birthday, which was an anomaly for this firm. Back then. All our interns were at least twenty.'

'Do you have a name, Helen?' The response came, causing Craft to grip the phone. Not the same name, but close enough. 'Do you recall anything about him?'

'You bet I do! Despite his young age, he was an accomplished liar and a thief.'

Craft looked at the few words she had written It was not proof, according to Thompson's way of thinking, but she was more than satisfied. 'If the company still holds documentation which confirms what you have just told me, I would be very grateful if you would email copies to Headquarters, for the attention of DCI Thompson.'

'Of course.'

'Thank you, Helen.'

Ending the call, she made another, to Wyatt the estate agent, and got a similar confirmation. Staring at her phone, call ended, she wondered how receptive Thompson might be to continuing the investigation based on the information she now had. Her phone rang. She reached for it. It was David Brown.

'Teigan, I've just heard what's happening at Headquarters. About Holdsworth curtailing your investigation. How are you and DCI Thompson?'

'We're fine.'

'I could not believe it when I heard that somebody else was taking over. What's he like?'

'A by-the-book type. No flare.'

'Oh. Well, that's that, I suppose.'

THIRTY-TWO

Craft arrived, seeing Thompson already inside reception. She had reconsidered her low opinion of his willingness to listen to the information she now had. She had to give it a try. Walking past him, she said, 'I must talk to you.' He watched her go, then followed. They came into the office, sat opposite each other. 'I have gone through every single piece of information we have acquired during this investigation and' – she gave him a direct look – 'I have a suspect.'

'Say again?'

'More than a suspect. Somebody who fits everything we've learned during this investigation.'

He waited. 'Give me a name.'

She did. 'Does that name remind you of anyone?'

'Yes, and it's crazy. How do you know?'

She pulled a file from her bag, opened it, took out the Harrison Marsh email. 'It's all here. Read it.' Taking it from her, he did.

'Enjoyed exerting power over females, despite young age, which has cast doubt on his performance in this first experience of employment in a London firm.' He looked up at Craft.

She nodded. 'That's right. At barely seventeen, he was the youngest intern they ever employed. Despite his young age, possibly because of it, Emma Matheson took an interest in him. My view has always been that the motive for her murder was expediency. Emma Matheson's involvement with him back then led to her suspecting that he was responsible for killing Phillip Marsh.' She paused. 'He was also stealing money from the company. Phillip Marsh had found out. I could not understand why Emma was killed so many years later, but it was obvious, once I really thought about it. She was experiencing hard times. She needed support, she needed money, and she believed *he* would help her because of what she knew about him. Emma was desperate. He did not share her view of the situation, but he knew he could not ignore her. So, he silenced her. Hid her body inside that house where it remained for years.'

Thompson gave a slow headshake. 'I'm not doubting what you're saying . . . I just can't believe he did this. He was more or less a part of the police.'

'What better way to use what he learned from his job to protect himself? He could access information, stay at least one step ahead. He stayed several years ahead, thanks to his concealment of Emma Matheson's remains.'

Thompson stared down at the sheet she had given him. 'The cold-hearted *bastard.*'

'You are right, Thompson. His attitude to women in general, including at least one he knew intimately, is devoid of pity.'

Thompson's eyes were fixed on the sheet.

'We also have to include a seemingly small offence which led me to a homicide more than a thousand miles away in Italy.'

'I'm impressed, Craft. I'd be more impressed if you had told me before this.'

'I doubted you would accept what I was saying. Now, I'm thinking how we might force his hand.'

'If you're suggesting putting yourself on the line to provoke him into action, my answer is no. The investigations I know about where that's been done didn't end well.'

She leant towards him. 'I have psychological skills and insights that officers do not have. I know what is required to present as trustworthy and plausible. We've now got just a few days left and I want to force his hand.'

'I don't want the responsibility of anything like that. What you would be doing is laying yourself right on the line. Putting yourself at physical risk. What might your partner's view of that be?'

Knowing Tom's likely response, she went with a not quite truthful answer. 'He would be supportive.'

They were silent for a couple of minutes. 'I don't like it,' he said.

'Specifically, what don't you like?'

'*Any* of it, but mainly putting you in danger. How confident are you?'

'I would estimate ninety-five per cent if it was planned well.'

'You're willing to put yourself on the line with somebody who's probably no stranger to surveillance tactics?'

She nodded. 'I've thought about it. You know the nature of these homicides. We must act. If Rollaston takes over, he has a long way to go to get to the stage we're at right now, which means there could be more deaths in the future. I'm aware that what I've told you is not direct, physical evidence, but what choice do we have?'

'You're not going into this alone.'

'May I take that as an offer?'

'Yes.' He watched her.

'I'll need back-up if all goes to plan.' She gave him a direct look. 'This has been my first hands-on experience of homicide investigation and I didn't want it—'

'I remember.'

'But my view has changed. I know that I can work with . . . that I can do it. I want to do more in the future.' She waited. 'Will you be glad to get back to what you usually do?'

He shook his head. 'In the short term, I'll take whatever I'm given but I'll make it known where I'm stationed that I'm up for more challenge.' He chose his words. 'This idea of yours is dangerous. Right at the sharp end of policing. You need to give it more thought.'

'I'm not a rule-follower.'

He shook his head. 'You don't say.' He stood. 'Come on.'

'Where to?'

'Bass in Forensics. We need his help.'

Thirty minutes later, Thompson was about to leave Headquarters. He turned to Craft. 'If this goes wrong, I could face dismissal for sanctioning it, but the personal risk to you is massive. You might want to discuss it with your partner. If you have second thoughts, phone me later.'

She watched him to his vehicle. He was right. She could not agree to it without confiding in Tom. She also needed to speak to David Brown.

Thursday 14 November, 9.25 a.m.

Craft came into the office, seeing Brown at his computer. 'Hi, David.'

He looked up briefly. 'Hey, Tig. How's it going?'

'Not so well. We don't have sufficient evidence to bring the investigation to a conclusion.'

'I'm really sorry to hear that, given the hard work you've put in.'

She sat near to him. 'I need some help. Can you help me?'

'That depends on the kind of help you're looking for. I'm here for just two more days, then I'm gone to a data-processing job in Yorkshire.'

'The reason I'm asking you, David, is that you are a "process" person. We both are. Two such thinkers are a real advantage.' She waited as he absorbed her words.

He nodded. 'In theory, I'm more than willing, but I would still have to put in the hours to complete my contract here.'

'If you agree to consider it, we could find some time after work hours. I'm happy to work around the commitments you have, but you're right. Time is short.'

He hesitated, then grinned. 'OK, smooth talker. When and where do we start?'

'I really appreciate this, David. I'll phone you and we can work something out, yes?'

Craft was alone in the office, her hands clasped at her mouth. She knew the questions to which she needed answers, but they had to be the right answers. If she did not get them, several lost lives would not be avenged and a killer would be free to kill again.

THIRTY-THREE

7.34 p.m.

She left her car, headed quickly for the house and rang the bell. Within seconds the door was opened and Brown invited her inside. She followed him into the sitting room, hearing a dog whining on the upper floor. 'Is your lodger at home?'

'Yes. He spends most of his time on his Xbox so he won't bother us. Fancy a drink?'

'Not for me, thanks. I would like to get started with a question for you, David.'

'Ask away.'

'Do you know a company called Harrison Marsh?'

He motioned her to a chair, took a seat himself. 'The only time

I've heard the name is when it was mentioned by you or DCI Thompson in the office. Why?'

'You never heard it before that in the course of your work?'

'No. Never.'

She opened her notebook, fanned pages, stopping at one. 'In your work for the police, you've been sent to many different forces and been involved in homicide discussions?'

'I have, yes.'

'As a data analyst you've been involved in homicides similar to those DCI Thompson and I have been investigating.'

He shook his head. 'Yes, from a data analysis viewpoint.'

'And you have a criminology degree.'

He nodded.

'David, I need you to help me link the homicides of Emma Matheson, Phillip Marsh, Alicia Franks, Lucy Greening and the attack on Penny Bristow.'

He looked hesitant. 'To be honest, Teigan, I'm still struggling to link any of those deaths to a specific theory or pattern. To me, they seem too different. I mean, one male, the others female, one of the females much older. I must admit, I don't actually see a pattern in any of it.'

'What about the Harrison Marsh link?'

He shrugged. 'I can see it for the Matheson woman and Phillip Marsh because they worked together, but where or what is the link with the other, younger victims? I don't get it.'

'Perhaps there wasn't one?'

He stared at her. 'So, what was the motive?'

'I was hoping you might have some ideas.'

He looked bemused, shook his head. 'During your discussions with Steve Thompson, I suppose I was a passive listener – you know, picking up what was being said but not reflecting too much on it.' He gave her a direct look. 'Tig, this is your chance to have second thoughts about asking me for help.'

'I think I might be asking the wrong questions.' There was a short silence.

He asked, 'What might be the right questions from your viewpoint?'

'I think those which relate to *what* this killer did and *where* he did it.'

He frowned. 'Sorry, I can't make suggestions or give a view on what he's done, but the issue of where – yes, I have one or two ideas. For example, Lifestyle Theory takes the view that some people may present as easy victims because of the choices they make in terms of, say, substance addiction. One of your victims was an alcoholic? From what I absorbed during discussions, it seems to me that the Matheson woman placed herself at risk of victimization from, say, any casual, ill-intentioned thief.'

'I understand what you're saying, David, but I am not keen on theories which imply blame to a victim.'

'We all make choices, don't we? Example: if an individual opts to run across a busy road, wouldn't you regard that as a choice which might invite an accident?'

'I suppose. Any other theories?'

'Just one, and I'm kind of bending this theory to suit the investigation. Deviant Place Theory suggests that an individual is more at risk if he or she is living in a bad neighbourhood, particularly if, for financial reasons, a move is not possible.'

'To me that sounds very similar to Lifestyle Theory, David. Placing the responsibility for outcome on to the victim.'

'Hear me out. Like I said, I'm kind of subverting this theory to fit. Think about it: Forrest Road itself is an expensive area in which to live, but it happens to be at the very edge of Forrest Park. If we accept that Forrest Park is "dangerous" in terms of the potential risk to those who might frequent it, particularly females, Emma Matheson's house was directly opposite it. The other, younger victims went there, in darkness and alone. I'm not victim-blaming, Tig. What I am saying is that that kind of area attracts deviant individuals. Which is why most females might choose not to frequent it. Those who do are knowingly placing themselves at risk of harm.' He waited, seeing her turning the idea over. 'Because I work away so much, I don't know these areas. If I was more familiar with these two crime scenes, it might help.'

'Neither of them is far from here.' She stood. 'I want you to see them.'

He looked up at her. 'You mean, now?'

'David, it might give you some insight into these homicides which I don't have.'

He thought about it. 'If I'm going to be of any use, I suppose it makes sense that I take a look at them.'

* * *

They were in Craft's car, heading for Forrest Road. 'Don't expect too much, Tig. I'll do all I can to help in the time I have left here, but I'm still doubtful that I can add anything, given both you and DCI Thompson have thoroughly explored each of these homicides.'

She paused to let traffic pass, then turned on to the next road. 'I'm asking for your views, David, because you've had no direct involvement in the investigation so you're unlikely to have preconceptions which might block your thinking to new ideas.'

'What about DCI Thompson?'

'What about him? He never wanted this investigation. Like me, his role here is almost finished.'

He hesitated. 'Tig, I'm more than willing to help wherever I can, but I wouldn't want to step on a DCI's toes.'

'You won't.' They came into Forrest Road. Craft parked opposite house number three and they both got out of the car.

She heard David's low whistle. 'That's some house.' He pointed. 'I'm assuming that's the one, given the builders' debris all around it.'

She nodded. 'Yes. Emma Matheson's last home.'

He gazed at it, then looked back at her. 'I've just realized what impressed me about your attitude to these homicides. You care, Tig. I'm not suggesting that DCI Thompson doesn't, but you are different and it shows in your commitment to the woman who lived here and the other victims.'

'Thompson would probably tell you that it risks clouding my judgement.' She shrugged. 'It did affect me. Emma had a very hard life in her later years, following which she lost her life to someone who—'

'Hated her?'

'No, David.' She shook her head. 'It is far worse than that. Emma was killed by someone who cared nothing for her at all, and for whom she had become a mere inconvenience. Something to be . . . tidied away.'

He took a couple of steps towards the house. 'I had assumed that whoever killed her had strong feelings for her, for him to do such a terrible thing. It stands to reason.'

Craft looked at him. 'What might those strong feelings have been?'

'I don't think I can answer that, but now I'm really thinking about it, have you considered at all the possibility that this was a burglary that went tragically wrong?'

'Don't be fooled by the house. She hardly had anything worth stealing. One aspect I am still trying to understand: why would this individual kill her then conceal her body inside? Why not take it away? Bury it somewhere, miles away?'

'Too risky.' He looked around, pointed to number three. 'I've just noticed – the Matheson house is the only one not concealed by trees.'

'It was, originally. The builders have chopped them down.' They got back inside Craft's car and headed out of the road, arriving within minutes at the edge of Forrest Park. They got out and stood looking at it a short distance away.

'Tig, you're not going to approve, but my immediate response on seeing it is to ask why the women who were killed here went into it alone?' He stared across at it. 'I think even I would have second thoughts about it, in the dark.'

'Perhaps because they were young, confident women who believed they were safe if they didn't stray too far from the road and the nearby houses.'

He turned to the houses. 'Did any of the residents along here report seeing or hearing anything?'

'No one confirmed it when spoken to by officers.'

'How could Sullivan, or anyone else for that matter, do such things?' he whispered.

She turned to him. '*Sullivan?*'

'Haven't you heard?'

'No. Tell me.'

'The new guy Holdsworth has brought into the investigation has his eye on Sullivan for the murders here and at Forrest Road.'

She stared at him. 'Since *when*?'

He shrugged. 'I think, in the last few hours.'

'How do you know?'

'Naz Sandhu told me. You didn't know?'

She shook her head. 'You're saying he's been arrested in connection with this investigation?'

'I haven't heard that, but . . .' He shrugged. 'Say what you like about the force, when it does move, it goes like a train.'

'It doesn't make any sense. Did Officer Sandhu give you any details?'

'She said there had been some breakthrough, some new evidence and everything has changed, that Sullivan is a suspect due to his whole demeanour towards females. Come on, Tig, you know that first-hand.'

'Yes—'

'And, whether he is guilty of murder or not, he's a *classic* misogynist. *I* know how inappropriate his attitude was to Officer Sandhu and I recall conversations between you and DCI Thompson about him.' He was silent, then, 'From what I've heard, the new investigation is being widened to another geographical area.'

'Where, exactly?'

'I'm not sure.'

'*Think,* David, it could be important.'

'Hang on. It was something like . . . Alney—'

'Olney Wood!' She turned and headed for her car.

He went after her. 'Tig! I don't have a clue where that is!'

'I do. I've seen it on a map!'

Arriving at Olney Wood, Craft parked and gazed out on trees in the meagre streetlight. David broke the silence. 'What are you thinking?'

'That it is too dark to go in there.'

'The moon is bright . . . hang on . . .' A sudden '*click*' and the slim Maglite in his hand threw light via the windscreen on to a row of sturdy trees. 'After we agreed to meet, I searched the records, looking for anything which might suggest a new line of inquiry. Do you know that at the start of his career Sullivan worked for the Met? It's a geographical link between him, Matheson and the guy she worked for in London. Place that in the context of his behaviour towards females – well, it convinces me. What shocks me is that he's managed to survive in the force for this length of time.' He got out of the car and headed to the trees.

Craft was half-out of the car, calling after him, 'David, wait!'

'We need to look at this place, Tig. The first time I heard it mentioned was by Sullivan, saying how much he loved being here. Now it's started me thinking.' He was walking away from her, his voice drifting back. 'We should at least take a look!'

She went after him, matching his quick pace through the dense trees, seeing him stop, one hand raised.

'*Ssshh!* Hear *that*?'

'I didn't hear anything.'

Gazing ahead, his index finger against his lips, his voice low, he whispered, 'I see a link between Olney Wood and Forrest Wood.' He turned to her, his voice dropping to a whisper. 'Don't you see it, Tig?'

'No, I don't. Tell me.'

He approached her. 'It's *you*.'

She backed away, began running, wanting to put distance between them. She could hear him coming after her, gaining on her. He caught her, swung her around, hitting the side of her head with the Maglite, pushing her down to the ground, his lips against her ear. 'How many people know about *dendrophilia*? Next to *none*!' His saliva hitting her cheek, she thought of Thompson, willing him here. 'I'll tell you something else I know,' he whispered. 'I know *what* you are. I know how you *think* – way, way outside the box.' He nodded. 'That's right, isn't it? I know you really, *really* well. Which means it's time you knew *me*.' One hand around her neck, he pointed. 'See this tree just here? No? I'll describe it for you. It's *so* beautiful with its reddish-brown bark, its leaves green all year round.' He reached out, his hand slowly, gently caressing its trunk, whispering, 'I want us to fully share our experience of it.'

Thompson was pacing, impatient. He had laid out his plan to Holdsworth on the phone and requested that he have several officers on standby, which had prompted a furious reaction.

'We need all those available, sir. That park is a big place.'

Thompson had managed to get Holdsworth's reluctant agreement, but it had done little to calm his growing concern. 'What's going on? I'm hearing *nothing*!'

Bass looked at him. 'We have a problem.'

'It's *Craft* who's got the problem. Just . . . fix it!'

'I don't think I can. He could be using a radio frequency jammer which blocks wires and bugs.'

Thompson clasped his hands to his head. 'Jesus *Christ*.'

Craft was aware that she was moving, being dragged over rough ground and tree roots. Pulled to her feet, her back slamming against something hard, again she felt his mouth against her cheek.

'The first time I saw you, I knew you were perfect.'

Her head dropped forward. He spun her round, slamming her

face against a rough surface. She felt warmth course slowly down her cheek.

'I know *exactly* what you are.' She felt his laugh against the back of her neck. 'Which means that we both know each other very, very well, don't we?' His hands grasped her clothing. 'We're . . . soulmates.'

Tom! Help me, Tom! She forced herself to focus, feeling the weight of him pushing against her, his mouth against her neck. *The wire . . . but it's too late . . .*

'We came together in your world,' he whispered. 'Now, I'm welcoming you to mine.'

Thompson's eyes moved quickly over Forrest Park. 'If she's here, we won't find her unless we search the whole area.' He took out his phone, not caring what Holdsworth had to say – they needed forty officers at least.

'Steve!' He quickly turned to Bass. 'I've established contact! I know where she is and it's not here!'

Craft's hand came up, trying to locate the searing pain in her head, her fingers wet, sticky.

'Welcome back.'

She glanced up at him, squeezed her eyes closed at the pain.

'Do *not* fight me again. I have tremendous regard for you, Tig, but we are natural enemies, you and I. In nature, our roles are predator and prey. A logical order I have always found comfortably unambiguous. Your logic is now making trouble for both of us. A *lot* of trouble.' He seized her by her coat, ripping it open, its buttons flying, his hand grabbing her by her sweater.

Neurons firing inside her head, she flailed at him, her bright fingernails at his face, gouging the skin around his eyes. '*You—*'

He gripped both her hands and threw her to the ground, his legs braced either side of her. She lay, words spiralling inside her head, disjointed, chaotic. *Bloody proof . . . kick . . . folded, tied . . . smashed face . . . severed hand . . . Tom . . . Penny wants her life . . . Tom . . . Tom.*

On a sudden rush of grief and broiling anger she kicked him between his legs, heard him wail, saw him double over, stagger backwards. On her feet, she lashed out again, looked for something with which to hit him. He was coming for her.

* * *

Time now a sliding, unreliable concept, she lay in implacable blackness, hands tied, something solid and unyielding around her. It moved and she saw moonlight. Seized by her coat, he pulled her out of the boot of the car and dragged her towards the house. Inside the hall, he threw her down. Grabbing her by her collar, he said, 'Do not *move*,' and threw her down again, causing her head to hit the floor.

Dazed, she lay on the floor, trying to track his movements. *Leaving the room? Drawer* opening . . . *jangle of* . . . *cutlery*. She struggled to her feet, her hands still secured, moved slowly, silently up the stairs. If his housemate was here, he might help her. Defend her? Pushing open the bedroom door, she saw a red setter lying listless on a fouled sheet next to a bowl of water. Nothing else.

Hearing movement in the hallway, she forced herself on to the next room, pushed open the door, stared at outdated wall decoration and more emptiness. He was on the stairs. Quickly closing the door on him, she stood listening, her hands at her mouth, trying to work out where he was. Thirteen stairs? She counted footfalls: seven . . . eight . . . nine . . . At twelve, she flung open the door, rushed the landing and kicked at his face, making direct contact with his jaw, sending him crashing down the stairs as the front door shattered into pieces around him.

Craft was inside one of the squad cars, its whirling lights striking her face. She closed her eyes. A door opened. Thompson's voice. 'How are you feeling?'

Picking up sympathy in his words, she began to sob.

'You did good, Craft. Bloody good.'

Fighting away tears, she reached inside her sweater, grasped a corner of adhesive tape and pulled it out. A small, black item was stuck to it. He took it from her.

'That gave us a bit of bother for a while.'

She pulled again at the top of her sweater, revealing a vivid red wheal on her chest. Another sob. 'I think . . . I'm allergic to latex.'

THIRTY-FOUR

Saturday 16 November, 10.45 a.m.

Recovered as much as possible and against Tom's wishes, Craft was ready to observe the man who only hours before was intent on destroying her. She looked down at the psychiatric report prepared on him. According to the psychiatrist, Daniel Browning aka David Brown, 'exudes a belief in his own invincibility, that the charges against him are derisory; indeed, he expresses no guilt and is incapable of recognizing the power of the evidence against him due to his significant psychopathology. During the entire evaluation, he has remained dismissive of all evidence and was highly motivated to engage in mind games with this professional.'

Thompson's index finger pointed at the report. 'He has refused legal representation and his current stance is that he's in charge of these proceedings. If you want my opinion, he's two stops past Barking.'

'You are saying he's insane?'

'Mad as a bloody hatter.'

'He is not.'

'That's because neither this psychiatrist expert, nor the one commissioned by the defence, has come out and said so, and now he sees himself in full control of this investigation and any future court proceedings. When his solicitor tries to discuss the case with him, he goes round the houses, admits nothing, regardless of the evidence against him.' He checked the time and stood. 'Right. I'm on. Keep watching.'

Craft switched on the monitor and an interview room somewhere inside Headquarters filled the screen. She watched Thompson enter the interview room, followed by the man she knew as David Brown, flanked by two officers. He looked relaxed, his tone breezy as he turned to one of them.

'Jim, isn't it? Thank you, Jim. This shouldn't take long, but keep my lunch warm if necessary, there's a good chap.' He came to the table, sat opposite Thompson. 'Steve, nice to see you again!'

Thompson's eyes were fixed on him. 'Daniel Browning, I need to check with you that your hours in custody so far have been comfortable and that you have everything you need.'

'That depends on the arrival of a one-hundred-per-cent wool blanket I've requested, but so far all else has been satisfactory.'

To Craft's eye, Thompson was looking surprisingly calm. 'I want to start this interview with—'

She watched the door open and an officer enter, carrying a tray supporting what looked to be coffee and three chocolate biscuits on a plate. Browning looked up at the officer and smiled. 'Thank you, Eddie. Very kind.' For Craft this was an object lesson in terms of Browning's undoubted psychopathy. Thompson was simmering. 'We'll start with – no thanks, no biscuits for me – your current perception of the charges against you.'

Browning took a bite of biscuit. 'I'm glad you've asked me that, Steve—'

'DCI Thompson.'

'Whoops! Sorry.' He sat back, smiled. 'My perception of the case is that it is entirely circumstantial.'

'Let's start with Professor Craft's statement which says that you physically attacked her in Olney Wood.'

Browning appeared to give the suggestion some consideration. 'That is patently untrue. I know she is a colleague of yours, Steve, but I must inform you that she is unfit to do her job.'

Craft's eyes were fixed on his face. She watched him lean closer to Thompson. 'Are you aware that she has significant difficulty in relating to people?'

Craft tensed.

'I refer to it solely to indicate that it is a significant barrier to her understanding others, plus any situation of which she is a part. I don't say this lightly, you understand. As you are aware, I have a psychology degree from Oxford so my opinion should carry weight. She is . . .' He sighed. 'How to put this kindly . . . not what you think she is. I assume you have noticed anomalies in the way she engages—'

'Professor Craft is not the focus here. Do you remember a young woman named Lucy Greening? When you met her, you identified yourself as "Gary Sullivan".'

'Did I?'

'Yes. What is your explanation for doing so?'

'I have no idea. But our paths have crossed before, Gary's and mine.'

The interview continued in similar vein until Thompson stood, glanced at his watch, gave the time. 'This interview is suspended for ten minutes.' He picked up the file and left the room, Browning watching him go. Raising both arms, he linked his hands behind his head and grinned at the officer standing next to the door.

Craft looked up as Thompson entered the observation room, dropping the file on the table. 'Why so brief?'

'I won't give him a platform to deny everything and make criticisms of involved personnel.'

'His being personal about me is entirely irrelevant.'

'I'm not providing him with an opportunity to slag you off.'

She stared at him. 'Slag me . . .? He is demonstrating to you that he is eminently sane and entirely fixed on game-playing!'

'So it's just me that's irritated?'

'I don't know.'

He sighed. She watched him leave the room.

Back inside the interview room, Thompson sat opposite Browning, whose eyes were fixed on him. 'This interview is now resumed in order to inform you that I am arranging for an identification procedure of you in connection with one serious offence which forms part of this investigation.'

'By whom?'

'The witness's name cannot be divulged, as well you know.'

'I refuse to participate.'

Thompson stared at him, aware that Browning was now in full game-playing mode. 'If you want my advice, Browning, you need legal representation. Interview concluded at eleven twenty-five.' On his way to the door, he said to the officer there, 'Take him back to his cell and tell your colleagues down there not to engage with him, got it?'

'Sir!'

Passing reception, an officer on duty said, 'Sir, your eleven forty-five visitor is already here.' He indicated the young woman. Thompson went to her.

'Miss Bristow, thank you for coming in this morning. My office is this way.'

Bristow turned to Thompson. 'I thought Professor Craft would be here. Where is she?'

'She is involved with another matter. Take a seat, please.'

She sat opposite, her eyes fixed on him as he said, 'You regard Professor Craft as a source of support to you?'

She nodded.

'We have to take great care when conducting investigations that there are no grounds for accusation of witness influence.'

She stared at him. 'Meaning?'

'We don't want to jeopardize in any way what we believe to be a strong case against Daniel Browning.'

'But I've come to *identify* him. Surely that's enough?'

'As of this morning, he is refusing to attend an identification parade.'

She was on her feet, staring down at Thompson. 'He can't *do* that!'

'Unfortunately, he can, but that isn't the end of the issue for us.'

She sat, her eyes glued to him.

'What we're planning to do instead is use a photograph for identification purposes. How do you feel about that?'

She thought about it. 'I've only just realized from being here that I was thinking this was my chance to face him. Prove to myself and him that I'm a survivor, that I'm strong, able to look at him without falling apart.'

Thompson nodded, suspecting that Browning knew this and would not give it to her. 'Are you willing to ID him by photograph?'

'Yes.'

'You do understand, Penny, that when we take the matter to court, you would be required to attend as a witness and that he will be there?'

She looked at him, chin up. 'I understand. It's what I want.'

He got to his feet. 'Would you mind staying in here for say ten minutes while I organize the photo?'

Getting a nod, he left the office and went directly to Forensics, seeing Bass at a workbench. 'You've got Browning's ID card. I need an enlargement of it.' Within minutes Thompson was looking at it, the subject full-face and sharply defined. 'That's just the job, Thanks.'

Penny Bristow looked up as Thompson returned to the office. 'Penny, we need to go to another room.'

She followed him there. Inside, he indicated a chair opposite him as another officer entered with a large envelope. 'Are you ready to do this, Penny?'

She nodded.

'This room is equipped with a recording device which is already activated. I'm about to show you a photograph of an individual. I want you to look at it, take your time, then tell me if you are able to identify him as the man who attacked you.' Thompson took the photograph from the envelope, placed it face down on the table. After a pause of some seconds, he turned it over.

She gave an involuntary gasp and reached out her hand, not making direct contact with it. 'Yes,' she whispered. Then, again: '*Yes.* It's *him,* that's the man I saw inside this building, the man who attacked me in Forrest Park, who hit me . . .' She covered her face with her hands, then pulled them away. 'I want to go to court and say it!'

Thompson said, 'You have identified Daniel Browning, also known to this force as David Brown.'

THIRTY-FIVE

Thompson was again facing Browning, who was regarding him with interest.

'I'm guessing you have some pithy questions for me, DCI Thompson. Shall we proceed?'

Thompson ignored the mocking bid for control of the situation. 'For the recording, the purpose of this interview of Daniel Browning, also known to this force as David Brown, is to share information available to this investigation and obtain his response.' He reached inside one of the envelopes. 'These are the ligatures and the white cord, the first of which were used to bind Emma Matheson's remains, and the cord to strangle her. What have you to say?'

Browning shrugged. 'I know nothing about such things.'

Thompson placed a single sheet of paper on the table. 'I'm now showing Mr Browning a statement made by a Mrs Turner' – he watched recognition register on Browning's face – 'who was a next-door neighbour to you and your mother several years ago.' He turned the sheet around. 'She states, and I quote, "His mother was a bit of a loner, but on the very rare occasions I was inside the house she would be doing handicrafts, you know, making items of jewellery, bits of shiny things threaded on to leather. She also made collages and hung them up around the house. To be honest, I did not like any of them. They looked depressing. As a person, Mrs Browning was not a familiar figure to other residents of the area due to her leaving her home very rarely—"'

Browning's hand shot out, seized the sheet, tore it into pieces and dropped them on the floor, his facial expression dismissive.

'We have a copy of that statement and it will form part of our evidence against you.'

'The woman is a liar.'

Thompson studied him. 'Tell us about Forrest Road, specifically house number three.'

'I know nothing about it.'

'Our inquiries have revealed that you owned it under the name of D-B Investments prior to it being sold at auction to a Bradley Baxter. We also know that at the age of seventeen you were working at a London company, Harrison Marsh Investments, as an intern. According to its records, you were the youngest they ever accepted. Your father persuaded Phillip Marsh to take you on. Tell me about that.'

'No comment.'

'According to what we've learned, you proved to be a big problem in those few weeks, stealing money and an even bigger one for Phillip Marsh, whom you killed by pushing him under a train because—'

'I categorically den— No comment!'

'He had evidence that you were stealing money from the company. I shall charge you at the end of this interview with his death. I also need to inform you that the Italian police are investigating the death of a girlfriend of yours, Suzette or Suzie Ross. According to what we know, you use both names for her. What is your response to that?'

'I've never heard of the woman.'

'You will recall a burglary at your house in recent weeks?'

'Yes. Which resulted in non-attendance from the local police.'

'That incident is classed as a false report. The apparent "disorder" inside your house was too tidy, Mr Browning. Too "careful".'

'If that's your view, I am not surprised that such offenses go unpunished.'

'We have evidence that not only was that "burglary" staged by *you*, due to accidentally dropping your front door key somewhere near to the house. You didn't want to risk us, the police, taking an interest in its Italian flag fob because of its connection to another homicide involving a girlfriend of yours—'

'This is pure fantasy!'

'—the investigation of which the Italian police are reopening.' Thompson paused. 'Do you have any comment to make on that information, Mr Browning? No?' He paused. 'You have a dog, a red setter which links you to brownish-red dog hairs recovered from Emma Matheson's remains—'

'Where is Buddy! What have you done with him?'

'I can see your concern about your dog. This is the first time I've seen you show concern for any living thing.'

'We recovered a plastic bag with reddish-brown dog hairs inside the space where Emma Matheson's remains were concealed. Something else that links you to her homicide.'

An officer standing by the door sprang forward as Browning got to his feet, his focus on the wall clock. 'My dinner should be ready very soon and I need to check that it conforms with my special diet.'

Thompson supplied the exact time, ended the interview, and Browning walked nonchalantly from the room, the officer's hand gripping his arm. Thompson knew that the catering firm had been instructed to supply wheat-and-dairy-free meals for Browning, guessing that he would eat anything if he were free. Thompson took a deep breath. Once a game-player, always a game-player.

Going into his office, he saw Craft, her eyes fixed on a monitor screen showing Daniel Browning being escorted to his cell.

She looked up. 'He *is one* piece of work.'

Thompson sat, his face showing how tired he was. 'Where did you pick that phrase up?'

'From working here. I've decided I need to commit some well-used phrases of police parlance to memory.'

He grinned. 'You don't need them. You've got your own versions.' He shook his head. 'I haven't finished with Browning but we'll get no admissions from him about anything, including his "friendship" with that bloody nightmare, Quirebell.'

'It doesn't matter. We both know what he did and we have other evidence from his house. My scarf. Lucy Greening's engagement ring. The letter written to him by Jerome Quirebell. Do you know how they became acquainted?'

Thompson nodded. 'A site on the Dark Web.'

There was a short silence.

Craft said, 'I've thought over the whole investigation. From the moment I met David Brown – which is how I still think of him – he showed such intense interest in our investigation. And I told him all that I knew. I should not have done that.'

'You'll get no criticism from me for that. You weren't to know what he was, back then. Nobody did.' He gave his face a brisk rub, looked at her. 'We've got solid evidence and he knows we have.' He looked up at her as she stood. 'You can have your scarf back, once these proceedings are over.'

'You are joking?'

'Yeah.' He stood. 'I need to give thought to my next interview with him.' He paused. 'It wouldn't surprise me if he pleads Not Guilty by Reason of Insanity.'

'He cannot do that.'

'He can, but it won't work.' He went to the door, his back to her. 'If an opportunity arose in future, how would you feel about us teaming up again?'

Her lips parted in a wide smile. '*Bloody*, yes!'

THIRTY-SIX

6.30 p.m.

Craft was home, Tom watching her push food around her plate. Half an hour earlier she had acted out for him what she had seen of Browning's interview, which involved her taking the parts of all those involved. He had watched and listened, understanding Browning's duplicity and her dogged commitment to the case. Since then, she had withdrawn into herself. He broke the silence.

'What is it, Tig?'

She looked up at him and shrugged. 'You know I got a call from Thompson a while ago? It was to tell me that as part of Browning's defence, he is intending to comment on my "social difficulties".'

'Surely that won't be allowed?'

'It only needs to be said and then . . . everyone will know.' She whispered, 'Help me, Tom. What shall I do?'

He reached for her hand. 'What he is intending to say about you – it's no one else's business, Tig. Yes, you struggle at times but you're highly capable in what you do. The investigation is proof of that.' There was a brief silence. 'My opinion has always been that it needs to be acknowledged because it's part of *you.* It *is* you, Tig. Why should you hide it?'

She looked across at him. 'You're saying . . . you think everyone should . . . know?'

'Why not? It's an integral part of who you are that shouldn't be judged, like the colour of your lovely blue eyes.'

'How would *you* feel if he says those things at the trial and the press is there?'

He grinned. 'I already know, don't I? It would make no difference to my feelings for you. You have shown *him* to be a pitiless killer whom you are helping to put away for good so that he can't hurt any other woman. That is what's important. Nothing else matters.'

Late January

Thompson was back at Headquarters for the press conference following the conclusion of Daniel Browning's trial. The office he had used here had been cleared, desks replaced by several rows of chairs now occupied by members of the press and the media. Fellow officers were also here looking jubilant. He took a couple of deep breaths. None of his prior homicide cases had excited anything like this level of interest. They were here to listen to his brief account of the investigation which had resulted in Daniel Browning being given several life sentences. Holdsworth was already facing them, expressing the force's 'delight' at the trial outcome. Hearing him wind down, seeing Holdsworth's eyes on him, Thompson was ready.

'So, all that remains for me to do is introduce the senior investigative officer, Steven Thompson, who is going to give you a brief overview of his investigation. Steve?'

Thompson walked to the front of the crowd, spoke for about ten minutes then, as hands were raised, said, 'There are two people who are going to assist me in answering the questions you have: Police Constable Naz Sandhu and forensic psychologist Professor Teigan Craft.'

Craft and Sandhu walked to Thompson as hands shot upwards. After thirty minutes, Thompson called a halt to the questioning. 'This has been a gruelling investigation for everyone involved. All I want to add is that we are pleased to have achieved the right outcome.'

Thompson paused, his eyes moving over the audience. 'Professor Craft has been central to this investigation and I am personally grateful to her for her professional insights on what has been a very complex case.' He sat down.

Craft looked at the audience looking back at her, their pens and phones poised. She had to do this. It was time. 'I am Teigan Craft and this was my first experience of collaborative work with the police.' She took a deep breath. 'I have been told that there is interest in my role within it, which was to provide psychological insight to the team.' She paused, reading from the sheet of paper she was holding. 'I am aware that there has been comment and speculation about me in the media, so I need to share a specific, personal aspect of myself.'

A quick glance and she saw anticipation on some faces, confusion on others. 'I find collaborative work difficult at times. My early years were similarly problematic. I did not know how people – relationships – worked. I had to learn how to play with other children, that it involved taking turns. Over time, I learned to interpret people's intentions, their emotions, their attitudes, mostly by close observation, active listening and analysing the cues I saw or heard. As an adult, I often feel bombarded still by information from my senses, which can be extremely tiring. Mostly I manage to do things which other people do without thinking.'

She looked up at them waiting, staring back at her.

'It is time for me to re-introduce myself. I am Teigan Craft, forensic psychologist, and I am neurodivergent.' There was a profound silence, most in the audience looking confused, a few intrigued. A slight tremor in her voice, she added, 'I am autistic. My partner, Tom, says that if there are any doubts about it, one glance at the regimentation inside my wardrobe, all hangers identical, all facing the same way, all spaced equally, should dispel them.' She looked up. 'That is my Tom making a sort of joke. That is all

I want to say. Except that autistic people are as different and individual as all of you.' She looked around the audience. 'When you have met one autistic person, you have met *one* autistic person . . . Thank you.'

Going to where Thompson was sitting, she took the chair next to him, eyes fixed on the floor. A few hands clapped, quickly turning into thunderous applause.

Holdsworth had provided drinks and snacks inside a meeting room for all those who had participated in the investigation. When Craft came inside, a cheer went up and glasses were raised. Head down, she went quickly to Thompson. 'I did it! You were right when you said they would understand.'

'I knew you'd play a blinder.'

She gave him a quick glance. 'I found the cheering and so forth difficult to manage. I just want to reassure you that if we ever collaborate in future, I shall appreciate your kindness and your humour – possibly.'

He handed her a glass. 'Without you, I doubt we would be having this conversation.'

'I realize how impulsive I am at times. It must have been very difficult for you, when you must follow procedure.' She paused. 'He left Emma . . . tidied away, didn't he? A mere loose end in his life.' Craft looked at him. 'Tell me now, what do you really think about us working alongside each other in future?'

He eyed her, thinking of all she had had to grapple with, manage in addition to the investigative challenges, yet she had still arrived at the right conclusion. 'I had an idea that there was something I didn't get about you. Want to know what I thought?'

'Go on.'

'I thought you were a spoiled only child.'

She nodded. 'That's something else I am.'

He laughed. 'Want another drink?'

'Well, I don't normally drink during the day.'

'I know. I've heard you spill most of it.' He waited.

She pointed at him. '*That* is a joke, like, if you are drunk you spill things. It *is* a little bit funny.'